MARIE ANTOINETTE, SERIAL KILLER

Katie Alender

is the acclaimed author of several novels for young adults, including *Bad Girls Don't Die* and *From Bad to Cursed*. A graduate of the Florida State University Film School, Katie now lives in Los Angeles with her husband and her daughter. She enjoys reading, sewing and eating delicious high-calorie foods. To find out more about Katie, visit www.katiealender.com

MARIE ANTOINETTE, SERIAL KILLER

KATIE ALENDER

■SCHOLASTIC

First published in the US in 2013 by Scholastic Inc.
This edition published in the UK in 2014 by Scholastic Ltd
Euston House, 24 Eversholt Street
London, NW1 1DB, UK
Registered office: Westfield Road, Southam, Warwickshire, CV47 0RA
SCHOLASTIC and associated logos are trademarks and/or
registered trademarks of Scholastic Inc.

Text copyright © Katie Alender, 2013
The right of Katie Alender to be identified as the author
of this work has been asserted by her.

ISBN 978 1407 14041 4

A CIP catalogue record for this book is available
from the British Library.

Printed by CPI Group (UK) Ltd, Croydon, CR0 4YY
Papers used by Scholastic Children's Books are made from
wood grown in sustainable forests.

1 3 5 7 9 10 8 6 4 2

www.scholastic.co.uk/zone

JUL 1 5 2022

For G,
my dearest girl

I

IN HER APARTMENT *high above the streets of Paris, Gabrielle Roux stood in front of the bathroom mirror, still wearing her daringly short purple dress and sky-high platform heels. The light glanced off her golden hair as she brushed it and thought back to the glittering party from which she had just come.*

There had been at least twenty girls there, and Gabrielle was sure that she had been the most beautiful and most admired. Six boys — at least one of whom had a girlfriend — begged for her phone number.

Of course, she wouldn't text back any of the boys. They just weren't good enough for someone like herself. After all, at only nineteen years old, she was already an almost-famous model. She didn't need to resort to stealing an ugly girl's not-cute-enough-and-not-rich-enough boyfriend. Once her Italian Vogue *cover came out, she would naturally start hanging out with people who were more worth her time and attention.*

Gabrielle wet a washcloth and gently removed her makeup, patting her high cheekbones. As she reached into the cabinet for her eye cream (it was never too early to protect her porcelain complexion), she scowled, catching sight of her arm. There was a dark smudge just above her wrist. She scrubbed her forearm with soap until the skin around the splotch was pink. When that didn't work, she used rubbing alcohol. But still the dark stain remained.

With an angry grunt, Gabrielle walked out of the bathroom — and froze.

All the lights were on.

But she hadn't turned on any of them — certainly not the light in the kitchen.

"Maman? Papa?" she called, irritation in her voice. Her parents were supposed to be out of town. It would be just like them to come home early and ruin her weekend.

But would they really return at two thirty in the morning?

There was no reply.

Well. She squared her shoulders, tossed her shiny hair, and walked toward the living room. Gabrielle wasn't scared of anything.

But as she reached the arched entryway to the luxurious sitting room, the skin on the back of her neck began to tingle . . .

And she knew she wasn't alone.

Ever so slowly, she turned around, expecting to see a stalker (preferably a smitten, handsome young man who'd broken in so he could proclaim his undying love).

But it wasn't a crazed fan.

A woman stood in front of her, wearing a long pale-pink dress with a wide-open lace-trimmed collar. Her hair was white and piled in frothy curls that extended nearly a foot into the air above her head.

Gabrielle stared. Clearly, her apartment had been invaded by some sort of crazy person — or was this one of her annoying friends in a costume, playing a joke on her?

The woman's cold eyes seemed to glow from within.

And Gabrielle realized that something was very wrong.

"Qu'est-ce que vous voulez!?" Gabrielle whispered. What do you want?

The woman's silence sucked the warmth out of Gabrielle's blood. Finally, she spoke in a low hiss. "La fille de la famille Roux."

Gabrielle opened her mouth to promise the intruder anything — all the money she had, her mother's jewelry, the keys to her father's car —

Before she could speak, a sharp CRACK filled the apartment. The mirror on the wall behind the woman shattered into jagged shards.

Gabrielle's eyes went wide as the largest piece flew across the room toward her.

And then her head fell off her body.

CHAPTER 1

YOU WOULD THINK it would be impossible to lose a large suitcase inside an apartment that was, itself, approximately the size of a large suitcase.

You would be wrong.

I'd searched my room, Mom's room, and my little brother Charlie's room (I'd had to sneak in, as things were still pretty tense after the morning's blueberry muffin incident), and had dug through the unpacked boxes in the living room — all with no luck.

"Mom!" I yelled. "Did Dad take all the suitcases?"

My mother was in her bedroom, trying to condense a walk-in closet's worth of clothes into her new closet, which was about three feet wide. "No," she said. "We have the big blue one and the little brown one."

"I've looked everywhere." I leaned against her doorjamb. "I can't find them."

Mom sighed. There were dark circles under her eyes, and she still had to work the closing shift at Macy's that night.

"Never mind," I said. "I'll call Dad."

"I know where they are."

The voice came from behind me. I turned around to see Charlie standing at the end of the hallway, smirking.

"Where?" I asked.

"Why should I tell you?"

"Because," I replied, "if I don't have a suitcase, I can't go to Paris tomorrow, and then you're stuck with me for all of Spring Break instead of having a nine-day sister-free bonanza."

"Good point," he said. "They're down in the garage."

I narrowed my eyes, trying to figure out if he was messing with me.

"In the storage closet," he added. "In the very far-back corner."

My heart fluttered.

"Have fun," he said, heading for his bedroom.

"Wait!" I stepped into his path. "Have I ever told you what a good brother you are?"

"Nice try." He moved around me. "Watch out for spiders."

"Charlie!" I cried. "Come on, please. I'd do it for you."

He stood up to his full height, five foot six — an inch taller than me, even though I was sixteen and he was fourteen. Suddenly, he looked like a young man and not just a twerpy boy. And when he spoke, he sounded world-weary, like he was the older sibling. "You would not, Colette."

Well, okay, no, I probably wouldn't. But admitting that

wouldn't help. "I'm sorry I ate your muffin, okay? I'll buy you more as soon as I'm back from France. Please —"

Charlie shrugged, slipping past me into his room. "It's not my problem you're scared of the dark."

"I'm not scared of the dark!" I yelled at his closed door. Then I stood in the silent hallway for a minute, formulating a new plan. "Hey, Mom?"

"Forget it, Colette," she said. "You'll be fine. It's not that dark down there."

Anger flared up inside me like an explosion. "I am *NOT* scared of the dark!"

Really — I'm *not* afraid of the dark. I'm just afraid of a lot of places that happen to *be* dark. What I'm scared of — what I hate — is feeling confined. Elevators, windowless basements, overcrowded public spaces . . .

And storage closets.

Five minutes later, I stood in the underground parking garage, looking at the cluster of doors.

The ceiling was low and seemed to sag — in fact, the whole garage felt like it was pressing in on me. The sound of water plinking into shallow puddles echoed from the far reaches of the structure, and the waiting cars were like sleeping monsters guarding the darkness.

A train whistle sounded outside on the tracks that ran about a hundred feet from our building. The sound, low and mournful, lent a chilling loneliness to my surroundings.

The key was warm and slippery in my clammy grip.

"Be rational, Colette," I said out loud.

You are a junior in high school. You are about to spend nine days in Paris, without your parents. You can handle one stupid little closet.

You know how, in fairy tales, the prince cuts his way through the deadly thorned vines, past piles of skeletons, to get to the dragon?

I felt like one of the skeletons.

The third door from the left had *203* written on it in what looked like goopy black nail polish. A gritty coating of rust on the knob turned my hand pinkish red, and the door squealed in protest as I pulled it open and peered inside.

The storage area was about four feet wide and eight feet deep, with filthy cinderblock walls. The sides were piled high with boxes and plastic storage tubs, leaving a narrow path all the way to the back. I stared at the suitcases, which were at the very bottom of the stack at the very far end.

Okay, no.

I would just have to pack what I could into my carry-on and do without a few extraneous items. Like, you know, shoes.

I considered begging Mom to come down, but that was basically hopeless. She was sympathetic to my claustrophobia up to the point where she decided I was just working myself up over nothing.

Dad would get it out for me. I felt a little twinge of guilt as I thought about my father. I still hadn't broken the news to Mom that I planned to spend the summer in New York City with him . . . and maybe stay there for senior year, too.

And then I heard a noise behind me.

Scritch, scritch, scritch . . .

I swung around and looked for its source — for the first time in my life actually *hoping* I'd see a rodent of some kind. But there was nothing, and immediately I imagined that someone had followed me down here and was hiding between the parked cars, watching me . . . waiting to pounce.

I could hardly breathe.

Scritch, scritch, scritch.

"Hello?" I called. "Who's there?"

And then I heard breathing. Soft but unmistakable, echoing lightly off the low ceiling.

Only the fear of being murdered could have made me do what I did next — I plunged into the closet and pulled the door shut behind me. Then I stood in the dark, holding on to the doorknob and wondering if there was a way to lock the door from the inside. If not, I'd just made things worse for myself.

A wave of nausea hit me, and I doubled over. Flashes of light seemed to blast through my peripheral vision, a familiar symptom of what I was feeling — pure panic.

Outside, footsteps approached. Someone pulled on the door from the other side.

I pulled back with all my strength.

"Colette?"

I paused. Was it a trap?

"Charlie?" I said.

"What are you doing?" he asked.

I let him open the door, and then I ran out of the darkness, plowing into him. I was on the verge of tears, gasping for air.

"Be careful," I said. "There's someone down here."

"Are you kidding?" He snorted.

Then I realized that there was no psycho on the loose — it had been my brother all along. I went limp in his arms.

"Jeez, it was only a joke," he said, holding me up. I could tell from the sound of his voice that he felt bad. Well, good. He *should* feel bad. "I came down to help you."

Now that the fear had passed, I was just humiliated. "Some help," I muttered.

"Move over," he said, wedging himself into the narrow opening. When he reached the back, he started unpiling things from the top of the luggage.

"Take this," he said, handing me an old cardboard box. "I'm afraid it'll fall apart."

I took it from him and watched as he unearthed the big blue suitcase and dragged it out of the closet.

He relocked the door. "Are you going to stand there all afternoon? Go."

I went. "It was nice of you to come down."

He shrugged.

"I'll do something for you soon," I said, smiling at him. "You scratch my back, I'll scratch yours."

My brother's mouth twisted in disgust. "You don't get it, do you?"

"Get what?"

The rattling of the suitcase wheels went quiet as Charlie stopped and looked at me. "You don't do nice things for people because you want to get something from them. You just do nice things to be nice."

"Yeah," I said. "And you're nice so people will be nice back to you. That's how the world works, Chuck."

"Your world, maybe." He rolled his eyes and started moving again. "Knowing your friends, I guess it's not a surprise."

I bristled at the mention of my best friends, Hannah Norstedt and Pilar Sanchez. "At least my friends have lives that don't revolve around role-playing games," I snapped.

"Oh, right. Hannah's and Pilar's lives just revolve around their cars and their bottomless credit cards."

I could have said his lame friends could pool all their money and be able to afford maybe the hood ornament off Hannah's Mercedes.

But I didn't — partly because he'd come down to help me, and partly because, now that we were poor, poverty jokes didn't seem all that funny. Besides, my insistence on staying at my private all-girls school, Saint Margaret's Academy, was possible only because Charlie had offered to leave Saint Bart's and go to public school (which is where he fell in with the War of Witchcraft people, or whatever it was called).

I followed him up the stairs. "So you're telling me that you came down here out of the goodness of your heart? That's actually kind of —"

Charlie glanced back at me, over his shoulder. "Not for you. For Mom. She was starting to guilt-trip herself."

Oh.

Not that we had the best sibling relationship, but I'd liked it better when I thought Charlie had helped for my sake, not for our mother's.

"Remember to send Mom a postcard as soon as you land," he said.

"I will."

"Seriously. I don't think you understand how important this trip is."

I turned to him in surprise. "This trip is the most important thing ever. How could I not understand?"

Had he not noticed the way I'd spent the past year thinking and talking of nothing else? How I'd switched to French after taking four years of Spanish, starting from scratch with a strange foreign language, just so I could qualify to go?

"I mean to *her*," he said. "Not everything is automatically about you. It's Mom's way of trying to make up for all the stuff that's happened."

"That's ridiculous." As if I blamed *Mom* that Dad had a midlife crisis and left her. As if I blamed her that we had to leave our old house and move into a cramped, dark little apartment. None of that was her fault . . . just like my wanting to go live with Dad wasn't my fault, right? First of all, given the choice, who in their right mind would choose Toledo, Ohio, over Manhattan? Second of all, I would actually be doing Mom and Charlie a favor — they'd have way more room if there were only two people living in the apartment.

"It's the truth." At the top of the stairs, Charlie set the bag down with a *thump*. "She's dying for you to have a good time."

"Well, that makes two of us." I held open the apartment door. "I'm dying, too."

He pulled the suitcase all the way into my room. As he

passed me on his way out, he looked down. "You're still holding that box."

I was. And it was a gross old box, too. The cardboard had gotten oily and soft with age.

"Just leave it in your room, and we'll put it back when we put the suitcase away," he said.

"Okay," I said. "And, Charlie —"

I was going to say *thanks*.

But he'd already closed his bedroom door.

*   *   *

Not to brag or anything, but I'm pretty ninja-like when it comes to putting together outfits and packing. So about twenty minutes later, I was finished. I moved the suitcase to the side of my room and started to prep my carry-on. First, I found the printout of our trip itinerary and read it over for possibly the billionth time.

Day 1	Afternoon — Arrive Charles de Gaulle International Airport. Check into Hôtel Odette. 8:00 p.m. — Dinner at Café Odette
Day 2	9:00 a.m. — Day trip to Château de Versailles
Day 3	9:00 a.m. — Le Louvre Afternoon — Free time
Day 4	9:00 a.m. — Basilique de Saint-Denis 1:00 p.m. — Notre Dame
Day 5	10:00 a.m. — La Conciergerie 1:00 p.m. — Champs-Élysées
Day 6	9:00 a.m. — The Catacombs 1:00 p.m. — Musée Rodin
Day 7	9:00 a.m. — Musée d'Orsay 1:00 p.m. — The Eiffel Tower

| Day 8 | 9:00 a.m. — Sacré Coeur
Afternoon — Free time |
| Day 9 | 4:00 p.m. — Depart for Charles de Gaulle Airport |

I felt a surge of excitement as I folded the sheet of paper and stashed it in my carry-on. The flight was the next morning, and I couldn't wait.

The old cardboard box was on my desk and as I reached past it for my camera battery, I caught a glimpse of the writing on the side:

Colette FOR LUCILLE *Leo*

Colette was my father's grandmother — I'd been named after her. Lucille was my father's mother. And Leo was my dad. So this box had been given to my grandmother from *her* mother, though it looked like Grandma had never even opened it. And then when she died five years ago, it got passed to Dad, who'd also never found the time to open it.

I wondered if I should call my father and get his permission to root through the box, but then I figured he wouldn't care if I just peeked inside to see if there was anything interesting.

Disappointment set in quickly. Great-Grandma Colette, who had apparently been sort of fabulous, had saved a bunch of mementos — flyers from nightclubs, cocktail napkins from restaurants, and ticket stubs from Broadway plays. But it was all "you had to be there" kind of stuff. I almost gave up, but I was too close to the bottom to quit. I lifted a stack of travel brochures and set them aside.

The very last thing left was a flat jewelry case.

The outside had once been sumptuous dark-red silk, but now it was worn and patchy, leaving a fine red fuzz on my fingertips. I opened the cover slowly, fighting the stiffness of the old hinges.

The inside was lined with black velvet, still thick and soft after who-knows-how-many years.

On the velvet lay a shining silver medallion with a tiny, intricate vine around its edge. At the top of the medallion was a simple hole where a black ribbon was looped, and in the center was an engraved key — the old-fashioned kind, with big square teeth. The round part of the key had a cutout in the shape of a flower with six spiky petals.

I delicately lifted the medallion and looked at the writing on the other side. I held it closer to the light, but all I could really understand was one word:

Iselin.

My last name.

I've spent enough time browsing antique and vintage stores to know that I'd stumbled across something unique — the kind of thing they keep locked up in the glass display cabinet by the register, not just sitting out with the old belts and costume jewelry.

This had obviously belonged to someone really important — or at least really rich.

It rested in the center of my palm, the size of a fifty-cent piece, heavy and cold.

I knew my father's family had come from France. Big deal — everybody comes from somewhere. But maybe being from an *important* French family would get me enough coolness points to make up for the fact that I had suddenly been plunked into a life of abject poverty.

I had a vision of myself visiting a museum in Paris, and an old curator spotting the medallion hanging around my neck. He'd get really excited and then tell me that my family had been noble and prominent. And the rest of the girls on the trip would gather around, and even though they'd be too cool to act impressed, inside, they all secretly would be.

Even Hannah.

Just last week I'd found the perfect white spring dress at the Salvation Army. I'd been planning to wear it with my black blazer and a pair of well-worn cowboy boots I'd picked up at a garage sale. All the outfit really needed was some little piece to tie it all together.

And I was holding that piece in my hand.

CHAPTER 2

"YOU'RE SURE YOU have everything?" My mother held my arm so tightly that my fingers were going numb. "Phone cards? Emergency credit card? Passport?"

Gently, I loosened her grip. "I checked three times before we left."

The unloading zone bustled with travelers. Mom's head whipped back and forth as she watched the crowds move by.

I took advantage of her distraction to pry off her hand completely. "Come on, Mom. You've had sixteen years to prepare for the day you'd have to set me free to walk fifty feet through an airport unattended."

"What if you can't find your teacher?"

"She's right there." I pointed through the window. "See? Surrounded by all those girls whose mothers *let them go inside*."

Mom's forehead creased. "I'm sorry, honey."

"Don't be sorry," I said. "Just unhand me, woman."

I'd intended to break the news about my summer with Dad at dinner the night before, but the right moment hadn't come along. So all the way to the airport, I'd had the words on the tip of my tongue, goading myself to stop being such a baby and spit them out.

And here was my chance. I opened my mouth to speak.

My mother interrupted me, her brown eyes shining. "Oh, Colette. I'm so excited for you. A week in Paris . . . just think of all the amazing things you're going to experience."

I almost said something sarcastic about how dopey she was being, but I choked the words back. Instead, I threw my arms around her and kissed the side of her head. To my horror, the beginnings of tears nipped at the back of my eyeballs.

"I love you so much," she said.

"I love you, too — now go, before you get a parking ticket!" I gave her a gentle push toward the car and turned away before she drove off.

Swallowing the lump in my throat as I walked through the automatic doors, I thought about Mom's excitement, her certainty that this trip would broaden my horizons.

Cheesy or not, I was sure it would be true.

I just had a feeling, down deep at the base of my stomach, or my heart or something, that going to Paris would change the way I looked at the world . . .

That it might even change my life. Forever.

*　　*　　*

I checked in with Madame Mitchell, our French teacher and chaperone, and then looked around for my friends.

"Hannah and Pilar upgraded to first class," Madame Mitchell said, seeing me scan the group. "They went through the priority security line, and they're waiting at Starbucks."

I nodded, trying to hide my disappointment. It wasn't a surprise or anything. Hannah and Pilar had probably never flown economy in their lives, and I couldn't expect them to do it for my sake. It was just kind of a bummer because it meant I'd be sitting in the back of the plane with a bunch of people I didn't know very well.

Once we got through security, we all swung by Starbucks. Hannah and Pilar sat at a little table, engrossed in their phones. Physically, my two friends couldn't have been more different. Hannah was tall and thin (like "Are you sure you don't have a size double-zero in the stockroom?" thin), with straight white-blonde hair, a perfectly turned-up nose, and sleepy green eyes. Pilar was five foot nothing, she would never be smaller than a size ten, and she had long, curly black hair and wide, anxious brown eyes.

They both lived in houses big enough to hold practically my entire apartment complex. They had both gotten fancy German cars for their sixteenth birthdays. They both had wardrobes big enough to stock a Banana Republic store (except they'd never shop somewhere so pedestrian).

Hannah's dad was the CFO of some gigantic corporation that sold everything from corn to military tanks. There were pictures on their living room wall of him with presidents and senators. He always "knew someone who knew someone," and Hannah had never heard the word *no* in her life.

Pilar's mother was Mariana Sanchez, a famous pop star who'd had a bunch of number-one songs from when my parents were in high school and then retired to Ohio with a herd of Grammys and gazillions of dollars. Pilar — whom I liked to call "Peely," to Hannah's supreme mortification — had inherited her mom's musical talent. She could play any instrument, and she had perfect pitch. The only thing she lacked was the stick-thin pop-star body, a point Mrs. Sanchez never let her forget.

Socially, they were la crème de la crème at Saint Margaret's Academy. Me? I'd been a nobody until the end of sophomore year, but at the start of junior year I'd managed to become friendly with Pilar. Then, over the next few months, Hannah had accepted me. By Christmas break, I was lumped in as one of their group. Now everyone in the whole school thought of us as an inseparable threesome. . . .

Except me. There was just something about Hannah that made you feel like your contract was always up for cancellation with her. But even with that ever-present uncertainty, the benefits of being her friend far outweighed the negatives.

Rationally, I knew I was a good match for them. Smarter than Pilar, but not as smart as Hannah. Thinner than Peely, but not as thin as Hannah (nobody was as thin as Hannah). My wavy strawberry-blonde hair fell past my shoulders, and my blue eyes were framed by short, unremarkable lashes. My face was heart-shaped, with a smattering of pale freckles across my nose and cheeks. People called me "cute" a lot more than they called me "beautiful." In short, I was pretty enough to hang with Hannah . . . but not pretty enough to upstage her.

"Ladies, we're all going to stick together as a group, starting now," Madame Mitchell said. At school, she was always put-together, but today, her brownish-gray hair had fallen out of its clip, and her reading glasses were sliding down her nose. She already looked like she'd been following a bunch of teenagers around for a week. "Everyone find a buddy."

There were nine girls, and Hannah and Pilar were obviously taken. I looked around and locked eyes with Audrey Corbett, inwardly groaning.

Audrey was nice, but if I had to be her buddy, I'd never hear the end of it from Hannah. There was this stubborn clueless-ness about Audrey that was totally bewildering in someone so smart. Take her outfit. She was traveling to Paris, France, for heaven's sake — wearing a pair of gray sweatpants and an Ohio State University sweatshirt. Her skin, a dark, rich brown, didn't need foundation or concealer — but would it have killed her to put on a little lip gloss every now and then? Her hair was divided into two Afro-puffs, which might have been cute if it had been at all ironic or self-aware — or if she were seven years old. But no, you just got the idea that she had been looking for the fastest way to put up her hair. She wore a pair of tortoise-shell plastic-framed glasses and — most appallingly — ginormous white tennis shoes.

But if we were stuck with each other, then so be it. We'd been on the Academic Games team together freshman year, so I knew Audrey's personality was better than her fashion sense.

"Hey, Aud, want to be my buddy?" Brynn Peterson, wearing her hair in two long brown braids, snuck up beside her.

Something flickered across Audrey's eyes as they met mine. . . . Was it haughtiness? Defiance?

Whatever. Let her and Brynn frolic around Paris together looking like second graders.

I turned to find someone better.

No luck.

"Audrey and Brynn . . ." Madame Mitchell made a note in her book and looked down at me. "So I guess we're buddies, Colette."

"Oh, joy," I said. And then, realizing how that must have sounded, I opened my mouth to retract it.

"Don't bother." Her voice was flat as she clicked her pen shut and put it in her pocket. "It's written all over your face."

On the walk to the gate, Pilar and Hannah came up and flanked me.

"Here." Pilar handed me a cup. "I got you a latte."

"It's a trap," Hannah said. "She's trying to load you up on caffeine so you can't sleep on the plane."

"It's the best way to beat jet lag!" Pilar protested. "Staying awake on the flight is the only way to feel human when we land."

I glanced at Hannah, who shook her head, her green eyes wide with warning.

"Thanks," I said, taking the coffee.

"Oh, you're not going to drink it. I can tell." Pilar grabbed the cup back and dropped it into the nearest trash can.

I laughed, but inside I was kind of horrified that she'd thrown away a perfectly good six-dollar coffee.

She looped her arm through mine. "Aren't you excited? Is this really your first time out of America?"

"It really is," I said.

"How is that possible?" Hannah asked. "I thought your family was going to Italy over Winter Break."

"That fell through," I said.

What I didn't say was that our Italy trip went *poof!* the day my parents' marriage went *poof!*

I'd never had to think about money in my life, but after my parents' divorce, it was suddenly a huge thing. When Dad first left and Mom was forced to get a job at the Royal Hills Mall, I'd just started hanging out with Hannah and Peely, and at the time I'd been too embarrassed to say anything about it. Then, when we had to sell our house and move into our shoe-box apartment, I still hadn't breathed a word about it to my friends. The hardest part was, so much time had passed that it would be weird to say anything now. Mom spent the whole year scrimping and working extra shifts just to send me to Paris, and I had to pretend like it was no big deal.

"No Italy trip and no car," Hannah said. "I think your parents are trying to torture you."

"Can we not talk about my parents? I want to think about Paris." We were literally minutes from boarding. My stomach tingled with anticipation.

"Exactly," Hannah said. "Who wants to travel with their family, anyway? We'll have way more fun by ourselves."

She smiled then, her thousand-watt smile that made you feel

like you were being bathed in warmth. Hannah was the most incredible combination of beautiful, witty, and nice — when being nice worked to her advantage, that is. It was what made her so popular and sought-after.

And I got to be her friend. Sometimes it kind of blew my mind.

We stood in a jittery group at the gate, and Pilar started listing off all the qualities of the ideal French men she was sure we'd meet: artistic, sensitive, brooding, and, most of all, absolutely mind-bogglingly handsome with soul-twisting gorgeous accents.

"You make them sound like vampires," I said. "You really think we'll have a chance to meet guys?"

"You have to make your own opportunities," Hannah said.

"Actually," Peely said, "Madame Mitchell said we have a new tour guide this year — since the old one retired — and he's in college and he's supposed to be super cute."

Hannah looked disbelieving. "You're trusting a teacher's taste in men? She's like forty."

"Just because she's old doesn't mean she can't tell the difference between cute and not cute," Pilar huffed. "Watch. He'll be adorbs."

"In that case, I call dibs," Hannah said. Hannah always got dibs.

"You can have the men — I'm not going to Paris to meet anyone," I said. "I'm going for the . . . Frenchness."

"Then the men will all be drawn to you by your captivating aloofness." Pilar lifted her nose in the air and tossed her curls.

Hannah looked mildly annoyed by the suggestion that anyone other than her could captivate a man. "We'd better go. They just called first class."

Pilar grinned and leaned in to air-kiss my cheeks. "Bon voyage, Colette! See you in Paris!"

II

PIERRE BEAUCLERC SAT *at the sidewalk café, drumming his fingers on the table as his father droned on about family honor, pride, and keeping up appearances. Apparently, "borrowing" a parked police car and driving it around the city didn't fit into his father's idea of what the heir of the Beauclerc family should be doing with his time.*

Pierre's tie felt like it was strangling him. He loosened it with a sigh. He'd already been lectured that morning, by the judge (who, after accepting a bribe from Monsieur Beauclerc to go easy on his son, decided to at least make it look like he was being tough on the young man). Why did these useless people think their words mattered to someone like him?

He was twenty years old, tall and slender, with silky black hair. He looked like a movie star, and he not only knew it but also used it to his advantage on a regular basis.

He snapped back to attention as his father stopped talking. All the old man required from Pierre was a few bland apologies and an insincere promise that it would never happen again. They'd been through this a half-dozen times, for a half-dozen different offenses, and though his father always threatened to cut off Pierre's allowance, it had never happened — and never would happen. Pierre knew his father actually admired his brazenness, and, after all, the law could always be bought.

Now he smiled winningly at his father, called him Papa, and cracked a joke that made the old man grin, recalling his own youth.

Pierre and his father finished their cups of café au lait and left some coins on the table. With a good-natured hug, the two parted. Pierre paused to check his reflection in the plate-glass window, pleased with everything about his appearance except for a dark stain on the skin of his wrist; some filthy person must have brushed against him at the courthouse. He'd wash it off later.

He cut through an alleyway toward the parking lot where he'd left his motorcycle, whistling as he walked, kicking litter out of his path and then imagining how handsome he looked doing so. If only there were a pretty girl around to watch.

He didn't see the woman who stood in his path until he'd already kicked an empty bottle in her direction.

"Oh!" he exclaimed, preparing to shout at her for being so careless.

But then he saw two things at once: first, that the woman wore a huge, elaborate dress — like something out of a history book, and second . . .

. . . that the bottle he'd kicked passed right through the dress, landing on the ground behind her with a clink.

"Qui êtes-vous?" he demanded. In his fear, he lashed out. "Vous avez l'air ridicule!"

She didn't answer. She only stared at him. He'd been wrong, of course — if anything, she was the opposite of ridiculous.

Pierre felt a chill travel up his spine, and for reasons he couldn't understand, he wished he hadn't insulted her. Her silence was terrible, and yet Pierre felt that were she to speak, it would be even more terrible.

Then, at last, she did speak.

"Le fils de la famille Beauclerc," she whispered.

Confused, Pierre said, "Oui?" He was the son of the Beauclerc family. But how did the strange woman know that?

He took a step back, glancing over his shoulder to see if there was an easy place to run. He needed to get away from her.

He was in luck. Just to his left was an old metal fire escape, attached to the side of an abandoned building. He ran toward it, intending to leap up and grab hold of the ladder.

But his foot landed on the bottle he'd kicked, and he slipped and fell backward. He found himself on his back, staring up helplessly at the woman in the dress.

After gazing down at him, she moved away.

Pierre breathed a sigh of relief before he noticed that the entire fire escape above him had come loose from the wall of the building.

And he had just a moment to realize what was happening before the rusted old handrail dropped down and separated his head cleanly from his body.

CHAPTER 3

I'M IN PARIS.

Just thinking the words made me feel like I'd been waiting my whole life to be able to say them. Determined to savor every detail of the trip, I took a long, deep breath. . . .

Unfortunately, as we were standing in the shuttle bus pickup area at the airport, I got a lungful of French exhaust fumes.

The flight had been as agonizingly long as I'd suspected it would be. I'd been stuck in a middle seat between a girl who took approximately fifteen bathroom breaks and Madame Mitchell, who snored like a freight train. I hadn't been able to shut my eyes for more than twenty minutes at a time.

But none of that mattered. We had landed safely, pushed through the mobs in baggage claim, and were about to start our drive right into the heart of Paris.

"Now," Pilar said, stifling a yawn, "where are my delicious French men?"

"Oh, look, here's one for you," Hannah said. *"Yummy."*

The man in question was our van driver, who was neither mind-boggling nor soul-twisting. He was about nine hundred years old, shriveled and wrinkled with a massive fluffy white beard. On his head he wore a cable-knit cap, and his beady eyes watched us with a hefty dose of wariness as we clambered into the van.

"Everybody, she is in the vehicle?" he asked.

A chorus of yeses answered him.

"Oui, merci beaucoup," Madame Mitchell said in her clearest French-teacher voice, giving us all the stink-eye.

As this was a trip for students of the various French classes, chaperoned by the French teacher, we were supposed to be immersing ourselves in the language. But we were all too tired to even think or speak in English, much less French.

The van doors slammed shut.

"Are you all right, Colette?" Hannah asked. "You look a little gray."

I *felt* a little gray. The combined effects of lack of sleep, an airplane-quality turkey sandwich, and being packed into a crowded van made my body buzz with anxiety.

"Why don't we switch seats?" Pilar asked. "I've seen Paris before."

I was on the verge of agreeing when Hannah spoke up. "It's not like she doesn't have nine days here. No one can be that excited about seeing the side of a highway."

"Yeah, thanks anyway," I said to Peely. "But switching places would be a logistical nightmare."

As we drove on, it seemed Hannah was right — from what I could see of it, the highway was pretty much like an American highway, complete with unimpressive views of normal-looking buildings and untended grassy hillsides.

But when we passed into the city, the whole world changed. I momentarily forgot to feel ill, craning my neck in the hopes of glimpsing some famous French sights.

"À la droite, la Seine," Madame Mitchell called from the front seat. We all looked out the right side of the van, where the River Seine cut through the middle of the city. I'd seen it a million times in movies, usually in a scene where the two main characters take a romantic nighttime stroll. But that was nothing like seeing it for real — the way the light reflected off the choppy water, sunken between two centuries-old stone walls and crossed by magnificent bridges with carved stone railings and ornate sculptures.

"Et à la gauche, la cathédrale de Notre-Dame."

On the left loomed Notre Dame, the massive cathedral. Its two towers stretched through a foggy mist toward the cloudy sky.

The van came to a jerky stop, sending all of us slamming into one another.

I tried to see out the front window, but there were too many heads in the way. Girls in the rows ahead of us strained to look, and finally Audrey turned around.

"It's a roadblock," she said. "Police cars."

"Oh, goody," Hannah said. "Stuck like sardines in a can. What a way to spend our first night in Paris."

"We'll be moving again soon," Madame Mitchell said.

But we weren't. We sat in the same spot for nearly a half hour. The air inside the van was getting stuffier. My breath was growing quicker, and my fingers were ice cold.

Madame Mitchell looked a little green, too. She leaned forward. *"Pardon, monsieur,"* she said to the driver. *"Savez-vous pourquoi nous nous sommes arrêtés?"*

The driver, who didn't seem interested in participating in our language immersion process, replied in English. "My wife call. She say there is another murder."

The word *murder* settled over the van for a moment, until Hannah broke the silence.

"Wait — *another* murder?" she asked. "When was the first one?"

"Last night," the old man said. "This one is same, my wife say."

The blasé tone of his voice sent a chill up my spine.

"The same how?" In her curiosity, Madame Mitchell forgot to *parle français*.

"The same for the head," he replied cheerily.

The van was quiet.

"What about the head?" Hannah asked finally.

"The head." He drew one finger across his throat, like a knife slicing it. "She is cut off."

My heart stopped beating for a second.

Pilar's eyes were as big as tennis balls. "She is?" she asked faintly.

Hannah had hauled out her phone and was looking online, thanks to the gazillion-dollar international data plan her father had shelled out for. She and Peely were the only girls in our group with working phones.

"Oh, here it is," Hannah said, and read out loud. "'Serial killer on the loose in Paris . . . Gabrielle Roux, up-and-coming model . . . Pierre Beauclerc, son of . . . some-French-name-I-can't-pronounce Beauclerc.'"

"A model?" Pilar asked. "That's terrible."

Audrey peered at us, one eyebrow raised. "Only ugly people deserve to be killed?"

Hannah waved her off.

Alarmed voices rose up like a bunch of yelping puppies. Brynn wore an expression of worried disbelief. "Are we going to get . . . like . . . murdered?" she whispered.

Madame Mitchell turned around. "Calm yourselves, ladies. I'm sure we're all quite safe. However, this is a good reminder of how important it is to stay together as a group."

"Or you'll get murdered," Hannah added.

"No!" the teacher said. "*Honestly*, Ms. Norstedt."

Hannah gave me a wicked grin, and I couldn't help grinning back.

That was the thing about Hannah — she could be really funny.

But that was also the thing about me when I was around Hannah. I laughed at her jokes, even when some deep, dark part of me didn't think they were very funny at all.

* * *

Eventually, we detoured across a bridge and turned onto a road that led us into Saint-Germain-des-Prés, the neighborhood where we'd be staying. It was made up of dozens of little avenues, all connected like a spiderweb.

It was everything I'd pictured Paris to be — chic boutiques, little cafés, flower shops, and open counters selling baguettes. The narrow cobblestone roads bustled with people who hopped onto the itty-bitty sidewalks to avoid our van.

We pulled to a stop on a tiny side street, hardly more than an alley.

"Hôtel Odette," the driver announced with a weary sigh.

"You get the idea that these were the worst hours of his life," Pilar said.

"I bet he'd rather quit than drive us back to the airport," I said.

"I know being in the van is great and all," Hannah said, "but could you two please move?"

After I got my suitcase, I stopped to look around.

The buildings were made of stone or smooth plaster and held little storefronts under apartments with curtains fluttering in their windows. I'd never been to a real city where you could just run downstairs and find grocery stores or a café. It felt so connected, so alive, as if the place were feeding off the energy of the people who lived in it.

And the people were magical.

I could have sat on a bench and watched them for hours — there was just something so perfectly *Parisian* about them. Even the little old ladies walking their tiny dogs had an extra "something" — a scarf or a pair of red boots or a baby-blue trench coat. The women dressed with great care but not the faintest trace of fussiness — they never looked overdone or like they were trying too hard. I was immediately inspired and ran through a mental list of the clothes I'd brought, planning modifications to look less like a girl from Ohio and more like a young mademoiselle from the sixth *arrondissement*.

"Nice, right?" Pilar looked up at the buildings around us. "This is my favorite neighborhood in the whole city."

"I love it," I said. It was mid-March, and the air was still crisp and cool, with a brisk breeze coming from the river. It ruffled my hair and brushed against my cheeks.

"I knew you would," she said, leaning her head on my shoulder. "I always thought you were like a French person. You have that *je ne sais whatever*."

I *felt* like a French person. I closed my eyes and inhaled the mingled scents of spring flowers and smoky sweetness from the tea shop two doors down. Even though I was in a foreign country halfway across the world, I felt weirdly like I belonged here . . . like I'd come home.

"Come inside, girls," Madame Mitchell said. "Let's get settled."

Passing through an elaborate wrought-iron gate, we entered the tiny hotel. Inside were marble floors and fancy old chairs. To the right was a small restaurant with a sign that read CAFÉ ODETTE, and to the left was the reception desk. Madame Mitchell made a beeline for it.

"Norstedt, Sanchez, Iselin," she called a minute later. "Come get your room keys."

We were the only people staying three to a room — but that was because Hannah's dad had decided that only the penthouse suite was good enough for his little princess. I'd be sleeping on the pullout sofa, but I didn't mind. I wasn't paying any extra, so I didn't have any reason to expect a bedroom of my own.

The clerk held out a little envelope marked *501*, with three keycards inside, and Hannah snatched it from her.

"Meet in the café at eight for dinner," Madame Mitchell said. "Peterson and Corbett, come get your keys."

Hannah, Pilar, and I started for the elevator — something I hadn't considered. The penthouse was on the fifth floor. My mind raced for an excuse to take the stairs, but I couldn't think of one.

Finally, the door slid open. My heart sank even farther — it was the smallest elevator I'd ever seen, about the size of a bathroom stall.

"Come on," Peely said. "We'll squish."

I hesitated.

"Colette?" Hannah said.

Just then, I heard voices behind me. Audrey and Brynn were rolling their bags over, talking animatedly about the city. I half-stepped out of their way, and they got into the elevator before noticing that I was standing there.

"Oh, sorry," Audrey said, seeing me. "We'll get off and wait."

"Nah, forget it." I rolled my bag over and shoved it in with the four of them. "Can you just get my bag, Peely? I'll take the stairs."

"Sure," Pilar said.

I took a second to catch my breath, and then I started the long climb.

When I reached the top, Pilar stuck her head out of a door and waved. She'd left my suitcase in the hall, near the elevator, so I took it with me. Still panting, I dropped onto the sofa.

"That's why you're so thin, Colette," Hannah said approvingly. "That, and you don't just snack on whatever's sitting around."

Pilar had already unwrapped a piece of chocolate from the fancy welcome basket on the coffee table. When Hannah turned away, she tossed the chocolate into the trash can. "Let's explore," she said.

The penthouse was gorgeous, fit for a president or a queen. There were two bedrooms, each with a king-size bed piled with lush covers and overstuffed pillows, and its own bathroom, updated with gleaming white tiles and modern chrome fixtures. The living area was huge, with an additional bathroom off to the side and a beautiful flowered couch that converted to a pullout bed — the one I'd be using.

It was incredible. And Hannah and Pilar, used to being fabulously wealthy, moved around it like they owned the place.

While I, as usual, felt like a complete fraud.

*   *   *

The cost of the trip included meals from the *prix-fixe* (fixed-price) menu in the hotel's café. This was great for me, since I wouldn't have to spend every meal thinking about cost. But for Hannah, who never stopped to think about the *prix* of anything, much less care if it was *fixe*-d or not, this was a fact worth sighing over.

"So say a person *didn't* want to drown herself in fat and carbs?" she said, staring dejectedly at the menu. "What then?"

"I'm sure you can order from the regular menu," I said.

"Yeah — *if* a waiter would ever bother to come by," she replied. "I meant to warn you, Colette. The service in France is dismal. And the waiters hate Americans."

Our waiter wasn't dismal, nor did he seem to hate us — that is, until Hannah started bossing him around. Then he gazed down at us with a glare of disdain and took our orders without even the slightest hint of a smile. When he set our plates down with a series of unceremonious *thunk*s, I gazed at the food.

I'd ordered a spinach and cheese quiche. Mom made quiches sometimes because they were pretty simple — a bunch of eggs in a pie crust.

But, with all due respect to my mother's cooking, her quiches were nothing like the one in front of me. This one was orangey golden, its surface a perfectly burnt brown, flecked with the green of the spinach. The crust was crispy but buttery. I cut a slice and took a bite.

"Oh," I said, my mouth full of food. The rich salty, cheesy flavor hit my tongue. "Oh my word."

"Is it good?" Pilar asked, eyes wide. She'd let Hannah peer-pressure her into ordering a salad.

I scooped a bite onto my fork and handed it to her. When she popped it into her mouth, her eyes closed, and she made a happy little *hum* sound.

"You two act like you've never seen food before," Hannah said, carving at the grilled fish on her plate.

"I haven't," I said. "Not food like this."

She looked at me archly. "Just be careful — you don't want to fly home with your belly hanging over your waistband."

"My belly already hangs over my waistband," Pilar said. "Can I have another bite?"

I put half the quiche on a bread plate and handed it across to her, and we ate in near silence, relishing the flavor. Hannah clearly disapproved, but she didn't say another word about it.

Even she couldn't resist the dessert plate made up of cookies and *macarons*, colorful French pastries with a sweet filling sandwiched between two fluffy discs. Delicious and completely addictive. And then the waiter brought over a tray of cheese — soft, melty, creamy cheese that practically collapsed on itself when you sliced it — and we all ate that, too.

By the time the meal was done, Hannah had the same food-glazed look in her eyes that Pilar and I did.

"I'm totally not sorry," I said, heading back toward the stairs.

"Me, neither," Peely said. "But I'm taking the elevator."

"Who am I kidding?" Hannah said, laughing. "I'm not sorry, either. I'll start my diet tomorrow."

When we got to the room, Hannah suggested we sneak out to some local cafés. But Pilar was already changing into her pajamas, and I couldn't stop yawning. So we decided to call it a night, and a few minutes later, I was snuggled under the covers of the pullout couch.

Despite the fact that I hadn't slept in more than a day, I lay awake for a while, staring at the ceiling. *The French ceiling*, I thought. I didn't want to waste one minute of my trip not remembering that I was in Paris — that the food I ate was Parisian food, that the people I met were actual French people, and that the ground I walked on was the most magical and romantic ground in the world.

The only thing that wasn't absolutely perfect was a tiny, nagging sense of unease about something — but I couldn't put my finger on what it was. So I turned onto my side and closed my eyes, resolving to put any unnamed worries out of my mind for the next eight days.

CHAPTER 4

"WHO ARE WE waiting on?" Madame Mitchell asked.

We were in the hotel lobby, ready to walk to the Saint-Michel station, where we'd catch a commuter train to our first official French destination: the royal palace at Versailles.

"Hannah and Pilar," Audrey said. "Surprise, surprise."

Although the way Audrey presented herself to the world physically was cringe-worthy, you had to admire the way she spoke her mind without worrying who she ticked off.

Madame Mitchell turned to me, pushing her reading glasses up onto the bridge of her nose. "Any idea when they'll be down?"

As if I had any influence over them? I shrugged.

It had taken me about fifteen minutes to get ready — I wore a gray sweater, a cream-colored corduroy skirt, a pair of gray tights, and knee-high dark-brown walking boots. Based on what I'd observed on the street yesterday, I kept my hair simple, pulling it back in a low bun, and my makeup minimal — pale-brown eye shadow, light blush, and pink lips, no mascara. My only accessories were a pair of small silver hoop earrings and the medallion I'd found in the old box back home. It hung from its ribbon around my neck.

I'd tried to convince Hannah and Peely that French women were lower maintenance than your typical Ohio prep-school student, but they both insisted on performing their usual elaborate grooming rituals.

"Versailles has been there for almost four hundred years," Hannah said, plugging in her flat-iron as I hurried to load my day bag. "I'm sure it can wait another few minutes."

Finally, I gave up and left them so I could eat breakfast and meet the rest of the group by nine.

They came strolling into the lobby together at 9:14. Hannah had meticulously straightened her hair and wore gobs of makeup. She was in one of her doubtless brand-new outfits, a dark-blue minidress with a flared skirt and wide bell sleeves, paired with four-inch heels and a Marc Jacobs handbag the size of a small car.

Pilar had gelled her curly hair into a bazillion shiny ringlets and wore a pair of skinny jeans with a voluminous bright-pink poncho-style top. On her feet were three-inch cork platforms.

"Are you going to be able to walk in those shoes, girls?" Madame Mitchell asked, one eyebrow raised.

"I hope so," Pilar said. "These are the lowest heels I brought."

Hannah flashed a disdainful smile. "I can walk in anything."

But after two blocks, we all had to stop and stand around for ten minutes while Hannah went into a shoe store and bought a pair of knee-high flesh-toned boots. At least after that, we could move at a normal pace.

"This is ridiculous," Hannah said, coming up alongside me. "They need to repave these streets so people can wear real shoes."

"Oh, sure," I said. "Hundreds of years of history should totally get covered up so you can wear your Jimmy Choos."

I'd meant it as a joke, but her sharp look stung me like a hornet.

"They weren't Jimmy Choos, Colette," Pilar said, a gentle rebuke in her voice. "They were Louboutins."

"At least Pilar and I don't look like we just rolled out of bed," Hannah said hotly.

I didn't let the comment bother me too much. She was only angry because she'd been forced to admit she was wrong. Looking around, it was obvious that I blended in, while Pilar and Hannah stuck out like a pair of overdone poodles on a hiking trail.

"Where are we going, anyway?" Hannah's voice was sour.

"To the train station," Pilar said. "It's not much farther."

Hannah rolled her eyes. "Well, I've got my clodhoppers on now, so that doesn't matter."

I cast a glance at Hannah's "clodhoppers," which had probably cost four hundred dollars.

"I think we should turn left here," Audrey said. She was walking next to the teacher, directly in front of us.

Madame Mitchell followed Audrey's advice without a moment's hesitation, which made Hannah murmur, "*Loser*," under her breath. Pilar laughed, and I stayed silent — but I could tell by the way Audrey's shoulders went rigid that she'd heard what Hannah said.

* * *

The Saint-Michel station served both Paris's subway and the commuter rail lines. We stopped near the antique art deco METRO sign while Madame Mitchell looked around for our tour guide.

Someone tapped me on the shoulder, and I found myself looking into the bright-blue eyes of a guy a few years older than me.

"*Pardonnez-moi, mais c'est un groupe d'élèves étrangers qui fait une visite guidée,*" he said.

"What?" I said. "I mean . . . *pardon*?"

His eyebrows went up in surprise. "Oh, you are with the group. I thought you were French. I was telling you that you were mixed in with a bunch of Americans."

I stared at him, not knowing what to say. He thought I was French! An actual French person *thought I was French*. He gave me a quick smile and walked over to Madame Mitchell.

"Girls!" she said. She flapped a red handkerchief above her head. "*Écoutez! Voici votre guide!*"

"That's him? *That* is our hot French tour guide?" Hannah's face fell. "I want my money back."

It was true that this guy looked nothing like the way you'd imagine a dashing European university student to look. I guess we'd all been hoping for Pilar's vampire — someone tall and slim, with an angular jaw and sexy, unkempt hair. Someone pale and artistic. Someone French-looking. Our guide had tan skin and neatly groomed dark blond hair. He wore a red hoodie, a black T-shirt, and jeans. His shoes, gray Pumas, weren't bulky white sneakers, but they weren't exactly sleek leather oxfords, either.

"Mesdemoiselles," Madame Mitchell said, *"Je vous présente Jules Martin."*

Jules Martin. Only she pronounced his name *Zhool Mar-tahn.* Which, I had to admit, seemed a little exotic for the boy standing in front of us.

There was nothing wrong with him, exactly. He just looked kind of . . . American.

Hannah crossed her arms, disgusted. "What a waste of time."

"Bonjour, ladies," Zhool said.

"At least his accent is cute," Pilar whispered.

"So we're supposed to tour Paris with our eyes closed?" Hannah replied.

"Yes, definitely," I said. "That's the best way to see the city."

Zhool glanced over at us, and his expression made me suddenly ashamed. It was this glazed look that told me he wasn't seeing us as people but as a stereotypical group of silly teenage girls. I half-pivoted away from my friends, but it seemed like too little, too late.

He led us down into the station. I was nervous when I saw that we had to go underground, but soon we were in a wide-open terminal. Madame Mitchell passed out our tickets, and we all sat together on the top level of the train.

Hannah took the window seat (another unspoken Hannah rule: if there was a window seat, she got it) and Peely sat next to her. I went to the next row back and sat down, picking up a newspaper some commuter had left behind.

As I folded it, I caught a glimpse of the headline: BRUTALITÉ! L'ASSASSINAT DE DEUX ADOS DES FAMILLES DISTINGUÉES!

Right. The murders our van driver had mentioned. I shivered as I glanced at the photos of the two victims, Gabrielle Roux and Pierre Beauclerc. Gabrielle was gorgeous and Pierre was alluring in the way we'd hoped our tour guide would be. I squinted at their faces for a moment, trying to figure out why they looked familiar.

Then Pilar turned around. *"Comment allez-vous?"* she trilled.

"She's *bien,*" Hannah said, turning around us. "What else would she be?"

I tried to smile. *"Très bien."*

But I felt like the faces on the folded-up newspaper were watching me, all the way to Versailles.

* * *

It was a two-block walk from the train station to the palace. Jules spent much of it walking backward, talking about the French monarchy. "Versailles was originally a hunting lodge, until King Louis the Fourteenth — the Sun King — moved the royal court and French government here in 1682."

"Do I have lipstick on my teeth?" Hannah asked, tugging my sleeve.

"Of course, the monarchy was abolished during the Revolution, beginning in the year 1789, when the Jacobins stormed the palace and captured the royal family."

Pilar stopped for a second. "Hang on, there's a piece of gravel in my shoe."

"King Louis the Sixteenth and his queen, Marie Antoinette, were both imprisoned —"

"Have you ever been out here, Pilar?" Hannah asked.

"No, I —"

"*Shh*," I said to them both, and they were quiet.

"— beheaded," Jules said. He paused. "Any questions?"

"You don't seriously care about all this boring stuff, do you, Colette?" Hannah sniffed. "We're not supposed to be *learning*."

Jules went on talking, but I gave up trying to hear him. Instead, I let Pilar lean on me because her feet were already sore, and I held Hannah's purse while she dug through it looking for her eight-hundred-dollar Bulgari sunglasses.

But when we turned the corner and the palace came into view, even Hannah was struck dumb. It was as big as a shopping mall and covered in ornate stonework and metal accents, with wings the size of slightly smaller shopping malls on either side. In the center was a gigantic cobblestone courtyard that had once, Jules said, bustled with the activities of the royal court. Separating us from the palace grounds was a fence of gleaming yellow-gold, impossibly vivid against the pale-blue sky.

I looked from one side to the other and thought, *My family might have come here. Maybe they even walked on these same cobblestones.*

"In front of us is the main palace," Jules said. "Behind it lie the world-famous gardens. Farther off, you will find the private residences of the king and queen, Le Grand Trianon and Le Petit Trianon. Past Le Petit Trianon —"

His voice faded out of my mind as I tried to imagine what it would be like to cross the bumpy courtyard in a horse-drawn carriage, knowing that when the carriage stopped, there would be an army of servants to help you out . . . carry your things . . . bow down to you. . . .

I could practically feel the weight of a gown on my hips, a powdered wig on my head.

"Earth to Colette," Hannah said. "We have to go get our tickets."

"Right," I said, snapping out of it.

After we crossed through the metal detectors, Madame Mitchell gave us the okay to split up, but threatened us with certain death if we failed to meet back by the entrance at 5 p.m. on the dot.

"Are you listening, Hannah and Pilar?" she said.

"No," Hannah said under her breath. But Pilar nodded and gave the teacher a thumbs-up.

Then we were on our own. Hannah declared that first we would walk through the main house (only *she* could look at this place and call it a "house"), and then we'd venture onto the grounds when the day got a bit warmer.

The wings contained a series of rooms, one leading to the next like links on a chain. You could imagine someone spending a whole morning lounging on the brocade sofas and satin chairs as they waited for their audience with the king. The walls were covered in jewel-toned panels of silk, with huge oil paintings and carved marble busts everywhere.

Hannah didn't linger; she entered a room, looked around, and then started for the exit on the other side. I tried to take a few pictures, but it was hard to keep up with her pace.

Finally, we stopped at the entrance to a grand expanse of a hallway.

"The Hall of Mirrors," Pilar said, reading from her map.

The room was as long as a football field, lined with gigantic mirrors, soaring arched windows, and classical statues. Hanging from the ceiling must have been forty crystal chandeliers. Thinking of the work that would have gone into creating such a place made me feel still and silent.

It was a work of art, a masterpiece that you could actually walk right into. And once upon a time, people had lived here, walked through it as they discussed their dogs, or what they were having for dinner, or who'd looked fat in her ball gown the previous night.

I felt a tightening in my chest, a sharp spike of intense sadness — almost like nostalgia, except it was for a life I'd never lived.

"So," Hannah said, suddenly turning on us, "I didn't want to say anything before now, but I talked to my dad this morning, and everything's settled."

Settled?

I glanced at Pilar, to see if she was in on it — whatever *it* was. But she seemed lost, too.

Hannah wore the beginning of an incredibly self-satisfied smile. "Next Saturday" — she paused for what felt like five minutes — "we're coming to a party here."

A party? *Here?*

"Whose party?" Pilar asked.

"It's being given by the embassy," Hannah said. "And Dad's friend got us on the list. Just the three of us."

"No way," Pilar said. Then she gave a little hop and then a bunch of hops that ended with her arms around Hannah's shoulders in a tight hug. "No way, *no way*, are you serious?"

Hannah backed out of the embrace. "No, I'm joking. Of course I'm serious. It's Saturday night, and it's a costume ball, and we're going to have a limo come and pick us up at the hotel — I mean, whatever French people consider a limo."

Pilar stared at her, open-mouthed.

Hannah turned to me. "Well, Colette? *You* usually have something to say for yourself."

"It's . . . it's going to be amazing." I was still in shock. My voice sounded like someone had let the air out of it. "I can't believe it."

Hannah, gratified by my reaction, deigned to give me a warm smile.

"And only for my besties," she said. "Remember that. Because you guys are special."

Hidden in her compliment was a buried threat. Specialness, in Hannah's eyes, was something that could be taken away as easily as it had been granted.

One thing was for certain — I was going to spend the week on my best behavior.

We continued through the Hall of Mirrors. Knowing we would be coming back to Versailles for a gala event made every gleaming surface glow that much brighter. My skin prickled with excitement.

At one point, I found myself alone in a quiet stretch of the room, apart from Hannah, Pilar, and the tourist groups. I stopped and looked into the mirror, wondering how many countless people had stared into it over the centuries. I let my eyes focus on its clouded surface rather than my own face, and was overcome for a moment by a dizzy, disoriented feeling.

A flash of movement behind my reflection brought me back to the present, and I caught a glimpse of a woman in full period costume among the crowd. Her pale-pink dress was almost ridiculous in its proportions — wide from the front and narrow from the sides. It was impeccably adorned with ruffles and bows and gathers and lace. Her hair was piled high on her head, small tendrils hanging down, with a jaunty little V-shaped hat placed in such a way that three massive white feathers arced over her right shoulder.

"Wow," I whispered, turning to get a better look at her.

But when I scanned the room, she was gone.

Then a massive wave of tourists approached like a wall of water. I could imagine the poor woman trapped in the center of the group, mobbed by people eager to add *Picture with costume character* to their list of French accomplishments, as if this were Disney World.

Pilar called my name from the exit doorway, and I hurried to catch up.

I couldn't stop thinking about the woman as we continued through the rest of the main palace. And even though I knew Hannah would tell me to forget about her, I kept checking behind us to see if she'd reappeared.

I was desperate to see her up close. Not just because of her clothes, which I would love to get a closer look at . . .

But because of what I was almost positive I'd seen around her neck . . .

A medallion, just like mine.

*　*　*

The lush green grounds were as impressive as the palace itself. They stretched on as far as the eye could see. A wide gravel path ran down the center, bordered by trees whose branches were groomed into impossibly straight vertical lines. The view was broken up by spraying fountains and enormous ponds reflecting the sky.

Hannah, Pilar, and I stopped for lunch at a little open-air restaurant next to the reflecting pool. I ordered a ham-and-brie baguette, creamy cheese and salty ham sandwiched between two pieces of bread so crusty they scraped the roof of my mouth. As we ate, we saw the rest of our group pass by us and start down the side road that led to the Grand and Petit Trianons — the king and queen's private residences.

"I'm gonna hit the ladies' room," Hannah said.

Pilar stood up, too. And then they waited for me, as if we were chained together.

"I actually need to ask Madame Mitchell something," I said. "I'm going to try to catch them, okay? Then I'll double back."

"They must be halfway there by now," Hannah said. "Just wait for us at the Grand Trianon."

"Okay," I said, although that wasn't even where I wanted to go. "But what if I don't find you?"

"I'm going to pee my pants," Pilar said. "I think I drank too much coffee."

Hannah looked exasperated. "Colette, we'll either see you there or we won't. Now, if you'll excuse us, Pilar needs to potty."

I nodded and started down the path, trying to look like I was rushing to find our teacher.

But as soon as Hannah and Peely were out of sight, I slowed down and felt a small, triumphant glow.

Because I wasn't trying to catch up with anybody. I was just trying to get away from my friends. Managing to do so with Hannah's express permission was like a bonus.

I couldn't explain why, but I wanted to be alone.

And now I had the whole afternoon to myself.

* * *

I followed the long, tree-lined path toward Le Petit Trianon. The building was beautiful, but it was small and boxy and almost plain. I mean, certainly not small relative to where *I* now lived, but to people like Hannah and Pilar, this place might not be completely awe-inspiring.

Inside, I got the same impression. Compared to the all-out opulence of the main palace, it felt cozy and intimate. There was still plenty of grandeur — plaster carvings on the walls, floors of checkerboard marble tile, and a chandelier hanging above the grand staircase — but also a vibe of privacy and closeness. You could see how a person would feel more at home here, like she had her own little space.

There were hardly any tourists, so I had time to linger, stopping in each doorway to look around before wandering into the next room. The air was still, but there was an underlying energy. It felt quiet . . . but not empty.

Kings and queens walked here, I thought, looking over what had once been a billiards room. As I turned to move on, I caught a flash out of the corner of my eye — a shape moving outside the window.

I peered through the glass but saw nothing except a flock of sheep grazing on a distant pasture and a pair of old ladies wandering down a winding dirt path.

But I could have sworn I'd seen a pale-pink dress.

As I stepped back from the window, I noticed that it had an elaborate metal handle with a lock.

And carved on the lock was the same spiky flower that was cut out of the key in my medallion. Checking the other windows revealed that each one had the same fancy lock, and on each lock was the same flower carving.

I felt my throat tighten almost imperceptibly.

I headed upstairs, following a path through a series of little rooms — dining rooms, game rooms, music rooms — and stopping at the queen's bedroom.

Every piece of fabric — the curtains on the windows, the bedspread, the drapes around the bed, and even the chairs —

featured a white background with tiny sprays of little blue flowers, each petal ending in a delicately spiked fork.

It wasn't *exactly* the same as the design on the medallion — it was missing the key. But the flower being featured so prominently definitely raised my curiosity. Had the Iselin family — *my* family — had some real connection to the royals?

A door to my left led to a small, square room with walls of light blue, decorated with white carvings like the frosting on a cake. There didn't seem to be any windows, but on each wall was a large gold-rimmed mirror.

I stepped into the room and saw myself reflected a million times. I spun in a slow circle, taking in the smell of polished wood and that hard-to-pin-down scent that just meant "old." As I completed my turn and glanced at my reflection, I froze.

The face in the mirror wasn't my own.

The eyes were set a little wider, there was a widow's peak in the center of the forehead, and the lips were fuller. I was so captivated by the odd sight that I hardly had time to realize that it wasn't just the face that was different — *none* of what was reflected was me, unless I'd somehow changed into a floor-length black dress.

I stumbled backward, and for a moment the mirrored room was like a funhouse. I lost my bearings and couldn't tell one wall from another.

Just as my mind began to reel, footsteps came tramping up behind me — a guided tour making its way through the building.

"Here we have Le Cabinet des Glaces. . . ." The guide's voice was flat and bored, and it jerked me back to reality. I was more than happy to move aside so the people on the tour could shuffle in and look around. "This room was specially designed so that the windows could be covered, as you see, by floor-to-ceiling panels that could be raised or lowered."

"What would be the purpose of that?" I asked.

The woman frowned at my butting in on her precious tour without permission.

"Privacy," she said. "And to have better light at night."

"For secret dalliances," said one of the old ladies in the group, and her friends giggled.

Ew. Old ladies and secret dalliances were definitely two topics I didn't need mixing together in my brain.

I turned to go when one of the tourists lifted her camera and snapped a photo of me.

"Look, it's the girl from the picture!" she said, showing the image to her friend. The friend said, "Oh!"

What picture? What were they talking about? I felt a knot of unease in my belly, but before I could get up the nerve to ask the woman why she'd randomly snapped a photo of me, the group moved on.

Wait till Mom heard that the strangest people I'd met in Paris were a tour bus full of old American ladies.

I passed back through the flower bedroom and went downstairs. Outside, I came upon a crisscrossing network of footpaths. A map on the wall showed that they led to something called Le Hameau.

A five-minute walk left me standing at the edge of a tiny fairy-tale village. There were houses and mills and a tiny duck pond, pink-flowered shrubs, and footbridges with rough wood handrails. It was basically the last thing you'd expect to find on the grounds of Versailles — the polar opposite of the palace itself.

I walked toward the biggest building. Its windows were blocked with wire mesh, and the door looked like it hadn't been opened for years. Peeking through the dirty glass, I could barely make out a black and white tile floor.

Behind the house was a garden, with fat heads of cabbage growing in neat rows. The garden was freshly tended, almost like someone was living there. There was also a round turret attached to the house, with a barred metal gate blocking off its entrance.

I got the odd feeling that I'd somehow traveled back in time. I half-expected to see a peasant woman come out of the house carrying a heavy wooden bucket to fetch water from the well.

As I looked around the garden, the eerie sensation hanging over me like a veil, there was a sound:

Creeeeeeeak.

It sounded like something very old and very stiff being opened for the first time in a hundred years.

And turning around to look, I saw that the gate to the turret had crept open a few inches, revealing the spiral staircase inside.

The locks were obviously there for a very specific reason — to keep tourists out. This was only a fluke, caused by a change in the atmospheric pressure or something, and it wasn't my place to explore inside the fragile old building. Feeling highly virtuous, I walked forward, intending to close it and then report the malfunction to the next employee I saw.

But as I went closer to the open doorway, the back of my neck prickled. I felt an almost magnetic pull toward the stairs inside.

It couldn't *really* hurt to go in for a second and see the place from a different perspective . . . could it?

I pushed the gate another two inches and slipped inside, stopping at the base of the stairs. Shafts of sunlight, glittering with dust particles, poured in through small rectangular windows. A little round ceiling soared twenty feet above me, supported by wooden beams like the spokes of a wheel. And carved between each pair of beams was a pale-blue spike-petaled flower, almost too faint to see after centuries of existence.

Versailles was turning out to be a creepier place than I'd imagined. Feeling slightly nervous, I reached up and fidgeted with my medallion. It was cold against my hand.

I heard a footfall behind me and spun around, prepared to apologize and try to weasel my way out of the situation —

But I was alone.

And the gate had closed when my back was turned.

Figuring I'd had my extra allotment of tourism-based thrills, I stepped toward it and pulled. It wouldn't open.

I let out a nervous laugh before wrapping my hands around the bars and yanking.

Nope.

Momentarily stunned, I gave the bars a fruitless shake before taking a step back.

I wasn't worried that I'd starve or anything — I mean, this was a major tourist attraction. Somebody was bound to come by before too long. But what would be the consequences of having gone inside this forbidden place? Would I be kicked off the palace grounds? Banned for life?

What if I couldn't come back for the party?

Why had the gate worked two minutes earlier and suddenly gotten stuck? The hinges seemed to be in decent shape — not rusted over or anything.

I sighed and looked around, noticing for the first time that there was a door *inside* the turret — one that led directly toward the ground floor of the building. But when I put my hand on the doorknob and tugged, it didn't budge.

A rustling sound came from above me. I glanced up toward the ceiling and saw a sweep of movement over the banister — almost like an arm, the way you'd reach out to steady yourself as you went up stairs.

Was someone else in here with me? Had somebody else gotten stuck, too?

"Hello?" I called. "Who's there?"

I took a few tentative steps up — testing my weight on each plank before I moved to the next. The last thing I needed was to go crashing through a French national monument.

"Bonjour?" I said. "Hello?"

Silence.

I could keep climbing and see if there was another way out — but if there wasn't, and someone came by to find me in an off-limits part of the cottage, I could be in major trouble . . .

which would seriously irritate Hannah — and possibly doom me to the social blacklist.

Peer pressure got the better of me, so I turned back.

At the bottom of the stairs, I stopped.

The barred gate was still shut tight — but the second, inside door was wide open.

Beyond it lay an expanse of small black and white tiles. It was the same room you could barely see through the dingy front window, and it looked like it hadn't been touched by a human in a hundred years. A few pieces of broken furniture, thickly blanketed with dirt and grime, were pushed up against the walls.

I felt that same weird, magnetic urge to go inside. It was the same strange feeling I'd had since arriving in Paris — that I somehow belonged in the city. And now it was telling me I belonged inside this strange room. But taking that step seemed like it was going too far, in more than one way.

So I stopped short of the threshold. On the far side of the room was a massive hearth, the kind where you'd find a fire with a giant pot of soup boiling over it.

Painted on the wall above the hearth was yet another flower.

My heart thumping, I backed out into the stairwell and closed the door just as another sound came from above me. I glanced up, and it took me a moment to process what I saw.

The woman in the pink dress stood on the landing at the top of the stairs, looking down over the railing. Her eyes were burning-bright, and her medallion dangled from her neck.

"*Bonjour*," I said. "Where did you come from?"

She didn't reply.

She just kept staring at me.

"*Je suis . . .*" I mentally searched my meager French vocabulary to find the words to express my stuckness. "*Je suis ici?*"

I am here?

Nice, Colette.

Her expression didn't change.

And next to me, the interior door opened again. By the time I glanced into the tiled room and then back up at the landing, the woman was gone.

Was I supposed to follow her?

I almost stepped over the threshold — but once again something held me back. Instead of going in, I reached for the doorknob and closed it.

Suddenly, I was interrupted by a flurry of voices and turned to see a tour group outside the turret, looking in at me.

"What are you doing?" the tour guide asked me in English, horrified.

"I'm stuck," I said. "I can't get out!"

The guide stepped forward, a deep frown on her face. "How did you get *in*? That area is absolutely unauthorized."

"The gate was open," I said. "I thought it was part of the tour."

"This gate? Impossible. It is never unlocked." She grabbed the bars and tried to push the gate but had no luck.

Finally, I tried one last time.

It swung open easily.

I darted out and slammed it shut with a *CLANK!*

After giving me a dirty look, the guide went on with her tour as if it had never been interrupted by a juvenile delinquent like myself.

"This was Marie Antoinette's private cottage," she said. "To get away from the pressures of court life, she would put on a simple dress and come here, tend her garden, play with her children, and spend time with her closest friends."

One of the people in the group, a teenage boy, walked up to the gate by the stairwell. I held my breath as he pulled on it.

It didn't budge.

"You can't go inside," the guide said, shooting me a death glare. "You'll have to try to peek through the windows. That's as close as anyone gets anymore."

"Anyone but the ghosts," the boy's mother said, winking.

"Oh, yes," the guide said, sounding tired. "I forgot about the ghosts. They can come and go as they please."

* * *

Still jittery, I left Le Hameau, passing a little farm with baby goats playing in their small paddock. The afternoon was quiet, the paths deserted. The dirt crunched beneath my boots as I walked. A light, cool wind lifted the hair on my arms and chilled my skin, until I pulled my sleeves down over my palms.

I walked all the way back to the main château, stood in the center of the courtyard, and turned in a slow circle. I felt out of it, almost dizzy.

Soon the group started to gather. Miraculously, Hannah and Peely showed up on time.

"Where have you been, Colette?" Hannah asked.

It was an innocent question, but the answer was complicated. Should I admit that I went off by myself? Should I tell them about getting locked in the turret? I couldn't tell if getting stuck in a two-hundred-year-old stairwell was cool or uncool.

"Just around."

"Did you go to the gift shop? I spent like fifty euros!" Pilar reached into her bag and handed me a black beret, a tin of candies with a picture of the palace on it, a silk scarf, and a postcard.

I passed the other items back to her and stared at the postcard, a portrait of an alabaster-skinned woman wearing a square-necked ball gown and high, powdered wig, surrounded by her children. I flipped it over and read the caption.

LA REINE MARIE-ANTOINETTE ET SES ENFANTS

Then I flipped it back over and looked at the picture once more.

Pilar was babbling on about the beret, but I wasn't listening to her.

I kept looking at the postcard until Peely lifted the card from my hands and put it back in the bag.

I could still feel the cardstock against my fingers. Most of all, I could still see the face — that unmistakable face: long, narrow, with a prominent chin and dark, piercing eyes.

I could picture it as well as if I'd spent hours looking at her.

Because I kind of had.

The woman on the postcard was the same woman I'd been seeing all day —

Marie Antoinette. The dead queen of France.

CHAPTER 5

I DON'T BELIEVE in ghosts. I don't.

I don't, I don't, I don't.

But I also couldn't shake the feeling that I'd seen one.

As we boarded the train back to the city, all I could think about was the woman in the dress. Her silence, her medallion — *my* medallion — around her neck. And that piercingly intense look in her eyes . . . as if she had something she wanted to say to me.

Hannah and Pilar were sitting together, a few rows up. When I plunked into my seat, I'd been too distracted to notice how far away they were.

I didn't even notice when someone sat down beside me.

"You are very thoughtful," Jules said. "Did you like Versailles?"

"Yes," I said, blinking back to reality. "It's beautiful."

"I agree," he said. "Although, of course, it's hard to admire it so much when you think about the difficulties of building it and the peasants who were basically treated like slaves."

"But living there must have been amazing."

Jules cocked his head. "Actually, for anyone but royalty and the very top noble families, it wasn't all that wonderful. Conditions for the rest were often very humble."

"Why did they stay, then?" I asked.

"Because the king required it," he said. "He wanted to keep them close by to ensure that they weren't plotting against him. They came to the palace and tried to seek the king's favor when they could, and then spent the rest of their time in elaborate court ceremonies designed to keep them bored and quiet."

"Keep your friends close and your enemies closer," I said.

"Exactly," Jules replied.

We rode for a few minutes without speaking, but the silence wasn't nearly as awkward as I would have expected it to be. With nothing to distract me, my thoughts turned back to the ghost.

"What do you know about Marie Antoinette?" I asked.

Jules looked surprised. "Well, all of the things I explained this morning, to start."

I felt a warm flush creep up my cheeks. "I'm sorry. I couldn't hear you."

He shrugged. "She was born in Austria, married the dauphin — Louis the Sixteenth — at fourteen years old . . . became queen when her husband rose to the throne after the death of his grandfather . . . known for being frivolous and wasteful, out of touch with the people of France . . ."

"And then they killed her, right?"

"She was tried and executed during the Revolution," he said. "She was sent to the guillotine and beheaded. It is said that she maintained great dignity in the face of death."

At the sound of the word *beheaded*, I tugged my sweater a little tighter around my shoulders. "What about the little village?"

"Le Hameau? It was like a playhouse for her. She and her friends would go there and pretend to be peasants. They would tend the gardens, milk the cows . . . of course, the cows had to be scrubbed clean before the queen could touch them."

"Well, naturally," I said. "Who would touch an unscrubbed cow?"

Jules looked at me then, and the moment lingered — as if, for the first time, he was really seeing me as an individual and not just one of the pack.

"What about the flowers?" I asked. "The spiky ones all over the place?"

He looked confused. Then he handed me his notebook. "Can you show me?"

As I took his pen, our hands brushed lightly against one another, and I didn't dare look up — I was afraid he'd be able to see me blushing.

After I drew the flower, with its forked, spiky petals, Jules looked at it and smiled.

"Ah, *le bleuet*," he said. "The cornflower. Marie Antoinette's favorite."

That sent a torrent of thoughts through my mind. Could it just be a coincidence that I had a medallion with the queen's favorite flower carved as part of the design — and that I'd seen her ghost?

I'd *maybe* seen her ghost.

I probably did not see her ghost, said the rational part of my brain.

"Why do you ask?" Jules asked.

"Colette!" I looked up to see Hannah standing in the aisle. "I found you a seat next to us."

The interested expression on Jules's face disappeared like a bird taking flight. He glanced up at Hannah. "No need to switch seats. Our station is the next one. Don't forget your camera."

He was gone before I had a chance to say good-bye.

Hannah slipped into the seat he'd vacated. "It figures," she said. "First we get the only French nerd as our guide, and then we waste our whole first day a million miles from the city. It's like they're *trying* to make us have a terrible time."

"We have seven more days," I said, not bothering to say that I didn't consider Versailles a waste at all.

Hannah sighed. "You're a hopeless optimist."

"I'm just a realist," I said, wondering if a realist would ever believe in ghosts. "We have to stay with the group, right? I mean, what else are we going to do?"

Hannah's eyes flashed wickedly, and her mouth curled into a smile that seemed to change the whole shape of her face into something sharp and dangerous. "What are we going to do? We're going to find our own good times, that's what."

* * *

Sneaking out of the hotel that night proved ridiculously easy; there was a private exit through one of the penthouse bedrooms, and Hannah had tipped the desk clerk fifty euros not to mention it to Madame Mitchell. Once we were all dressed and ready to go, we simply waltzed out the secret door and down the stairs, and left through the back door of the café.

Hannah's plan included taking a taxi across town and slinking into a dim, smoky café called La Dominique. It was crowded to the point that you could hardly push your way through.

"Where did you hear about this?" I asked Hannah, trying to sound cool but feeling my stomach going *flippity-flop, flippity-flop*. My fingers nervously toyed with the medallion around my neck.

"I read about it in *Vogue*," she said, leading us to a table wedged into a tight corner. "Apparently a ton of models and photographers hang out here."

I almost pointed out that our coming to a café that was crawling with internationally acknowledged beauties might have demonstrated a tiny bit of overconfidence, but I bit my tongue. Then I thought about the young model who'd been murdered — what was her name again? Had she come here? I tried to shake off the morbid thought.

Hannah ordered us three coffees, and then we people-watched — Hannah looking right at home, Pilar trying desperately not to look like she was trying desperately to look cool, and me, squinting against the din and the crowds. When the waitress brought our drinks, we all stared — there were three tiny coffee cups, each on its own saucer with three sugar cubes and an itty-bitty spoon. They could have been straight out of *Alice in Wonderland*.

"Um . . . what exactly did you order?" Pilar asked, taking one and peering down into it. The coffee was dark brown and smelled like a whole Starbucks shoved into one large sip.

"Café noir," Hannah said, trying to look snooty but faltering for a moment. "Because it's dark outside."

Then, because she'd rather stab herself in the eye with a stick than admit she was less than perfectly in control 100 percent of the time, she dropped her sugar cubes in, stirred it up, and drank the whole thing in one gulp.

Her eyes popped open for the briefest moment — but then she narrowed them in triumph and looked at me and Peely.

We obediently followed her example. It was like getting a shot of coffee straight into your artery. My head had already been reeling from the noise and the bustling crowd — adding a jolt of caffeine made everything twice as bad.

"Are you okay?" Pilar asked, tugging on my hand.

My heart beat like a snare drum, and my breath felt like it was snagging on something in my chest. And the people seemed to be one big wall, closing in around me —

"Colette, if you sit there looking like you're about to vomit all over yourself, you're really going to hurt our chances of meeting cute boys," Hannah said.

Her voice was like rusty razor blades in my ears.

"I'm fine," I said. "Um . . . I'll be back in a minute."

Clutching my purse to my chest, I took a deep breath and plunged through the crowd as if I were diving into a poisonous swamp. I muttered, *"Pardon, pardon, pardon,"* as I went, but I didn't dare slow down to let anyone actually move out of my way. I must have bumped into a dozen French fashionistas. The music and conversation swelled into a single force that pushed in on my ears, and the smoke and dirty looks stung my eyes.

To my left was a door under a glowing green sign that read SORTIE. That meant "exit," right? I turned sharply, smashing into a pair of models, who swore at me in French as I passed.

The door slammed shut behind me, leaving me in instant stillness. Off in the distance, a plaintive car horn cut through the clear, chilly air.

I paced back and forth, trying to clear my head and catch my breath.

I was in an alley — not really very different from the regular streets we'd walked earlier in the day, only it was too narrow for cars to pass and its edges were dotted with trash bins and empty wooden crates. About fifty feet to my right was the road where the taxi had dropped us off; to my left, the alley curved away out of sight.

I cast a wary look at the door through which I'd exited. The mere sight of it made the hair on my arms stand up.

I can't go back in there.

But what was I going to do, wait outside all night?

I leaned against one of the stone walls. The night air seeped through my pale-gray cashmere sweater, and my royal-blue faux-fur shrug was definitely more for looks than for warmth.

There was no getting around it — I had to go inside.

I started one last round of pacing, complete with lots of deep breaths, as though I could store fresh air in preparation for the suffocating smallness awaiting me in the café. But just before turning for the door, I heard a sound.

It's amazing how fast your brain can tell you that something is very wrong.

My brain, for instance, immediately told me: *GHOST!*

I hurried away from the sound, farther down the alley. I figured that as I rounded the curve I'd find myself on another brightly lit street, surrounded by people out to have a good time.

Only I didn't. I found myself staring at more of the same — a dark, narrow alley.

Now the sound was so close I could easily tell that it was footsteps.

I broke into a run. I'm a decent runner, so I probably would have been fine — if I hadn't tripped. In my defense, I was running blindly down centuries-old uneven cobblestones wearing a pair of Hannah-approved shoes with three-inch heels.

Just as I started to vault to my feet, someone grabbed my shoulder.

CHAPTER 6

"LET ME GO or I'll scream!" I said.

"*Non*, please do not scream."

At the velvety sound of the voice, I looked up and saw a boy — I mean, a man . . .

Or maybe more like a god or something.

It took my eyes a second to adjust to looking at him. He was strikingly, mythically gorgeous, like a lion that had been turned into a human. He had sparkling golden eyes and waves of honey-colored hair. He looked vaguely familiar, but that was probably because he looked like every gorgeous movie star I'd ever seen, all rolled into one even-handsomer form. I was so distracted by his beauty that I couldn't stop staring.

"*Bonsoir, mademoiselle*," he said. "I am Armand Janvier."

He extended his hand, and I let him pull me off the ground.

"I'm Colette. Colette Iselin."

His eyes, which already looked like the sun setting on a pool of liquid gold, got even sparklier.

Oh, help.

"Are you hurt," he asked. "Won't you come back to the café?"

How did he know I'd been in La Dominique? Had he followed me?

No. There was simply no way someone like him would follow someone like me anywhere. Much less out of a café full of models on a freezing-cold night.

"No, thank you," I said. "I'm just meeting my friends. They'll be wondering where I am —"

"But your friends are still inside," he said.

I stood dumbly for a moment.

His laughter was rich and colorful. "Colette, I mean you no harm. Come with me."

"But why?" I asked.

He leaned closer. My breath got shallower and my legs started to feel numb.

"Because," he said softly. "You and I have something in common."

I wanted to ask what it was, but I couldn't find the words. I felt my mouth open and close like a fish.

"Come," he said, resting his hand lightly on my shoulder. "It's too cold out here. There will be time for explanations later."

So I followed him to the front door, past the doorman, who nodded respectfully to us, and back into La Dominique, which was as full of crushing, sweaty bodies as it had ever been.

"This way." Armand aimed me toward the left side of the room, where a dark-red velvet rope separated a large table from the rest of the café. He moved the rope aside so I could go in.

It all happened before I had a chance to figure out what was going on. And then I realized that we were in the VIP section. Hannah and Pilar were already seated at the table, looking like they'd won front-row seats at Paris Fashion Week.

Armand pulled a chair out for me and effortlessly pushed it in as I sat down. Then he went back to the head of the table.

Hannah slinked into the seat next to him. "That's Colette," she said. "She's one of my friends."

Then she started talking about herself, throwing in carefully calculated references to her family's cabin in Aspen and their condo in the Caribbean. Armand seemed to lap it all up.

I turned to Peely. "How did this happen?"

"He just, like, saw us from across the room and invited us to come sit here! Isn't that *amazing*?" She looked like she might swoon. A waitress appeared with a tray full of café noirs. Pilar grabbed one and downed it.

"He asked you to sit with him?"

"All three of us! He noticed you'd gone outside so he went out to get you. Talk about chivalry." She leaned in closer, practically vibrating from the caffeine coursing through her body. "Hannah called dibs, though, so be careful."

The warning was completely unnecessary. In the first place, no way would someone who looked like *that* ever be interested in me. In the second place, it would never even have occurred to me to make a play for Armand before Hannah had made it clear that she was done with him.

And from the looks of things, she was just getting started.

For the next two hours, their heads were never more than inches apart as they whispered and laughed. Hannah was aglow — I'd never seen her look so beautiful. And Armand looked like a handsome prince out of a fairy tale. They were a perfect match.

Pilar and I talked to Armand's friends, a mix of girls and guys almost as gorgeous as he was. They were really nice to us, too, although that might have been an act of obedience to Armand's wishes rather than the goodness of their hearts. They asked us about America and answered our questions about France.

I kept looking for opportunities to talk to Armand. It began to seem like I would never get one, as long as Hannah was around. Not that I would be foolish enough to try to get him to like me. What I wanted to figure out was *why* — why he'd selected us, when there were clearly older, more sophisticated, and more exciting people he could have welcomed into his roped-off paradise. What had he meant, saying that he and I had something in common?

Finally, Hannah *excusez-moi*'d herself to *la toilette*. And I made my move.

"How's it going?" I asked, planting myself in the chair next to Armand.

"Très bien." His eyes were lit from within, a sign that he was thoroughly under Hannah's spell. When she wanted to be, she

was enchanting, bewitching. It was where her power came from — her ability to reel people in and then, if it suited her, turn on them and treat them like they were nothing to her.

"Is tonight a special occasion?" I asked. "Or do you always reserve the VIP section?"

He shrugged, grinning. "I like the privacy."

"Isn't it . . . expensive?" I asked, catching myself too late to stop the question.

"Hey, it's just money." He smiled at me in a way that meant, *Right?* And I realized that he assumed we were all wealthy. Probably because of the glaring extravagance of Hannah's fur minicape. Or the way Pilar talked about her grand piano and her antique square piano and all the other pianos she was thinking about buying.

"Well, thanks for inviting us to sit with you," I said.

"Of course," he said, flashing his white teeth. "I had to, when I saw you."

"How did you notice us, out of everybody else here?"

"Not you," he said, swirling his finger around to indicate Pilar and Hannah's empty chair. Then he pointed at me. *"You."*

I sat for a moment, completely shocked.

And then he reached up and touched my arm in a motion that made my whole body feel tingly and warm. I thought for a second he was trying to hold my hand — and a warning sign flashed in my brain, in all caps, saying, *DO NOT DO THIS. HANNAH WILL MURDER YOU.* But I was too busy melting to stop him.

"I noticed *this.*"

Then I realized that he hadn't been reaching for my arm —
he was holding my medallion.

"My medallion?" I said. "What is it? What does it mean?"

He touched my arm again. And this time, it was a deliberate,
lingering touch. It took my breath away.

"It means you're special," he said quietly. "Like I am."

"Special," I repeated. "Really?"

"Yes. And perhaps soon we will have a chance to talk more
about it."

Suddenly, a tiny mug appeared inches from my face.

"Hey, Colette. Have a coffee." Pilar's words held a hint of
approaching danger — Hannah. So I yanked my arm away
from Armand and scrambled back to my own seat.

Hannah slipped down next to Armand. "Did you miss me?"

"Bien sûr." He lifted her hand to his lips and kissed it. "Of
course."

I was dying to ask Armand more about the medallion, but
with Hannah latched on to him, it would be impossible. They
resumed their conversation, Hannah glancing around the room,
collecting bits of other people's envy like seashells.

III

ROCHELLE DUBOIS LEANED *against the pile of pillows on her bed, pouting. Monique, her childhood friend, sat at the foot of the bed, tears streaming down her face.*

The tears offended Rochelle, who did not wish to be made to feel guilty for something that she thought of as "following her heart" (which sounded better than "stealing her best friend's boyfriend"). Was it her fault that Giancarlo had grown bored with Monique? Was it Giancarlo's fault that Monique had gained fifteen pounds, while Rochelle had stayed thin and beautiful?

And now she and Giancarlo were — well, if not exactly "in love," at least interested in each other.

Rochelle had decided to take the high road and be honest with Monique about it, and look what that had gotten her! Une catastrophe totale. Just a bunch of sobbing and carrying on about betrayal and friendship and blah blah blah.

"Je te supplie," *Monique blubbered.* "Je te supplie, Rochelle!"

Rochelle turned away and rolled her eyes. Begging? That was really taking things too far.

She picked up the phone and texted Giancarlo to let him know that things were going worse than predicted. MONIQUE = PATHETIQUE.

He replied: C'EST DOMMAGE.

Then she set the phone down and opened her bedroom door, calling for the old butler. He appeared a minute later, peering in at Monique with a worried look on his face.

Rochelle ordered him to take Mademoiselle Poirier home; she wasn't feeling well.

The old servant gave Rochelle a dirty look as he practically pried Monique out of the chair and herded her into the hallway, his ancient arm wrapped around her shoulder.

As soon as she saw the family's BMW pull away from the curb with Monique safely loaded into the backseat, Rochelle smiled and stretched her arms. At last she could relax and enjoy her day. The best part was, she and Giancarlo didn't have to sneak around anymore.

Although, without all the sneaking around, he already seemed less fun. He used too much hair gel. And his cologne smelled like shoes.

Well, maybe it would be a short fling. But Rochelle was determined to enjoy herself nonetheless.

She went out to the kitchen to get a snack, taking the loaf of bread out of the pantry and grabbing a long serrated knife from the drawer by the sink. She set them on the butcher-block countertop and turned to get the cheese from the tray in the corner. As she did so, she caught sight of a black smudge on her arm. Had some of Monique's dripping mascara gotten on her? Disgusting.

When Rochelle turned back to the counter, what she saw made her jump and drop the cheese, which fell to the ground with a sickening splat.

A woman stood in the kitchen with her, wearing an elaborate ball gown that looked like it came from the eighteenth century.

"Mon dieu!" Rochelle exclaimed.

The woman stared down her thin, imperious nose at Rochelle.

Rochelle put on her best snarl, the one she used on bouncers who wouldn't let her into clubs, or waitresses who took too long with her food.

"Qu'est-ce que vous voulez?" she asked, a challenge in her voice.

But the woman didn't answer the question, didn't tell Rochelle what she wanted. Instead, she pointed to the counter.

Rochelle looked to see what the woman was pointing at —

And just as she turned her head, the large knife sailed through the air, straight toward the softest part of her neck.

CHAPTER 7

JULES WALKED BACKWARD in front of us. "Probably the most celebrated work of art on display here at the Louvre is Leonardo da Vinci's *La Joconde*, or as it is commonly known, the *Mona Lisa*."

Hannah rolled her eyes and yawned. "Kill me."

"It's famous," Pilar said. "Don't you want to see it?"

"I've been to Paris seven times without being dragged into this tourist hole," Hannah said. "I'm supposed to celebrate now?"

"If you like art, I guess," I said.

"I like art as much as anybody. I'm the one who talked my dad into buying that painting in our foyer, the one of the purple horse. And that was like twelve thousand dollars."

As Hannah spoke, she slowed, and we slowed with her. She would have been completely happy to go back outside and sit on a bench for the four hours we were scheduled to spend inside the museum. But I glanced ahead at Jules, who was involved in a conversation with Audrey.

"Um . . . I think I'm going to catch up with the group," I said.

"Why?" Pilar asked.

"Curious, I guess," I said. "I don't get to a lot of art museums."

Hannah closed her eyes as if my very words were giving her a migraine. "Whatever."

I pulled away from them and dodged the groups of tourists to rejoin the others.

We crowded into a smaller gallery where the *Mona Lisa* hung on the wall. I had to admit, the painting wasn't as impressive as I'd thought it would be. It was small — smaller, in fact, than most of the posters I'd seen of it. I fought my way to the front of the room, where a low barrier kept the crowds several feet away from it. With the pulsing group of bodies moving behind me like pounding ocean waves, I wasn't eager to linger and absorb the painting's more subtle merits. I found myself pushed up against the barricade with some guy's giant camera stabbing me in the arm, and the air in my throat seemed to thicken.

"Here, Colette, this way," Jules said, taking me by the shoulder and leading me to a patch of open space.

"Thanks," I said, breathing deeply and trying not to show how relieved I was.

"How are you today?" he asked. "Tired?"

I looked at him in alarm — did he know we'd snuck out last night?

"The second and third days are usually the worst for jet lag," he said.

"Oh," I said. "A little. But I had three cups of coffee with breakfast. That should keep me going for at least another hour."

He smiled.

You couldn't deny he had a nice smile.

After the whole group finished with the *Mona Lisa*, we moved through the rest of the halls, which were lined with paintings. Jules walked ahead to deliver his spiel, but I noticed that he kept glancing at me, as if he wanted to see if I was listening.

And I was.

When we paused to choose one of the cafés to eat lunch in, I looked around at the paintings nearby.

"Oh, hey!" I said, to nobody in particular.

On the wall hung a portrait of a young man sitting at a desk. He wore a black jacket, white ruffles showing at his collar and wrists. His face had that round, glowy look I'd seen in countless portraits that day — but what drew my attention was the cuff he wore on his forearm.

It was a burnished silvery-gray, like it was supposed to be metal. And clearly visible on its surface was an engraving of a key, with small pointy cutouts in it that went all the way through the metal.

"*Le duc d'aubusson*," Jules said, appearing at my side and looking at the little label next to the painting. "Philippe Roux."

I pointed at the cuff. "That's a cornflower, right? Do you know what the key means?"

Jules squinted and leaned closer to look. "It seems to be a mark of some organization or affiliation."

"Like a club?"

"Perhaps," he said. "Or a family alliance. The nobility of France were very closely connected to one another. This was painted in the 1780s, just before the Revolution."

My heart pounded. Could my medallion date back that far? I'd left it in the hotel suite that day, deciding it didn't go with my outfit. But as I stared at the man's luminous face, I wished I had it with me to compare with the symbol in the portrait. One thing seemed certain — the medallion had something to do with this duke.

Holy cannoli. What if I was secretly a French duchess? Even Hannah, with all her father's connections, couldn't claim to be nobility. Mr. Norstedt once joked that his grandfather had a reindeer farm in Sweden.

And could it go even further than that? I thought of the spiky cornflower I'd seen in Marie Antoinette's bedroom. If I had seen the queen's ghost — was it because I was a part of an alliance that had something to do with the royal family? And if Armand knew about the medallion, did that mean he knew about the club it stood for? Was that why he thought I was special?

I felt a little breathless as we entered the cafeteria — maybe this trip really *would* change my entire life.

* * *

On the walk back to the hotel, I found myself next to Jules. "What are we doing this afternoon?"

He held his hands up. "Whatever you like. It's a free afternoon. You could take a nap."

"A nap?" I repeated. "I'm in *France*. . . . I'm not taking a nap. Got any better ideas?"

Was I imagining things, or did he shoot an approving look in my direction? "If I were you, I would spend some time in the city. Get to know the real Paris. Walk around, see the architecture and churches. . . ."

I had a hard time imagining Hannah and Pilar consenting to a walking tour. "My friends might not be completely on board with that."

"Do you have to do everything your friends do?" he asked. "You left them today, didn't you?"

Yes, but . . . "I'll see how they feel about it, I guess."

"I will make a deal with you," Jules said. "If you decide to go out walking and your friends won't go, *I* will go with you."

"Really?" I asked, surprised. "But don't you have the afternoon off?"

"Yes," he said. "So I can do as I please. And that's why I said *if* your friends won't go with you."

He was smiling.

"All right," I said. "But I think I'll be stuck."

"Like the courtiers at Versailles, right?" he said. "Bored and quiet."

His words wriggled under my skin and itched at me. "Give me a second, okay?"

I made my way to the back of the group . . . and then fifty

feet farther than that — and found Hannah and Pilar practically dragging their feet.

"So . . . what do you guys want to do for the rest of the day?" I asked.

Peely yawned. "I need sleep. I was up all night."

"That's because you drank about a gallon of café noir last night," I said.

In the midst of the most amazing city in the world, Hannah managed to look bored. "I'm tired of wandering around like a loser. I'm going to rest until Armand calls."

"Did he say he would?" I asked.

She gave me a displeased little smirk. "Colette, give me some credit."

"What about you?" Pilar asked.

I tried to replicate Hannah's bored look. "Well . . . I'm not that tired. I guess I'll find something to occupy myself with."

"Have fun," Hannah said, in a voice that said I could fall into the Seine, for all she cared.

* * *

I ran upstairs to the suite, changing into a pair of walking shoes and grabbing my medallion. I wondered why Jules had offered to show me around. Was it possible that he liked me? Like, *liked me* liked me?

Boys were a bit of an enigma to me. I'd been out on a few dates over the years, but as Saint Margaret's Academy was an all-girls school, it wasn't like we were constantly awash in a sea of eligible guys. I spent some time around my brother's friends, but they hardly counted. While I wasn't a prize catch, I knew that my social tier at least exempted me from having to stoop to finding romantic companionship in the Chess Club.

When I asked Madame Mitchell if I could go walking with Jules, she raised her eyebrows but said it was fine. Then I went out to the front of the hotel, butterflies in my stomach. What if Jules tried to hold my hand? Should I let him? Did I like him?

Would I really even consider someone like Jules if Armand was interested in me?

Newsflash, Colette: Armand didn't exactly spend the evening wrapped around YOU. Actions speak louder than words, and Hannah was getting the action. I just got a few mysterious words.

"Hi," I said to Jules, feeling shy. "Are you ready?"

"In just a moment," he said. "I hope you don't mind, but I invited someone else."

Before I had time to react, I saw Audrey stroll out of the hotel, backpack on, wearing a blue-and-white Saint Margaret Snowy Owls sweatshirt over a white polo and massive athletic shoes on her feet. Her giant camera hung from a strap around her neck. She couldn't have looked more like a tourist if she'd tried.

I could barely contain my horror. Jules had invited *Audrey* to walk around and see the city with us? I tried to force myself to be expressionless as she trotted over.

"Hi, guys! Thanks for letting me tag along."

And then he smiled at her — the same smile he'd used on me.

I felt a flare-up of wounded dignity. For a second I considered letting them do their little Paris walkabout alone. Then I realized that the alternative was to sit around and watch Pilar sleep and Hannah pout. As insulted as I felt, I wasn't going to sacrifice my time in France just to spite someone else — even if they deserved a little spiting, in my humble opinion.

"Would you like to do anything special?" Jules asked.

Audrey shrugged. "Whatever you want is good with me. I just needed to get away from Madame Mitchell for a while."

I tried to hide my surprise. I thought girls like Audrey couldn't get enough of teachers.

But I guess my face gave me away, because she sighed and said, "Every single thing we do or see, Madame Mitchell has to talk about all of the other times she's seen or done the same thing. 'I was here two years ago and it was *raining*!'"

Jules laughed. "I noticed that. Yesterday, when she told the story about losing her scarf . . . I think she missed the entire Hall of Mirrors."

"I know!" Audrey laughed. "I'd like to spend one day of this trip living in the moment, if possible. Well, a half day."

I was mildly jealous that they had an inside joke between them, but I tried to dismiss the feeling.

Jules turned to me. "What about you, Colette?"

"Actually . . . I do kind of have something I'd like to do. If it's okay with Audrey." I fished the medallion out of my purse and held it out for them to look at. "I'd like to learn more about this."

Jules gently took it from me and turned it over. "That's the symbol from the painting of the duke. This is very nice. Where did you find it?"

"It belonged to my dad's family."

Jules handed it to Audrey. "The noble and loyal are bound together through time," she murmured.

"Is that what it says?" I asked. "I couldn't read it."

"It's in Latin." She flipped it over. "How beautiful, Colette. It looks so old."

"Thanks," I said, slightly mollified by their admiring words. "I thought it might be cool to learn more about it. I know the flower is a cornflower, like the ones in Marie Antoinette's bedroom in Le Petit Trianon. And Jules thinks it might symbolize a club of some sort. But that's all I know."

"All right," Jules said. "Let's see what we can find."

"Cool," Audrey said, smiling goofily. "We have a mission. . . . I feel like Nancy Drew!"

And I sort of felt like I should give up everything I'd been working for and join the Chess Club.

CHAPTER 8

WE ENDED UP in the library at Jules's university. Audrey pored over an old, illustrated guide to French family crests, while Jules paged through a giant book called *L'Alliance Noble*. I sat at a computer, pretty much at a loss. I'd tried googling *Iselin*, along with *key*, *cornflower*, and *queen*. But nothing of interest had turned up in the results.

I randomly clicked on a link that took me to a local news site — and my breath caught in my throat. The huge headline was in French, but I could understand it, more or less — it was about the murders. Apparently, there'd been a new victim, a glamorous-looking girl named Rochelle DuBois.

As I stared at her photo, a creepy feeling of déjà vu settled over me. Why did I feel like I'd seen her curly red hair and deep blue eyes before?

After a minute, I shook it off and decided to try more research.

I typed *Armand Janvier* into Google. I came upon his Facebook page, but not much else.

Jules appeared from around the corner. "Your name is Iselin, correct?" he asked. "That's French."

I liked the way it sounded with his accent: *ees-eh-LAHN*. His pronunciation was unique and fancy. Most people in America pronounced it like *Iceland* without the *∂*.

"Yeah," I said. "My dad's parents were born here."

Jules peered at the screen before I could minimize the window. He frowned. "Armand Janvier? Why are you searching for him?"

I looked up at him. "You know Armand?"

The frown deepened. "Unfortunately, yes. We go to university together. Do *you* know him?"

Before I could answer, Audrey came over with her notebook and set it down next to me, open to a page with a bunch of small sketches. "I've found a bunch of family crests with cornflowers and a bunch with keys. But none with both cornflowers *and* keys."

Her drawings were done in ink, with sketchy lines. They were evenly spaced on the page, and each one had a French surname scrawled below it.

"Oh, wow, those are adorable," I said. "It looks like something from Anthropologie."

"It's more like genealogy," she said. "But thank you."

"No, I meant . . ." Had she really never heard of the store? "You could frame that. It's like the ultimate souvenir."

"They're just copied out of books." She pressed her lips together in a shy smile. "You can have it, if you want."

One of the thrift stores I went to all the time had a cool selection of old picture frames. I could paint one shiny red and hang the sketches on the wall in my new bedroom.

"Seriously?" I asked. "Yeah. Make sure you sign it."

She looked pleased as she leaned down, signing *Audrey L. Corbett* in her tiny, neat handwriting. Underneath that, she wrote the date and *Paris, France*. "Ta-da," she said. "You weren't just messing with me, were you?"

"No," I said. "Why would I do that?"

"I don't know," she said. "I guess maybe you wouldn't. But Hannah would."

"No, she wouldn't," I said.

Audrey cocked her head. "Anyway, you're not like Hannah."

I'm not?

And then it occurred to me that Audrey thought that was a compliment.

She turned away and checked the time on her watch. "I need to get going soon. I told my mom I'd video-chat with her before she leaves for work."

I followed her and Jules through the streets, past little pâtisseries with their windows full of colorful pastries, brightly colored flower shops, hole-in-the-wall bookstores . . .

You could see why people called it the most romantic city in the world.

But following behind Jules and Audrey, who laughed and pointed to things and talked about history like it was a reality show they were both totally into, I felt utterly alone.

* * *

When we reached the hotel, Audrey gave us a cheerful wave and hurried inside.

Jules called, *"Au revoir!"* to her and then looked at me.

"Well . . . *au revoir*," I said. *"Merci beaucoup* and all that."

He nodded and half-turned, like he was going to start walking away. Then he swung back. "What now? More research? Or do you need to go see your friends?"

"They're probably still asleep," I said. "I'll hang out in the café and read or something."

He seemed vaguely uncomfortable. "Would you like to keep walking? Unless you're tired."

"Aren't *you* tired?" I asked. "I mean, tired of being a tour guide?"

Jules smiled. "Walking around isn't being a tour guide. It's just being a person."

So we walked. We must have covered five or six miles. We went down by the river, and past Notre Dame Cathedral. We walked through Le Marais, a neighborhood full of old stone walls with doors painted bright red or cobalt blue, hanging lanterns, intricate iron scrollwork on the gates and under the windows, and window boxes overflowing with sumptuous flowers.

We passed corner cafés whose signs were almost overgrown with ivy and tiny shops selling everything from toys to bicycles to wigs. We stopped at a street vendor to buy crêpes, steaming hot thin pancakes covered in cinnamon that somehow manage to simultaneously melt in your mouth and fill it with a thousand crunchy sugar crystals.

And we talked the whole time. Jules told me about his classes and asked about our school. He'd led enough tour groups to know how American high schools work, but I'd never heard anything about high school in France. It sounded insanely hard, with really long days, lots of classes, and a big, terrifying test at the end.

"There must be a lot of pressure on you," I said.

"Mostly I think the pressure comes from myself," he said. "What about you? Is there a lot of pressure?"

"Sort of. Not the same kind. The school part is easy compared to the rest of it. I mean, I know I'll get into a decent college. It's just managing things in the meantime that gets hard."

"What kind of things?"

I hesitated for a second. "Well . . . my friends. Trying to make sure I don't say or do something wrong."

"How can you say the 'wrong' thing to your friends?"

"That's just how it works," I said. "You want people to like you, so you worry about what happens if they don't."

"And what does happen," Jules asked, "if they don't?"

"Then you're alone. And miserable."

"I don't understand," he said. "Is it worth being friends with someone like that?"

How could I possibly explain what it was like to navigate a school day without any allies? To face someone like Hannah every day with no backup save Pilar, who was also looking out for herself?

"And why are you worried?" he went on. "I always see you with Hannah and Pilar. You are safe, no?"

"You're never completely safe. There's always a risk."

"You make it sound like a spy movie," he said, smiling.

"If only it were that simple."

We were passing a tiny park, a circle of benches surrounding a fountain. I plopped down on one of the benches, suddenly feeling like I needed to rest.

"I know it probably sounds stupid," I said. "But I still have a year and three months of high school left. Spending that much time without friends would be horrible."

"Just because you don't have *those* friends doesn't mean you don't have any," he said. "What about Audrey? She's very nice."

"Yeah, she is, but . . ." My voice trailed off. "We did actually used to hang out a little. We were on the Academic Games team in ninth grade."

"Academic Games?"

"You're a team and you compete against other schools. . . . It's for, like, math and science."

"*That* sounds like a lot of pressure," Jules said.

I smiled. "No, it's fun. I mean, we didn't always win, but it wasn't the end of the world." I sighed. "But then when I started to hang out more with Pilar, I kind of ran out of time."

"You ran out of time for fun?"

I shot him a sharp look, but his eyes were twinkling. He was teasing me. "I ran out of time for clubs and things."

Jules shook his head. "I have to say, Colette . . . I like Audrey. I think she would be a better friend than the other girls."

Technically speaking, having a friend like Audrey, who was loyal, funny, and not afraid to be herself, *was* better than having a friend like Hannah, who was a ticking time bomb — or even

Pilar, who was so paralyzed by her need to fit in that she would sell you out in a second if she had to.

But in reality, if I were to wake up one day and find that I was suddenly back in Audrey's social circle, that Hannah and Pilar wouldn't even take a millisecond to notice me in the halls — I'd be devastated.

I couldn't even say why. I knew it made me sound shallow and horrible.

Jules seemed to sense my inner turmoil. "Perhaps this is just something you need to figure out for yourself."

"Perhaps," I said.

We sat and watched the people walk by. At one point, a woman walked up to us, looked at me, and asked me something in French.

I opened my mouth to apologize, but Jules spoke to her. She said, "*Merci*," and walked away.

"She wanted directions," he said. "See? I said before you look French."

"If you knew how much I cared about that," I said, "you would think I was crazy."

"You don't want to look French?"

"No." I was running out of patience with myself and tired of trying to say the right thing. "I'm, like, pathetically desperate to look French."

Jules let out a gentle laugh. "Colette, you spend a lot of time thinking about things that should not matter to you."

"I know," I said. I glanced at Jules. "Does that make me a bad person?"

"No," he said softly. "That's how you know you're a good person. Because it makes you unhappy. You are thinking about it and fighting it. A lot of people don't think about it at all."

I wasn't sure why, but I felt my cheeks get warm. "You think I'm a good person?"

"Is that as important as thinking you look French?"

"Almost." I couldn't help smiling. But then I remembered everything else we'd been talking about and my smile faded. "I'm sorry. It's just been such a weird year."

"Weird how?"

And then, without meaning to, I told him everything — how my dad freaked out and left us. How we suddenly had no money, and how my mom worked at a perfume counter at Macy's to pay the bills, and how I was on scholarship but nobody knew it, and how desperate I was to leave Ohio and spend the summer in New York with my dad, and how my little brother thought I was a superficial monster most of the time, and how I couldn't tell any of this to Hannah or Pilar.

And then I realized how completely dumb it sounded that I couldn't talk about my problems to the people I was supposed to be the closest to.

"You know what?" I said finally, shaking my head. "The more I talk, the worse it all sounds." I checked my watch. "It's actually getting kind of late. Maybe we should head back."

Jules's blue eyes were thoughtful. "If you like."

"I need to be at the hotel's café for dinner or I'll have to pay for it myself." I smiled, embarrassed, but suddenly feeling light and free, unburdened by all my secrets. "I'm completely broke."

"I know a place we can go for dinner," Jules said.

"Broke," I repeated. "It means, no euros in *les pockets*."

"It's very inexpensive," Jules said. "I get a discount."

I have to admit — the idea of spending more time with Jules, as opposed to going back to the hotel and doing the keep-Hannah-happy tap dance, sounded pretty good.

"Well, okay," I said. "But I need to call Madame Mitchell."

"Here," Jules said. "Use my phone." He scrolled back through his recent calls to a number labeled MITCHELL.

I took the phone, but stared at it for a moment. "Um . . . are we, like . . . allowed to do this?"

"To do what?"

Uh. "To do things together — alone?"

Jules's mouth twisted into a very adorable half smile, half concentrated frown. "I don't know, actually. . . . I have never asked."

Oh, what the hey. I dialed.

Madame Mitchell answered with her most nasally accent. *"Bonjour?"*

"Hi, it's Colette," I said. "Can I skip dinner at the hotel and eat with Jules?"

"Oh. Well." She paused for a few seconds to think. "All right. Try to be back by eight thirty. Come by my room and check in so I don't have to send out *les gendarmes*, okay?"

I said good-bye and handed the phone back to Jules. "Now . . . where's this magic restaurant that serves people with no money?"

CHAPTER 9

"*SALUT!*" JULES CALLED, pushing open the door.

Instantly, a rich, spicy aroma wafted out into the hallway.

The restaurant that serves broke foreigners? Jules's family's apartment.

"*Salut*, Jules," called a voice that was young, sweet, and female.

Jules ushered me inside. I looked around the small living room, which was decorated with nice — but older — furniture, a lot of plants, and dozens of framed photographs of family members.

A girl who looked a little older than Jules stuck her head out from a doorway. She had a mop of short brown hair and round wire-framed glasses. Over her clothes, she wore a floral apron, soft and faded from years of use, and in her hand was a wooden spoon.

"Ah!" she said, and then she started speaking French at me.

"*Non, elle ne parle pas bien français,*" Jules said.

"Oh," the girl said. "Hello."

"She thought you were French!" Jules said in a stage whisper. "Good job! You fooled another one!"

I elbowed him in the side. *"Bonsoir,"* I said, not sure if I should try to shake hands or what.

"Colette Iselin, this is my sister, Mathilde. Mathilde, this is Colette. She's visiting from America."

Mathilde's eyes lit up and she grinned.

"Sois sage," Jules said, a warning in his voice, and his sister's eyes seemed to flicker with mischief.

"Nice to meet you," I said.

"Here, would you like to set your things down?" Jules asked, directing me to the piano bench before she could say anything else.

Mathilde disappeared back into the kitchen.

"It smells amazing," I said.

"She is a genius at cooking," Jules said. "She's training to be a chef. What are you making tonight, sister?"

"Pot au feu," she called. "And there is enough to share with *la jolie américaine.*"

Jules made a clucking sound, and — was I imagining it, or did he actually blush?

"What is *pot au feu*?" I asked. "Not that I'm picky. I'll eat anything."

"It's a beef stew," Jules said. "Very traditional. Would you like some water?"

"Sure," I said, and he went into the kitchen. I heard him talking in hushed, urgent French to his sister, who laughed a little as she answered him back. When he reappeared with a glass of water, he looked even more flustered.

"So your whole family lives here?" I looked around. I hoped my voice didn't convey the surprise I felt. The apartment was tiny.

"Yes, and this is where my father grew up," Jules said. "His parents moved out to the suburbs when my mother and father were married."

"Are you going to live here the whole time you're in college?" I asked.

He shrugged. "I don't see why not."

I thought of all the kids I knew, who were champing at the bit to leave their parents behind and go away to school.

"Want a tour?" Jules asked me.

"Aren't you tired of giving tours?" I said.

"This will be a short one." He led me down a short hall. "My parents' room . . . Mathilde's room . . . my room . . . the toilet."

He went so fast I didn't really have time to get a good look at anything, so after nodding at the bathroom, I turned back and gave the door to his bedroom a light push. There was a twin bed pushed up against one wall, a dresser next to the bed, and a desk by the door. The walls were covered in posters of bands — Radiohead, the Pixies, the Beatles, Metallica . . .

"You like a lot of different music," I said.

"What?" He grinned. "You think French people only like jazz and accordions?"

"Pilar can play the accordion," I said. "It's pretty amazing. She can basically play anything."

"Really? Pilar?" he said. "I would not have guessed she had any hidden talent."

"She's just insecure," I said. "Her mom has always made her feel short and fat."

"That is a shame," he said.

"Yes, it is," I said, turning to look over his bookshelves. Most of the titles were in French. A lot of them were classics, and the whole bottom shelf was textbooks. There was no TV in the room, just a set of small iPod speakers.

"Very nice," I said.

"Is it like American boys' bedrooms?"

I turned to see that his grin had turned impish. "I wouldn't really know," I said airily. "I don't make a habit of visiting boys' bedrooms."

"Don't you have a brother?" he asked.

"Oh. Yes. It's sort of like his room. Only he has a giant computer and a bunch of chessboards." It was actually smaller than Charlie's room, I noticed. And Jules seemed to have spent his whole life living there without being traumatized by the lack of square footage.

We went back out and Jules showed me the kitchen. Mathilde stood over her pot on the stove like a mother duck over her ducklings. Jules and I sat at the dinner table and watched her cook.

"Colette . . . you like Paris?" Mathilde asked.

"Yes," I said. "I love it."

"What is your favorite part, so far?"

"Versailles." It was true, in spite of the strange things that had happened to me there. People still like roses even though they have thorns, right? So I could still like the palace even though it was potentially full of ghosts. "But today was nice, too."

"Where did you go today?"

Without meaning to, I looked at Jules. He gave me a shy smile and tried to sound casual as he said, "We walked around."

Mathilde didn't miss a chance to shoot him a sparkling look. "Alone? Just the two of you?"

"Hey," Jules said. *"Occupe-toi de tes oignons."*

"What does that mean?" I asked.

"He told me to mind my onions." Mathilde tried to hide her smile as she went back to stirring. "All right, I will stop asking questions."

I thought it was totally funny and sweet, the way she teased him. I never joked with Charlie that way — as if we were friends, on the same level. Furthermore, she was actually interested in what Jules did. And he was clearly proud of her cooking.

What were my brother and I doing wrong?

A few minutes later, their parents came home, and then we all sat around and talked until it was time to eat. Monsieur Martin's English was terrible, but he loved testing it out on me. And I tried to answer in French. By the time he and I limped through an entire conversation, Mathilde and Jules were crying with laughter.

The food was served on mismatched plates, all different brands and patterns that somehow looked like they were created to be mixed together. Along with the stew, there were green beans and steaming red beets.

I was aware that everyone was waiting for my reaction, so I was determined to fake it if necessary.

It wasn't necessary.

"*Mon dieu*," I said, after taking my first bite.

"She says, 'Oh my God!'" Monsieur Martin crowed, delighted.

"It's good?" Mathilde asked.

"It's unbelievable," I said, finishing the bite. The meat, salty and tender, broke apart in my mouth, and the broth was sweet and fragrant. I could have eaten a bucketful. Mathilde rewarded me with a smile, and then everyone stopped staring at me and turned to their own dinners. Monsieur Martin had brought home a crusty baguette wrapped in wax paper, and we each got a hunk of bread to dip into the broth.

Madame Martin took a bite of hers and then closed her eyes with a happy sigh. "She has only twenty years, but she cooks like my grandmother."

Jules smiled at his sister, who smiled back at him, beaming with pride. It was such a warm, personal moment that I almost felt embarrassed having seen it.

The whole meal took about an hour and a half, with everyone talking and laughing and taking their time, lingering over a platter of cheese and then cups of coffee. Even back in the days when my family ate dinner together (at Mom's insistence), we'd never been like this. It was always Dad hurrying to finish so he could go check his work email, and Charlie trying to catch glimpses of the TV in the next room, and me with my earbuds in, making a point of ignoring everything. We'd say grace, scarf down our food, and be out of there in twenty minutes.

None of the Martins seemed to want to be anywhere else, or doing anything else, besides just sitting around with one another and hanging out.

"So what else do you have planned for the week?" Mathilde asked, pouring cream into her second cup of coffee.

"Whatever Jules has planned," I said, and then I blushed. "I mean, because he's the tour guide."

Jules was smiling at his plate. "Museums, historical sites, the usual."

"Oh, there is one cool thing," I said, remembering. "My friend Hannah got some of us invited to a party at Versailles next Saturday."

Jules turned to me. "I didn't know that."

"Yeah — we have to go rent costumes and everything." Although where I'd get the money to rent one, I had no idea.

Mathilde brightened. "I know where you can find a dress. My school did an exhibition last year, and the costumes are in storage."

"Oh, thanks," I said. "I'm not sure. . . . Can I let you know?"

"Of course," Mathilde said. "How fun. A costume ball . . . do you need a date?"

Jules shot out of his chair. "I'm getting more coffee. Does anyone want anything?"

Mathilde grinned. "All right, we can talk about something else."

By the time the meal was done, I was strangely, achingly homesick for my mother and brother.

"We'd better get going," Jules said to me, after we'd carried our dishes into the kitchen and handed them to Monsieur

Martin, who stood at the sink wearing Mathilde's floral apron over his work clothes.

I thanked them all for their hospitality, noting the glint in Mathilde's eye as she told me to come back *anytime*.

When the apartment door clicked closed behind us, it felt like we were leaving some special, enchanted place.

"Your family's great," I said.

"Yes," he said. "Though Mathilde can be a . . ." He said some French word I didn't understand, but it made me laugh.

"It's just cool that you guys are friends," I said. "My brother and I are never like that. If we're talking, we're fighting."

Jules pursed his lips and opened the main door for me. We stepped out into the twilight. "You must talk about the wrong subjects."

"I guess so," I said. "But . . . it's more than that. It's like we're so different that one of us has to be wrong."

"About what?"

"About everything. We don't like each other's friends, or music, or ideas about what's a worthwhile way to spend time." And it suddenly seemed so silly. Why couldn't we both be right?

"I'm sorry for you," Jules said. "My sister is my best friend. We fight sometimes, but . . . I don't know what I would do without her."

We walked for a while without speaking, just soaking in the sights and sounds of the night. The cafés were setting up their heaters, and dinner patrons were beginning to crowd the small tables. Golden light poured out of shop windows, and a mix of

French voices floated on the cool air, rising and lowering in lively conversation.

I didn't really let myself think about Jules, about the fact that he'd voluntarily spent his whole day with me and taken me home to dinner, and that his sister had teased him about me.

I did take his words from earlier — *you're a good person* — and let them tumble around in my head like rocks being pushed along the floor of a river, until they were smooth and shining.

But the rest of it — and what it might mean — I pushed to the far reaches of my mind. Instead, I focused on the glow of the streetlamps, accenting each cobblestone with its own little half-moon of light.

In what seemed like a tenth of the time I expected it to take, we were back at the hotel. I took a deep breath and turned to face Jules.

"I'll see you in the morning, then?" he asked.

"Of course," I said.

And then there was a pause. One of those really, really long pauses where both people feel like there's something to say, only neither of them is willing to be the one to say it.

What was it I wanted to say to Jules? What would I say if I weren't afraid?

Thanks for listening to my secrets? Or *Thanks for making me feel . . .*

How, exactly, did he make me feel?

Like a whole person. A person who didn't need to change anything about herself to be okay. Essentially . . . the opposite of how I felt 99 percent of the time.

But would I ever say that? Not in a million years.

"Thanks for dinner." I burst the bubble of silence before it turned into something dangerous. "See you tomorrow."

I pivoted and started to head into the hotel, feeling proud of myself for getting us onto safe ground.

But Jules stopped me. "Colette," he said.

I hesitated before I swung back to look at him.

He was smiling. "I had a very good time with you today."

"Okay." I smiled back. And then I went inside.

"Okay?" Is that really what I just said?

I took the stairs to the third floor and knocked on Madame Mitchell's door. She pulled it open and checked her watch. Three minutes early. "How was dinner?"

"Great," I said. "Authentic French cuisine."

"I must say," she said, raising her eyebrows a little, "I don't know that I've ever had a girl in my group get along so well with the tour guide. Of course, for the past six years we had Monsieur Delacorte, and you'd have to be not only blind but also pretty much out of your mind to find him attractive."

I wasn't sure whether to blush or laugh. "Anyway, thanks for trusting me."

"Oh, I wasn't worried," she said, waving her hand. "I know he's not your type. Besides, I'm sure your friends don't approve, so it's not an issue."

As I climbed up to the suite, I couldn't get her comment out of my head. She hadn't said it in a mean way, or as if she were trying to call attention to some giant flaw — she'd said it like it wasn't a big deal at all. As if everyone in the world knew I didn't take a single step without the approval of Hannah and Pilar.

Well . . . do you?

I didn't have time to answer the question — or even think about it — before I opened the door to the room.

"There you are!" Pilar said.

"Where have you been?" Hannah demanded.

I took a second to hang my bag in the closet before I faced them. "Hi," I said.

"Seriously," Hannah said.

"I was out."

"With?"

What would happen if I said, *Mind your onions*?

I didn't dare find out.

"With Jules," I said. "And Audrey."

I threw the Audrey thing in because I didn't want them spending too much time thinking (or asking) about what Jules and I did all day by ourselves. It was a calculated risk, and it seemed to work.

"Ugh, really? Why?" Hannah looked up at me, a cross expression on her face. But then she started telling me about a store she and Pilar had found that sold both brands of jeans she'd been hoping to buy, and I knew I was off the hook.

CHAPTER 10

"AAAAAANNND LOOK OVER here," Hannah said. "Another dead person. What a shock."

I cringed. Hannah was in rare form that morning. Even Peely had tried to shush her once — we were in a church, after all — and was rewarded with a look that might as well have been a slap. So now neither of us said anything.

We were at the Basilique de Saint-Denis, where the kings and queens of France were buried. I was glad it was on our itinerary. As time passed since our day at Versailles, the rational part of my brain began to get the upper hand, insisting (to my relief) that I hadn't really seen a ghost. Getting a look at the final burial site of Marie Antoinette and her husband seemed like a good way to reinforce that. Once I could assure myself that the queen was safely stowed away in a massive stone casket, I'd stop thinking she was following me around.

All the remains were in giant marble boxes, like above-ground coffins, and atop each one was a lid that had a sculpture of the occupant in a state of eternal rest, lying down, hands pressed together in prayer. It was amazing how different they all were — and how well-preserved, even though some of them were about eight hundred years old.

At the feet of most of the men were lions, and at the feet of the women were dogs. Many of the dogs were sleeping, some were holding the women's robes in their mouths . . . one had even caught a rabbit. Considering how morbid the whole place was, they were pretty adorable.

Finally, we came upon the memorial for Marie Antoinette and Louis XVI.

As I looked up at the sculptures of the late king and queen, instead of the sense of reassurance I'd been hoping for, I immediately felt ill at ease, like there was a trickle of freezing water running down my spine.

"This is different," Pilar said in a hushed voice. "They don't look peaceful, they just look . . . sad."

All of the other memorials featured people in peaceful repose. Marie and Louis, on the other hand, were depicted kneeling at prayer benches — looking the opposite of restful.

Louis was praying, and he looked sort of resigned. Marie clutched her chest, staring down at the floor like her heart was breaking. The carvings were amazingly elaborate, with intricately draped fabric and royal crests made of stone.

Brynn gazed up at them. "Why don't they get to lie down?"

"A good question," Jules said. He spoke loudly enough for the whole group to hear, but still in a tone that had a hush to it. "This memorial was constructed in 1830. It contains only the partial remains of the king and queen. So they are not technically at rest here. Also, their positions represent the tragic circumstances of their deaths."

They are not technically at rest here.

My stomach tightened. I turned away.

"Around the corner," Jules was saying, "you will find the mummified heart of Louis the Seventeenth, the son of Marie and Louis, who died in captivity at the age of ten during the Revolution. His heart was preserved after his death — which was typical for the hearts of royalty — and confirmed to be legitimate by DNA testing in the year 2000."

"Now *that* actually sounds interesting," Hannah said.

Mummified heart? No, thanks. I was already having stress-induced hallucinations of a ghost in a ball gown. Seeing the shriveled heart of a ten-year-old boy wouldn't exactly nurture the cool, collected state of mind I was struggling to regain.

I started to walk away . . . but then I got the feeling that someone was following me.

Oh, God, please don't let it be the ghost.

Bracing myself, I spun around, my eyes wide and unblinking.

"*Bonjour*," Jules said, looking startled. "Are . . . you all right?"

I took a second to calm myself before I spoke. "I'm okay. . . . Just thinking about Marie and Louis."

"You don't want to see the heart?"

"No," I said quickly. "I really don't. Their tomb is bad enough."

"You know, it may not even be their actual tomb. There's a lot of controversy based on the fact that they were originally buried somewhere else, in the Madeleine Cemetery."

"Oh," I said. "But then they were exhumed and brought here?"

"Well," he said. "That is what some people say."

My spine tingled. "It's not true?"

"The problem is, when they removed the bodies, Marie was identified only by . . . this bone — *le maxillaire*?" Jules ran his fingers along his jawline.

"Her jaw?"

"*Oui*, the jaw. By a man who had met her twenty years before."

"That would be impossible," I said. "Wouldn't it?"

"Maybe so," Jules said. "It depends who you ask."

"So she's still buried there?"

He shook his head. "Probably not. The bodies from the Madeleine Cemetery were moved to another cemetery, the Errancis."

"So the queen's body could be at the other cemetery, and it could be some random person's bones in this vault?"

Jules shrugged. "Some people say the queen and king were buried in coffins, which made them easier to identify."

"What do you think?"

He smiled. "I wasn't there. It has been an ongoing argument for many years."

"Is the Errancis Cemetery one of the places we'll be going?" Even if it were an unmarked, mass grave, I could know that the queen had found some closure — the closure I'd been hoping to find at the Basilique.

"Ah, I'm afraid that is not so easy, either. The Errancis was closed after only a few years, and later most of the bodies there were taken to the Catacombs."

This was getting ridiculous. "Well, are we going to the Catacombs?"

"Yes, on Thursday." Jules looked at me out of the corner of his eye. "You are very interested in the queen."

"Sort of," I said. "But before you ask again, I really don't want to see the heart."

He smiled. "I understand."

A shriek of laughter came from behind us, and we turned to see Pilar, pink-faced, darting away from Hannah.

"How could you *say* that?" Pilar cried, her voice echoing off the stone walls around us.

I winced.

"I just think your mother would appreciate it," Hannah replied, in a voice that carried throughout the church, "since she loves you so much."

"Gross!" Pilar squealed. "No one's going to pickle my heart!"

They burst into laughter, drawing annoyed stares from other tourists.

Jules sighed and walked over to them. He said something in a low voice, and immediately, their grins disappeared. Pilar looked embarrassed and Hannah looked like someone had told her that her diamond earrings were made out of plastic. They spied me and walked over, Hannah venting under her breath.

"I *know* it's a church," she seethed. "Hello, I go to a Catholic school. I know how to act in a church."

Clearly not, but . . .

Pilar was glancing around, worried about who might be mad at her.

Hannah noticed. "You can relax, you know. Jules isn't God."

He was right, though. I looked over Hannah's shoulder and saw that he'd wandered away from us. I didn't blame him. I kind of wished I could walk away, too.

"You don't really like him, do you, Colette?" Hannah asked. "He's such a dork."

"I don't know, Hannah," I said, feeling tired all of a sudden.

Despite her insistence that there had been nothing wrong with her behavior, Hannah was much quieter for the rest of the visit — but she was quiet like a half-buried land mine.

* * *

As we were leaving the Basilique de Saint-Denis, Hannah pulled me by the arm away from the group. "We're not going with them. We're taking a taxi to a costume rental house to find something to wear to the party."

I wanted to say good-bye to Jules, but Hannah insisted that we hurry or risk missing our appointment.

The cab pulled to a stop outside of a warehouse-style shop for theatrical rentals. A sign on the door announced *PAS OUVERT AU PUBLIC*, which Hannah proudly translated as meaning "not open to regular people" as she rang the bell.

Inside was a wonderland of clothes. I drifted down the aisles, studying the hundreds of costumes. There were soldiers' uniforms, 1960s go-go dancer outfits, and long, elaborate dresses that could be straight out of a movie about Paris a hundred and fifty years ago.

I slowly made my way over to Hannah and Pilar, who stood in front of a rack of ginormous ball gowns. Some were the flattened bell shape I'd seen on the ghost — I mean, on the *woman*. The completely alive, nonghost woman.

An attendant glanced at each of us and pulled dresses in various sizes, hanging them on a smaller, separate rack. She grabbed one of the gowns and gestured for Hannah to follow her behind a curtain into the changing room.

Pilar and I waited on folding chairs and listened to Hannah's surprised exclamations of pain and discomfort.

"How much does this thing weigh? A hundred pounds?" she whined at one point.

Then the curtain parted, and Hannah stood before us in a pale-purple gown covered in clumps of pink ribbon flowers. Across the skirt were stripes of ivory lace, and the same lace flowed over the collar and poured from the sleeves.

"Voilà!" she said. "What do you think?"

"Wow," Pilar said. "It certainly plays up — um . . ."

What she meant was that the top was very tight and very — uh — encouraging.

"I know, right?" Hannah said. "That's what I like about it. Colette?"

"It's pretty," I said.

Hannah narrowed her eyes. "But?"

"But —" What I couldn't say was that it looked disturbingly

like something you'd expect to see on Little Bo Peep. "I think you should try the green one."

Hannah turned imperiously to the attendant. "Bring the green dress."

The woman closed the curtain without a word. There followed more whining and little yelps, plus Hannah's sharp admonitions of "Be careful!"

The curtain opened once more.

This gown was pale sage green, edged in a metallic gold lace. The fabric draped heavily over its wide hips. The skirt was made up of dozens of gathered scallops, and the bodice was constructed of horizontal pleats that opened up to a gauzy explosion of gold tulle at the neckline. Every element of the dress was carried out with ruthless attention to detail. Each pleat, each drape of the heavy fabric, was precise and perfect.

Hannah's pale-green eyes shone as vibrantly as emeralds.

"Colette?" she asked.

The words just popped out of my mouth: "You look like an evil queen."

Pilar gasped and shot me a scandalized look.

"I mean . . ." I couldn't think of how to say what I meant — or what I would have meant if I hadn't just said exactly what I meant, which was that she *did* look like an evil queen. The kind who keeps a bucket of poisoned apples right next to her cursed spinning wheel.

"Oh, I know what you mean." Hannah studied herself in the mirror, her lips pressed into a triumphant smile. "This is the one."

The woman helped her change out of the dress, then hung it on a rack near the small office.

"Pilar, your turn!" Hannah said.

A few minutes later, Pilar emerged through the parted curtains. "Oh my God, I can't breathe!"

"Wow, Peely!" I said.

She stopped short, mouth open. "That's a good wow?"

"Yeah," I said. "Turn around."

This dress was simpler than Hannah's — it had a smaller skirt, one that was just round instead of sticking out on the sides. But it looked like it had been made for Pilar. Its dark-red satin brought out the warmth in her skin and made her black curls look dramatic, especially in contrast to the white satin ruffle that encased the square neckline. The same style of ruffle, tight and neat-looking, adorned the ends of the sleeves. The back of the gown was bustled, the red satin slightly gathered to reveal an underskirt of black lace.

"It's perfect for you," I said. "It makes your waist look nonexistent."

"Nonexistent like a barrel?" Pilar asked.

"No, like a wasp," I said.

Pilar grinned at her reflection. If Hannah was the evil queen, then Pilar looked like the sweet, charming fairy-tale princess who the queen was determined to poison.

And it almost seemed like that was the case. Hannah was the only person in the room not infected by Pilar's happy smile.

"I don't know," Hannah said, shrugging. "It doesn't look very French."

The attendant drew back, horrified. "Eet ees *very* French!"

"Be reasonable," Hannah said. "I just don't think the color suits you."

Peely glanced at her. "But Colette likes it."

"Colette doesn't know everything about clothes," Hannah said, and I felt her glare out of the corner of my eye.

"Yes, she does!" Pilar said. But she looked doubtful.

"There must be something better," Hannah said, pulling me to the rack.

This was a test. Nothing would be better than the dress Pilar was wearing, and I wasn't going to outright lie and say so. I reached out and touched one that was a stiff purply-mauve material covered in starched lace of the same color.

"This fabric is really cool," I said lamely.

Hannah grabbed that dress and handed it to the attendant.

When the curtain opened, Pilar waited for our response.

The dull purple of the dress had just enough gray in it that it didn't bring out any of the warm tones in her skin. In fact, it was another dress that would have looked fantastic on Hannah's cool pallor. But on Peely it was nothing special.

"Great," Hannah said.

"I like the lace," Pilar said glumly. "Is it glued on?"

The attendant sniffed but didn't condescend to answer.

"I'm tired," Peely said. "I guess I'll take this one."

"Perfect," Hannah said. "Now Colette's turn."

As Pilar changed in silence, I went over to the rack to look at the other dresses. There was a teal one with a fitted, jacket-style bodice. I had a sense it would look good on me — too good for

Hannah's taste — and passed over it, reaching for a dusty tan gown that would completely wash out my complexion. But the attendant pushed in front of me, grabbed the teal one, and pulled me into the changing area.

Getting dressed was a squinchy, pinchy process, but I tried not to complain. After she'd buttoned the jacket, the woman looked at me, her eyes shining. Before I could step through the curtain, she grabbed me by the shoulders and aimed me at the mirror.

"C'est parfait," she whispered, pulling my medallion out and settling it over the crisp neckline.

It *was* perfect.

The jacket hugged my rib cage and cut in sharply at the waist, flaring in a short peplum over the top of the skirt. The color, like the ocean on a sunny day, made my skin look as radiant and luminous as the portrait of the duke at the Louvre.

I almost didn't recognize myself. Hannah's and Pilar's dresses, however pretty they were, still looked like costumes. But I looked like a girl who'd woken up in 1785 and put on her traveling outfit.

For a moment, I had the same disoriented feeling I'd experienced in the mirrored room at Versailles, like my eyes couldn't quite focus on my own face — and when they finally managed to, somehow it wasn't my face I was seeing. Once again, my eyes were wider and my lips were fuller, and my hair was piled up on my head in an elaborate updo. I reached my arm out to lean against the wall, and the attendant took me by the elbow and swung me around.

Suddenly, it was like the spell was broken. I could see again. And I could breathe again —

But just barely.

What was happening to me? Was I losing my mind?

Who was the woman I'd seen in the mirror, the woman whose face was so similar to my own?

I didn't have time to think. The attendant pulled the curtain back, revealing me to my friends.

"I don't like it," Hannah said immediately. The attendant sucked in an annoyed breath.

Pilar was silent for a moment. "Could you . . . turn around?"

I turned to let them see the back, which was just as perfect as the front, I knew.

Out of curiosity, I glanced at the tag hanging off the sleeve. *249 EUROS/SEMAINE + 100 NETTOYAGE*, it read.

Um.

There was no way on earth I could afford to pay 249 euros (plus another 100 for whatever *nettoyage* was). My dress for the winter formal at school had cost nine dollars at a brown-bag sale at the Women's League thrift store. The most expensive item of clothing I'd bought in almost a year was a shirt I got for nineteen dollars on clearance at the mall.

Too shocked to speak, I turned back to Hannah, trying to think of a way to get out of this.

"There must be something better," she said. "How about that beige one?"

That was too much for the attendant. "Actually, I'm so sorry. We are closing."

We all turned to look at her. She didn't look sorry, for the record.

Hannah scowled. "It's just one more dress."

The girl shrugged, palms up. "No time."

"Hello, we're wearing these to *Versailles*," Hannah said. "Colette's supposed to go naked?"

The woman blinked. I don't think she knew what the word *naked* meant.

I touched Hannah's arm. "Maybe I can come back . . . it's not a big deal."

"It's a huge deal," Hannah said hotly. "You can't just show up to an embassy party in a burlap sack."

Bristling, I wanted to tell her I wasn't in the habit of showing up *anywhere* in a burlap sack. But I swallowed the words and cast an apologetic look at the attendant. "I'll figure something out."

I saw in her eyes that we were united in our disdain for Hannah's hissy fit. "If you call, you can make an appointment for Wednesday or Thursday."

"See?" I said. "I'll come back." It didn't save me from paying 350 euros, but it bought me a little time. Suddenly, I remembered Mathilde's offer of a dress, and I felt a wave of relief. Maybe I could ask Jules tomorrow.

Hannah pulled out her well-worn Amex and paid for her own gown. As she folded the receipt and slipped it into her red patent-leather shoulder bag, she turned to me. "You know, you can be very passive sometimes. You really need to learn to stand up for yourself, Colette."

*　*　*

I was no expert on Parisian geography, but I knew the taxi was heading away from our hotel, not toward it. Not wanting to offend the driver, I leaned over and spoke quietly. "Hannah . . . do you know where we're going?"

Her smile was as mysterious as the *Mona Lisa*'s. "*Oui*, Colette. I know exactly where we're going."

But she wasn't going to share. All right, then.

Finally, we pulled to a stop on a small side street. Hannah paid and then scrambled out as if her seat were on fire.

This neighborhood was different from Saint-Germain — the boulevards and sidewalks were wider, the buildings were bigger, and the people walking by seemed like they were on their way to work rather than ambling around for the pleasure of it. Pilar and I followed Hannah warily as she led us down the street, looking at the addresses and names of the places we passed.

"There!" she cried, catapulting across the road, dodging traffic. She was headed for a park that occupied a whole block. Pilar and I hung back until the traffic light changed, and then we went after her.

A green metal fence surrounded the park, and in the center was a domed structure that looked like a small museum or church. There was a playground and some benches and a big old tree stump. But still nothing that would indicate why we'd come there.

As Hannah looked at me, her face lit up. And then someone's hands were over my eyes.

"Guess who?"

I was momentarily flustered by the sound of Armand's voice, and even more flustered when he took his hands away and I found myself on the receiving end of Hannah's most toxic glare.

But before Armand could see, her expression changed into one that was sweet and charming. *"Bonjour,"* she said, positioning herself between us.

He kissed her knuckles, and she was instantly under his spell.

"Hey, Armand," Pilar said, sounding slightly bored.

"Bonjour, Pilar," he said, and then turning to me, *"Bonjour,* Colette." Those liquid-gold eyes flashed.

I gave him a curt nod and turned to Peely. "Want to walk around?"

While Hannah and Armand wandered off, hands lightly linked, Peely and I went up to the big structure. Up close, it resembled a medieval monastery, with a long center corridor bordered by stone arches. The front had a big paragraph of French writing on it.

"La Chapelle Expiatoire," Pilar read.

"Chapel of . . ."

"Expiatoire means atonement," Pilar said. Then, seeing my face, she gave a good-natured huff. "Don't look so surprised, please. We played Sauguet's *Symphonie Expiatoire* at music camp last year. But that was about World War II. This is way older than that."

We studied the plaque and tried to work out what it said. The words I could understand seemed to suggest that this had been a burial place . . . but then it said something about *"transférées"*

129

to Saint-Denis. When I saw the words *Marie-Antoinette*, my heart jumped.

I stumbled backward. Wait. Was this the Madeleine Cemetery that Jules had mentioned?

I let out a long exhale, and my breath came out in a tiny cloud of fog. I suddenly wished I was back at the hotel with the rest of our group. Anywhere, actually, but right there.

"Can we go sit down?" I asked, my voice rising.

Pilar shrugged and followed me toward a metal bench near the exit. "Do you think the lovebirds will be back soon?"

"What's Hannah expecting from Armand?" I asked. "Does she think he's really serious?"

"He seems pretty serious to me," Pilar said. "And Hannah's never been more serious about anything in her life."

I didn't want to come out and say that I thought Armand was just toying with her. "But we're here for only a week."

Peely shrugged. "Hannah could easily talk her parents into sending her to a boarding school in Paris."

Hannah was one of the smartest people I knew. Would she really throw her life into total turmoil for a boy who'd whispered sweet nothings to her a few times?

"I've been meaning to tell you . . ." Pilar faltered. "I saw you and Armand the other night."

"That wasn't what it looked like," I said.

"Colette, I might be sort of dumb, but I'm not blind, okay? I can see what goes on in front of my face. And I'm just saying . . . be careful."

I thought about telling her she wasn't dumb, but that seemed beside the point. "I know. I'm not looking to make Hannah angry."

Pilar's eyebrows went up. "Angry wouldn't even begin to cover it. If Hannah thinks you're trying to move in on him, *you'll* be the one looking for boarding schools five thousand miles away."

The air was quiet around us, except for the sounds of cars driving by on the roads that bordered the park.

"Hannah's my friend," I said at last. "I would never do anything to hurt her. And I'm sure she feels the same way about me."

Pilar tried to turn away before her face betrayed her thoughts, but I caught the way her lips flattened into a hard, doubtful line.

We both knew what she was thinking — that Hannah would hurt me in a heartbeat if it came down to it. Especially if it had anything to do with Armand.

After a little while, Hannah and Armand appeared. Their hands were clasped, and he looked smug. Hannah was practically skipping.

"Ready to go?" she asked.

We found a taxi stand, and Armand pointed out his apartment — it had windows looking over the park. When a cab stopped for us, Hannah and Pilar climbed in.

"Oh, Colette," Armand said. "One moment, *s'il vous plaît*."

We all stared at him.

"Come here," he said.

I didn't want to go, but it was like an order. I slowly walked over to him.

He smiled down at me.

"You're going to get me in trouble," I said, my voice low.

"Don't worry about Hannah." His white teeth looked almost blue in the cool light. "I spent a whole hour talking to her just so I could spend one minute with you."

My heart was racing. "Why would you say that?" I asked, not daring to glance back at the taxi. "I don't understand what you're doing. Why do you think I'm special?"

Despite the cold, the gleam in his eye made me feel like I was on fire. "Because of Laclay."

"Laclay?" I asked. "Who's that?"

"Colette!" Hannah's voice was cold and rigid. "The meter's running."

I turned back to Armand. "I'm going now."

"You and I will have a chance to talk soon."

"I doubt it." I said, already stressed about Hannah.

"Colette, we're going to leave without you!" she snapped.

"You should go." Armand reached over to straighten the collar of my jacket, and I yanked away.

His laugh roared behind me as I hurried to the waiting taxi and climbed in.

"Au revoir, mesdemoiselles!" he called.

Hannah stared icily at the back of the seat in front of her.

"What did he want?" Pilar asked.

My mind raced for something, anything, that would explain Armand's actions.

"Yes, Colette, tell us," Hannah said through her teeth. "What did he want?"

"It's . . . a surprise," I said. "I can't tell you."

She narrowed her eyes.

"All right, fine," I said. "He wanted to know what size you wear. For a present."

That threw her off. She sat back, trying to look angry but unable to conceal her curiosity. "What do you think he's going to get me?"

"I told you," I said. "It's supposed to be a surprise. I've already said too much."

"All right," she said reluctantly. "Wait, did you tell him size two or zero?"

"Zero," I said.

"Okay." She looked relieved — but not as relieved as I felt that she'd bought my lie.

CHAPTER 11

WE ATE DINNER with the rest of the group at the hotel café. Hannah treated me exactly like usual — at least, that was what I tried to tell myself. Afterward, she and Pilar got into the elevator, and I hung back, trying to think of an excuse to take the stairs.

"Hey, Colette, hang on!"

I turned to see Audrey and Brynn coming up behind me.

"Oops, sorry," Hannah said, letting the elevator doors slide shut.

"Hi," I said, hoping they hadn't noticed Hannah would have had plenty of time to hold the elevator.

"Are you busy tomorrow morning?" Audrey asked.

"Um . . . just with whatever's on the itinerary."

Audrey nodded. "We're going to the Conciergerie at ten. But before that? Are you busy?"

Only a person like Audrey could make plans before ten in the morning and expect other people to have plans, too. "I don't know. Maybe I'll be . . . eating?"

"I want to show you something." Her face was lit up, like she had a big secret. "Will you meet me in the lobby at eight thirty?"

I shrugged. "Sure."

"Great!" She grinned, and then she and Brynn turned as the elevator returned with a soft *ding*.

They held the door for me, and I shook my head. "I hate elevators," I said. "I'm claustrophobic."

"Oh, okay," Audrey said. "See you in the morning."

When they were gone, I stood there for a moment, wondering what had made me spit out one of my deepest secrets to people who were basically strangers, when in eight months I'd never found the right moment to say it aloud to Hannah and Peely.

*　*　*

The next morning, I went down for breakfast at eight and found Audrey already there. Because there was no way not to, I joined her at her little table, and we ate our chocolate croissants together.

"What am I going to do without French food?" she asked, taking a big bite of the pastry.

"I wonder if you could melt a Hershey's Kiss on a regular croissant," I said.

"Blasphemy!" Audrey laughed. "Not the same at all."

She refused to say a word about the mysterious place she wanted to take me, even when we were on our way there. All she would tell me was that she'd spotted it the day before, when the group was walking back to the hotel.

We crossed the river and walked through the streets near Notre Dame, where the buildings were elaborately trimmed with stone and iron scrollwork.

"It's unbelievable," I said, gazing up at a doorway adorned with carvings of lions. "It's like somebody decided to take the time to make every single part beautiful."

"They were artisans," Audrey said. "They'd rather not build something at all than make it ugly."

She snapped photos and occasionally took out a small brown notebook and made a note or a sketch.

"Ugh," I said. "I keep forgetting to send my mother a postcard! She's going to kill me."

"Get one now," Audrey said. "You can buy a stamp at the hotel and mail it this afternoon."

So we stopped at a tiny storefront and I combed through the racks of postcards. I found one for Mom that was a photo of Notre Dame. Then I found one with a picture of the Paris city skyline for my father, figuring I could write something clever on it about New York.

"Oh, look," Audrey said, pulling a card off the rack. "Wow."

I leaned in to see the picture and then did a double take.

It was a painting of a woman sitting on a bench by a little pond . . . but not just any woman.

It was *me*.

Or rather, it was the not-me me I kept seeing in place of my own reflection. The same light hair, done up in an elaborate twist and covered in powder. The same full lips and wide blue eyes.

"It's crazy," Audrey said. "She looks *just* like you. Do you see it?"

I couldn't answer.

I turned the card over to read the caption, which was written in French and English:

ONE OF THE MANY PORTRAITS PRESERVED AT THE ROYAL PALACE AT VERSAILLES: *LA DUCHESSE*, PAINTED BY DIEGO ROSTANO, CIRCA 1786.

I remembered the old lady back at Versailles taking my photo and saying I was the girl from the picture. This must have been the picture she meant. So I wasn't just inventing this woman, dreaming her up. She was ... or had been ... real. Alive. Long ago.

"Are you going to buy it?" Audrey asked.

I forced a smile and slid the card back into its slot. "No," I said. "I don't need any more postcards."

I don't need that woman staring at me from my carry-on for the rest of the trip, is what I really meant.

We kept walking, my thoughts racing, until finally, Audrey stopped on a street corner. "There it is!" she said, pointing.

I stared at a tile set into the stone wall of a building. It was streaked with lines from centuries of rain, the carving on its surface rounded and softened with age.

But the design was unmistakable:

It was the key. The key with the cornflower in it.

I gasped. My hand automatically went to the neckline of my shirt, which the medallion was tucked behind — but something, a sudden shy feeling, stopped me just short of pulling it out.

"It's the thing from your necklace!" Grinning, Audrey reached into her bag for her travel journal and opened it, revealing the page on which she'd originally sketched my medallion. Next to it, in pencil, was a sketch of the tile. "We passed by here yesterday and it jumped out at me."

"What is this building?" I asked, stepping back and looking up at it. It was three stories tall with wrought-iron balconies and a steeply sloping metal roof.

"It looks like they sell camping supplies," she said, studying the sign hanging down. "But sometimes they have signs saying what they *used* to be."

We walked from one edge of the structure to the other but found nothing.

"Let's go inside and ask," Audrey said. "It's nine fifteen, but we can still make it back in time if we hurry."

"Are you sure?" I said. "I mean, I could always come back —"

"But this is important," she said, reaching for the door.

"How do you know?" I asked.

"I mean . . . it's important to you, right?"

"Oh. Well, yeah, kind of."

"So we'll go in."

We walked up to the counter.

"*Parlez-vous anglais?*" Audrey asked.

The clerk, a guy in his late twenties, made an uncertain face. "No so good."

In his halting English and our halting French, we quickly established that he knew absolutely nothing about the building's history. Audrey showed him the photographs she'd taken of the tile, and he shook his head.

Another employee, a girl who was apparently bored, came over. The clerk showed her the picture of the key, and they spoke to each other in French. I didn't understand a single word they said, until I heard the girl say, "Laclay."

"Excusez-moi," I said. "Laclay? Who is that?"

The clerk gently turned Audrey's camera so I could see the screen, and pointed at the image. *"La clé,"* he said slowly.

"The key," Audrey said. *"Clé* means key."

Suddenly, the female employee's face brightened. *"L'ordre de la Clé!"*

"What does that mean?" I asked.

"The Order of the Key?" Audrey said.

The girl cast a glance around the empty store, said something to the guy in French, and then beckoned to me and Audrey. "Come."

A mix of anticipation and uncertainty simmered in my stomach as she led us through a door marked ENTRÉE INTERDITE. We passed through a stockroom and made a left turn. There was an old wooden door tucked behind a pair of bikes, which the girl moved out of the way. She reached for the doorknob and yanked on it, hard, until it opened with a loud screech.

She held up a hand, telling us to wait, and darted away, returning a minute later with a camping flashlight still in its package. She flipped the light on and went through the door.

"Attention!" she called. *Be careful.* Just inside the door was a rather steep stone stairway.

I hesitated. Already, my heart was beating faster.

Audrey looked at me. "Are you okay? I can go down and see what it is, if you want."

"Um . . ." I looked down the steps into the gaping darkness. I hated to send someone else to do my dirty work.

Audrey didn't seem to mind, though. She descended halfway and stopped. "It's dark, but it's not small, if that helps."

It did. I could handle the dark, as long as I knew the walls weren't pressing in on me. The echoes of our footsteps off the room's distant edges made me feel better.

We were standing in a cellar of some sort. The store didn't appear to use it for anything, although when the girl swept her flashlight across the walls, I saw a collection of old brooms and a beat-up metal trash can.

"Aha!" The girl's triumphant exclamation reverberated around us. *"Ici* — here!"

Audrey and I came up behind her and looked at the spot on the wall illuminated by her light.

"Oh," Audrey said softly.

It was an engraved metal sign. At the top was the key design. Under that, it read, L'ORDRE DE LA CLÉ, MDCCLXXXI. EN SERVICE ÉTERNEL À SA MAJESTÉ LA REINE.

"What year is that?" I whispered, trying to remember my Roman numerals.

"One thousand . . . five hundred . . . two hundred . . . L is fifty, right? Plus thirty-one." Audrey sighed an amazed little sigh. "Seventeen eighty-one. In eternal service of Her Majesty the queen."

"The *queen* queen?" I asked, my pulse quickening.

"Let's see," Audrey said. "In 1781, that would have been Marie Antoinette. Wow."

I couldn't even speak. So "Laclay" wasn't a person. It was an organization. And now I knew for certain: it had something to do with me — and with the duke in the portrait — and with Armand . . .

And with Marie Antoinette.

The girl was smiling at us. Clearly, she'd gotten the reaction she was looking for.

Audrey took out her camera. "The Order of the Key. So whoever they were, they were devoted to the queen."

"But the queen died in the Revolution," I said.

"Yeah." Audrey started taking photos. "A lot of people died in the Revolution. Probably these Key people, too."

The girl who worked at the store wandered around the perimeter of the room, inspecting the walls with interest.

"Come!" she said. "Come, see. More!"

She stood with her flashlight pointed to another metal tile. The key symbol was at the top, and beneath that was a list of words. I knelt down to look at them.

They were names.

DUBOIS. BEAUCLERC. VOCLAIN. ROUX. JANVIER . . .

And ISELIN.

CHAPTER 12

WE HAD TO book it to the hotel to meet our group by ten o'clock. The whole way back, my thoughts were swirling. Had my family, the Iselins, really been members of this mysterious order? With Armand's family? The idea of having something in common with a person as awe-inspiring as Armand made me feel electrified.

In the lobby, Madame Mitchell did a double take when she saw me. "I thought you all weren't feeling well this morning."

"Oh," I said. "I don't know. I'm fine."

"I guess it's just Hannah and Pilar, then." The look on her face told me she knew Hannah and Peely were lying — but also that she didn't really care. I guess after teaching overprivileged girls for twenty years, you've pretty much heard it all. I kind of didn't care, either. If they wanted to sleep through the entire trip, that was their business.

Jules arrived and we began our walk. I didn't want to seem clingy, so I stayed at the back of the group. Finally, I fell into step beside him.

"Hey," I said.

"Good morning," he said. "How are you?"

"I'm really sorry about yesterday, at the Basilique. Hannah was . . . she just wasn't thinking."

"That is not your fault. You don't need to apologize."

"I feel like I should," I said. "I hope you don't think they represent all of us."

He turned to me, a small smile playing on his lips. "I don't think that at all."

I couldn't keep the smile from my face. "Okay, then."

I was on the verge of telling him what we'd learned about the Order of the Key, when Madame Mitchell turned and yoo-hoo'd at him, and he had to excuse himself and walk away. A little fountain of happiness sprang up inside me and I couldn't keep the smile off my face.

We bought our tickets and then went across a massive walled courtyard into La Conciergerie.

"During the Revolution, this was a notorious prison," Jules announced as we stood inside the vaulted room where huge stone pillars and arching stone beams braced the ceiling. "Many historical figures were held here prior to their executions, including Marie Antoinette, Madame du Barry, and Robespierre. Now, most of the building is used for judicial purposes."

All I heard was *Marie Antoinette*.

We walked through a hall filled with examples of eighteenth-century prison cells.

"Kind of tight," Audrey said, as we peered into a room that couldn't have been bigger than about six feet by six feet, with a rough wooden bench that served as a bed.

"Yeah," Brynn said. "Not the ideal place to spend a weekend."

"Or the last few months of your life," Jules said, coming up behind us.

"Did Marie Antoinette have to stay in a room like this?" I asked, sort of appalled. I mean, she *was* the queen. You'd think they'd have given her a little extra space.

"No, her cell was larger. But not very much larger. You will see a representation of it farther along on the tour."

I noticed that he stayed with us as we passed the other rooms, which were full of janky-looking mannequins that Brynn made hilarious comments about.

But we all fell silent as we crossed into the re-creation of Marie Antoinette's cell.

A shudder passed through my body as I looked at the items displayed behind glass. A rug. A cup. A water pitcher. Things the queen had actually held and used while she had been locked up, separated from her husband and children . . . waiting to die.

The room *was* larger than the other cells, but compared to the grand opulence of Versailles, Marie must have thought she was losing her mind. She had a small bed and a desk, with a short privacy screen to shield her from the view of the guards who were always sitting a few feet away.

I started to back away from the display, my palms growing sweaty.

To live there . . . to be stuck there, knowing you were going to die but not knowing what had become of your children . . .

"This is what you get when you tell people to eat cake," Brynn said.

"Marie Antoinette never said that," Jules said. "It's a famous misrepresentation. Actually, she was not even the first person accused of having said it."

"Then why did people believe it?" I asked.

He shrugged. "She was raised in utter luxury as an archduchess and then became a queen at a young age. She was spoiled and probably thoughtless in many ways. But I don't think she was bad in the way that an evil person might be called bad. She was devoted to charities, and she was a good mother who loved her children very much. But the people wanted to hate her."

"Why?" I asked.

"They needed a symbol," he said. "Somewhere to project their frustration. Marie Antoinette was a foreigner — she was born in Austria, she was independent, and she had extravagant taste. But she was falsely accused of many things and often used as a . . . I don't know how to say it."

"A scapegoat?" I suggested.

Jules's confused face was seriously cute. "A what kind of goat?"

"Scapegoat. It means . . . someone you blame when things aren't good."

"Then yes. She was a goat."

At the far end of the hallway was a small square room, lined with benches. Every wall had a sign on it, filled with columns of names of prisoners held there during the Revolution.

I went straight to the *I*s, steeling myself for the sight of one or more Iselins on the list. My own relatives, horribly condemned to die.

But I didn't find any Iselins. And when I looked for Armand's family, the Janviers, I didn't find any of them.

I tapped Audrey on the shoulder. "Do you still have the pictures you took this morning?"

She started scrolling back through her camera. "Yeah . . . oh, are you checking the names?"

I nodded, and then we went down the list together, looking for the rest of the families — Beauclerc, DuBois, Roux, and Voclain.

But we didn't find any of them.

"What do you think it means?" I asked.

Audrey shrugged. "That they were lucky?"

Still, I found it weird — that out of literally thousands of people, six whole families had escaped the guillotine entirely — and they just happened to be the same six families who were in the Order of the Key together.

We trailed down the hallway to the final room on the tour — a memorial chapel.

"This room was actually the queen's cell," Jules said. "It was turned into a memorial twenty-three years after she died, by King Louis the Eighteenth."

The chapel was beautiful, with a real altar and everything. It was dark and quiet, small but not suffocating. On one side was a portrait of Marie Antoinette dressed all in black; on the other was a small table.

As I turned to go back to the main room, I froze.

Standing directly across from me was the queen.

She stared at me, her eyes burning with the same intensity I'd seen at Le Hameau.

In the dimly lit room, she almost seemed to give off a light of her own — a ghostly light.

No. I don't believe in ghosts.

And then a tourist took a step toward the altar — and walked right through the queen's enormous skirt.

I staggered backward, running into a woman who said, "Watch out, hon," in a thick Texan accent.

By the time I got my feet back under me, the ghost — or whatever she was — had disappeared.

Audrey was by my side. "Are you okay?"

I wanted to nod, but I was too freaked out. Fortunately, Audrey just assumed I was having a claustrophobic meltdown.

"Come on, let's go sit. It's a little stuffy in here." She guided me back out to a bench in the hallway. We sat for a couple of minutes, and I tried to force myself to take slow, even breaths. The thought kept sliding back into my head that I should feel better, but then it was run over by the giant, screeching fact that I'd seen a *ghost* — an actual ghost. I'd come so close to convincing myself that I'd been wrong about what I experienced at Versailles . . . but there was no denying it any longer.

She really was a ghost.

My stomach turned over with a flop. I rested my head in my hands.

"You really don't seem okay," Audrey said.

"I think I really might not be," I said.

Her voice was calm, but I could hear the anxiety she was trying to cover up. "Should I get Madame Mitchell? Do you need a doctor or something?"

I tried to swallow the thickness in my throat but found that it wouldn't go away. Then I tried to tell Audrey that I was fine, but I couldn't say the words.

"Let's go outside and get some actual fresh air," Audrey said. "Wait here for a second."

As if I could go anywhere.

When she came back, Brynn was with her. "Is it a panic attack?" Brynn asked. "My mom gets panic attacks."

"Can you walk?" Audrey asked.

"No," I said. "I mean, yes, I can walk. No, it's not a panic attack. I don't think." Was it still called a panic attack when there was something actually worth panicking about?

Somehow, I got to my feet, and we walked all the way back to the exit and emerged into the courtyard.

A light, chilled rain had begun to fall.

Instantly, I felt better. Not 100 percent, but I could breathe again. Brynn and Audrey watched me as I stood in the rain, enjoying the cool mistiness and swallowing the sweet, fresh air.

After a minute, I turned back to them.

"Better?" Audrey asked.

"Way better," I said. "Thank you."

"Of course." She made a face like thanking her was kind of dumb. "Do you want to go back to the hotel? I can skip the Champs-Élysées. . . . It's just shopping."

"Maybe that would be a good idea." Spending a whole afternoon surrounded by stuff I couldn't afford wasn't quite as bad as being stalked by a ghost, but it was close. "I'm sure I can get there by myself."

Brynn pretended to be shocked. "Without your buddy?"

I half-smiled. "I guess I'll find Madame Mitchell and tell her."

She shrugged. "It's easier to apologize afterward than get permission before, right? We'll tell her you left. 'We tried to make her stay, but she karate-chopped us. Who knew Colette was secretly a ninja?'"

I grinned.

"You'll take a taxi, though?" Audrey asked.

"I'm okay to walk," I said. "I promise."

"Here." Audrey dug through her backpack. "Take my umbrella."

She insisted, so I took the tiny umbrella she offered. I still got wet, but it didn't matter. The rain made the city seem even more romantic — the people pulling their coat collars up and hunching under overhangs and striped awnings, and the gleam from the headlights on the wet cobblestones.

But even as I took in the loveliness around me, my thoughts were occupied with the ghost.

What I needed was to figure out why I was seeing her, when obviously no one else was. Did I just happen to be visiting places that were significant to her, or was she following me? Was it because of the Order of the Key? It couldn't be a coincidence that my ancestors had been closely connected to the queen and now I was seeing her ghost around Paris.

That made me wonder — would Armand be able to see her?

The trouble was, to ask him, I'd need his phone number. I couldn't exactly ask Hannah for it.

In the penthouse, Pilar let me in and then drifted back to the couch, where she was reading a fashion magazine. The shower was running in Hannah's room.

This was my chance.

"Have you seen my turquoise scarf?" I asked.

Peely looked up and shook her head.

"Did Hannah borrow it?" I turned to look at the closed bedroom door. "I told her she could. . . ."

"Go check," Pilar said. "She just got in the shower. She won't care."

I nodded and opened Hannah's door, my heart pounding. Her stuff was strewn everywhere, but I found her phone charging on her nightstand.

I scrolled through her texts. There were about six in a row sent to Armand, unanswered. It was a huge difference from the way Hannah usually was with boys — she was the cat, and the boys were the mice, getting batted around for fun. With Armand, she was a tiny white mouse . . . sending unanswered mouse texts to the big old cat.

I wrote down his phone number on a piece of hotel stationery and crammed it into my pocket, then returned the phone to the nightstand and went back out to the living room.

"Did you find it?" Pilar asked.

It took me a second to remember that I was supposed to be looking for my scarf.

"No," I said. "It must be somewhere in my suitcase."

"Oh," she said.

"I'm going to run downstairs and grab a sandwich. Are you good?"

She nodded, her eyes drawn back to her magazine. "Do you really think people are going to be wearing a lot of olive green this summer? They keep saying so, but honestly, I don't see it happening."

"Sorry," I said. "I don't know."

I slipped out the door and down to the lobby courtesy phone. I dialed Armand's number and got his voice mail.

"It's Colette," I said. "Please call me at the Hôtel Odette. . . . I have a crazy question for you."

* * *

Back in the room, Hannah was in a rage because Armand hadn't returned her calls or texts. Trying to avoid attracting her attention, I changed out of my rained-on clothes and borrowed Peely's laptop to see if I could find anything online about the Order of the Key. But every lead took me to a dead end. There were offhand mentions of the various families, usually in the context of accompanying the king on a diplomatic trip or being present at the signing of a treaty or whatever, but nothing that linked them together . . . and nothing at all that linked them to the queen.

At dinnertime, Hannah declared that she was going to order room service and watch the DVDs she'd brought from home. Pilar ordered from room service, too, but I said I'd go down to the café and grab some food.

"It's all the same food," Hannah said scornfully.

It's not the same at all, I thought. *It's free.*

I endured her eye rolls and made it to the café just as the waiters were making their rounds.

"Colette, over here." Audrey waved to me from the small table where she and Brynn were sitting. I wove through the tables and stood behind one of the chairs.

"Are you alone?" Brynn asked. "Sit with us."

"Yeah," I said. "But I'm not eating here. . . . I'm going to get my food to go."

I ignored their quizzical expressions but pulled a chair out and sat down.

"I love that dress," Brynn said. "Is it vintage?"

I nodded. I was wearing a simple black-and-white rayon dress, loosely cut, with buttons down the front, and over it, a short, structured black jacket. I'd found both of them at the thrift store. What Brynn (or Hannah or Pilar) didn't know is that my so-called vintage clothes weren't *designer* vintage. Most of them had labels from brands my friends would never be caught dead in.

"It must be so fun to shop with you," Brynn said. "Like a treasure hunt."

"I hate shopping," Audrey said. "I just wear whatever my grandmother buys me . . . except the dresses. I have like fifteen dresses in my closet gathering dust."

"I walk into the Gap, find a mannequin I like, and buy everything the mannequin is wearing," Brynn said. "Baa, baa."

"If I could figure out how to dress like Colette, I would try harder," Audrey said. "But what's the point? And I don't want to end up looking like I obeyed the corporate mall overlords. No offense, Brynn."

Brynn laughed. "I welcome the guidance of our evil corporate overlords."

"It's not that complicated," I said. "You just follow your instincts."

Audrey sighed. "Easy for you to say. My fashion instincts are defective. I don't know the first thing about what color goes with what pattern, or whatever."

"I could help you sometime," I said, without meaning to.

"Really?" Audrey was looking at me like I'd offered her a pony. "That would be really cool. It would make my mom's entire year."

I shrugged, but inside I was already wondering (a) what I'd just done, and (b) how to get out of it.

Before I could say anything else, the waiter came to take our orders. I asked for a ham and cheese quiche, and then Audrey started talking about French food, and nobody said anything else about clothes.

I was halfway through my meal before I remembered that I was supposed to be going back to the suite to eat with Hannah and Peely. I stopped short, my fork hovering in midair.

"What's wrong?" Audrey asked. "You look like you just saw a ghost or something."

Um.

"I was supposed to get this to go," I said. "I totally forgot."

"That's not a big deal, though, is it?" Brynn asked.

"Hannah's in a bad mood already," I said, starting to stand.

"At least finish eating," Brynn said. "She's got Pilar in her clutches; she can't be mad that you ate dinner, can she?"

I didn't answer. But not answering felt like making a giant confession about my friendship with Hannah.

Brynn and Audrey exchanged a quick glance, and that one little moment contained an eternity of shame and humiliation for me. A warmth spread up through my face, and I hoped the lights were too low for them to see me blushing.

"Colette, don't take this the wrong way . . ." Audrey spoke slowly, cautiously. "But do you really need Hannah in your life?"

The warmth reached my ears and turned to heat. "She's my friend," I said. "I know she's a little high maintenance sometimes, but you don't ditch people based on little flaws."

"Hannah would," Brynn said shortly.

Audrey gave Brynn a look. "Colette's right. You have to decide how much you're going to put up with."

I couldn't bring myself to make eye contact with either of them. "Thanks for letting me sit with you. I'd better get back upstairs."

I left my plate of half-eaten food and walked out of the café. But I made it only halfway to the stairs before someone moved into my path.

"*Bonsoir*," Armand said, smiling down at me.

I took a step back, Peely's warning echoing in my head.

"Hannah's upstairs," I said.

"I am not here to see Hannah," he purred. "You called me, so I came."

I stood up straighter, not letting my guard down for a millisecond. "You could have called me back . . . you know, on a phone?"

"It is time to tell you about *La Clé*." He gently took hold of my arm. "It will be better to do it face-to-face."

I looked up at him warily. "Like, really tell me, or just drop a bunch of mysterious hints?"

His laugh echoed off the lobby walls. One of the girls at the reception desk glanced up in curiosity and then popped to attention when she saw him. You couldn't blame her. He looked like a movie star.

"No hints," he said. "I will tell you everything I know."

I sighed. If Hannah came downstairs I'd be in huge trouble . . . but what were the chances of that happening? Still, I nudged him toward a little sitting area that wasn't visible from the elevators.

"Five minutes," I said. "I have to get back to Hannah."

"Don't worry about her," he said. "I will deal with that later. So what do you know about the order?"

I told him about finding the building and the names on the engraved plaques in the basement. "I guess that means our families knew each other."

"They were very rich, very powerful, and very closely tied together," he said. "They knew each other intimately."

The sound of the word *intimately* in his French accent sent shivers through me.

"But that was more than two hundred years ago. What difference does it make now?" I asked.

Armand clasped his hands, interweaving his fingers. "We are bound together. Our families are linked, and we can preserve that. We need to claim our birthright, and we must all act together to do so."

"What do you mean, claim our birthright?"

He unclasped his fingers and relaxed. "I did some research on you. Your father is Leo Iselin, heir of the Iselin estate, and the rightful owner of the title of *Duc de Broglie*."

Wait. My dad, a duke?

Seriously?

What did that make me? I guessed it made Mom a duchess (or ex-duchess), and since titles seemed to travel down the male side of the family, it made Charlie a duke, too.

I remembered the postcard with the picture of the woman who looked like me — the one the caption had called "the duchess." Did that mean she was an ancestor of mine?

I was in a daze. This would be seriously impressive to Hannah and Pilar. My mind began to trace the paths of all the fabulous possibilities that lay ahead of me. Spending the summer in Manhattan and having the paparazzi follow me around . . . my picture on celebrity websites — *"La Duchesse de Broglie made an appearance at a charity event last night, wearing vintage Chanel"* — being the It Girl, for once, instead of the It Girl's Struggling

Backup Friend. Maybe they'd even find some way to make a big deal out of me at the Versailles party.

Except —

"Does France even have dukes anymore?" I asked.

"No — but that is an unfortunate technicality, one that we can fix." He leaned forward. "My father is working very hard to restore my family's title. And if we can gather the members of *La Clé*, we have that much more advantage."

"But why?" I asked. "Who cares?"

He snorted. "I care! And you should care! It's about prestige, and pride in your family's history . . . your mother could be *La Duchesse de Broglie*."

I wondered if the customers at Macy's would be impressed that *La Duchesse de Broglie* was ringing up their perfume for them.

"We're special," he said, grabbing my arm. "We must return to the glory our families once possessed — *la noblesse ancienne*."

I had the sense to pull away.

"And what about the queen?" I asked.

He stared at me. "What do you mean? Why do you ask?"

"Because the order was in the eternal service of the queen — Marie Antoinette."

For the first time since I'd met him, Armand seemed ill at ease. He sat back and looked at me as if he was making up his mind about something. "How do you know this?"

"Because it's what the plaque said. That's why the symbol has the cornflower in the key shape — it was her favorite flower."

Armand shook his head.

"What?" I asked. "What's wrong?"

Had the queen appeared to him, too? Was he just hesitant to say it for the same reason I was — because it sounded crazy?

I decided to take a chance. "Have you . . . seen anything unusual lately?"

"*Oui.*" His eyes flashed, and he looked around like he wanted to make sure no one was watching us. Then he rolled up his right sleeve. "This was on my arm when I awoke today."

I looked down at his right forearm. On it was a dark mark, about two inches long. It was smudgy, but I didn't have to use my imagination to figure out what it was. A key. With cornflower-shaped cutouts.

"Is that a tattoo?" I asked.

"You can see it?" He stared at his arm. "I don't know what it is, but no one else can see it."

"Where did it come from?" I asked.

"I do not know. Do you have one?"

I shook my head, but he reached over and pulled up my sleeve for confirmation. All that was visible was my winterpale arm.

But had he seen the ghost? Or a slightly different version of his own face staring back at him in mirrors? Was there a portrait at Versailles of a man who resembled Armand?

"Perhaps yours will come soon," he said. "But now you understand that what I am saying is real — and important. Don't you see, Colette — it means we're truly connected!"

The air in the lobby seemed warm, and I began to feel dizzy — almost like one of my claustrophobic episodes, except it was from the thoughts closing in on my head.

Maybe Armand was special — maybe I was even special. But my family couldn't even come together for dinner, so how were we supposed to fight for anything? Clearly, Armand assumed my dad had tons of money, more than enough to lead the crusade to restore our — what had he called it? — *noblesse ancienne*? I opened my mouth to start explaining when I felt a hand on my shoulder, pressing down with more intensity than seemed necessary.

"Well, hello," Hannah said. "What am I missing?"

My blood went cold. I looked up into her icy green eyes and knew that I was in seriously dangerous territory. I pulled my arm out of Armand's grasp.

"Nothing," I said.

"We were waiting for you to bring your food back," she said, a psychotic-sounding little chirp in her voice. "And I got a strange feeling, so I decided to come check on you."

Somehow, while saying this, she managed to wedge herself between us.

"I ran into Colette outside the café," Armand said. "I was just about to call you."

"How nice that you two could spend some time together," she said coolly, "alone."

Armand didn't even blink. "Yes, it has been nice."

Hannah shot me a look that would have turned a fireball into a lump of ice. "I can't wait to hear *allllll* about it, Colette."

Armand grabbed her around the waist and pulled her down to sit on his knee. "Oh, you don't want to hear it. To be honest, even I was getting bored. We were just talking about our families."

Hannah, thrilled by his affectionate gesture, took the bait. "Your families?"

"Oh, yes," he said. "Didn't you know? Colette's family is one of the oldest and most influential in France."

"Really?" she asked, shooting me a curious look. "No, I didn't know that."

"She outranks us all."

"Rank?" Hannah's gaze lingered on me for a moment. Then she turned back to Armand. "What's your rank?"

"Well, it's very complicated . . . but one day I will be the *Duc de Valois*."

And boom — Hannah was hooked. Her eyes went wide and starry, and I knew she was imagining her future life as *La Duchesse de Valois*.

I took the opportunity to escape. "Okay, cool, see you guys later."

Armand shuffled Hannah to the side and stood up, reaching for my hand and kissing it with exaggerated courtesy. "We will talk again soon."

"Maybe."

"We are bound, Colette." Armand looked right into my eyes. "We are bound by blood."

I broke away and practically ran for the staircase.

When I reached the suite, Pilar let me in and asked if I'd seen Hannah. I nodded, breathless, and flopped down on the couch. Suddenly, the fact that I'd kept all of my stuff neatly packed in my suitcase seemed like a good idea, because I had a feeling that when Hannah got back I'd be kicked out of the penthouse and left to sleep in the hallway.

Finally, the door opened.

I braced myself.

"*Bonsoir, mes amies!*" Hannah trilled. She wafted into the room and sank down next to me on the sofa. "Colette, why didn't you say anything? This is such a *huge* deal."

"I . . . I guess I didn't really know," I said. What on earth had Armand said to her?

"What's a huge deal?" Pilar asked.

Hannah ignored her. "Armand said that technically the title would pass to the male heir, but that since it's modern day, you could potentially contest Charlie's right to —"

"It's not that simple," I said. "Did he tell you that titles don't exist anymore in France?"

"He said he's working to bring them back, and that you were going to help. And I told him I'd help, too — I'd make Dad let me go to school here and then I could do whatever he needs me to do."

"Also," I said, "why would I fight my own brother to steal a title from him?"

She laughed. "All you ever do is fight with your brother, Colette. Why not do it over something important, for a change?"

Peely's head went back and forth like she was watching a tennis match. "I'm still majorly confused, by the way."

"Just think . . ." Hannah said dreamily, the low lamplight casting a golden glow on her pale skin as she rested her head on my shoulder. "We'll be duchesses together."

CHAPTER 13

MY HEAD HURTS. I'm sweating. I try to move, but I feel sluggish, heavy. It takes me two tries to get to my feet. And then something is dragging me down, like a fifty-pound weight harnessed to my shoulders and hips.

The room I'm crossing is full of people. Soft music plays, but I can't see the musicians because I'm holding a fan in front of my face. I pause in front of a mirror and steal a glance at myself.

My wig is a monstrous mass of curls and bows and powder. That's why my head hurts. And the weight pulling me down? It's a dress of dove-gray taffeta that grips me around the waist like a boa constrictor and then explodes out from my hips.

It's midsummer, and the room feels stiflingly hot, especially as I'm wrapped in fifteen layers of fabric. I just want to find the exit and escape out into the evening air.

But I can't; there's someone I need to talk to.

I scan the room over the top of my fan, and I can tell something is wrong. Though we're gathered for a small party, the mood is tense. The guests are pretending to be festive, but something is off.

I keep walking. I bump into a servant girl with my skirt, and she turns to me and blushes.

"Pardon, madame," she says, curtsying.

Then people clear out of my way, and I find the person I'm looking for: a woman who reclines on a chaise, her head held high, her large eyes surveying the room with what I know is feigned interest. Her gown is the finest pale-pink silk, with delicate tufts of silk flowers sewn onto it. It rests low on her shoulders.

Around her neck she wears the most fragile-looking silver chain . . .

And from the chain hangs a medallion.

* * *

I woke in a cold sweat to sunlight peeping in through the closed curtains. I had an unsettled, unrested feeling, like I'd hardly gotten any sleep at all. I'd been dreaming, but I couldn't remember the details — only that there was something I'd been trying to do, and I hadn't been able to do it. The frustration lingered as I lay on the sofa bed and stared up at the crystal chandelier, running through last night's talk with Armand.

Even if I were a duchess, it wouldn't make a huge difference in my life . . . would it? I thought about Dad and how status-conscious he is. He'd jump at the chance to be the *Duc de Broglie* . . . and then I started to daydream about how maybe dukes weren't allowed to be divorced and he'd have to come

crawling back to Mom and beg her to be his *duchesse*. And then
we could all spend the summer in New York together.

One clear advantage of being part of France's *noblesse
ancienne* — it made Hannah treat me like someone who
approached being her equal. So I hadn't heard another word
about not coming back up for dinner, or even about my
unplanned meet-up with Armand.

When I heard Hannah's phone alarm go off, I got up and
took a shower. I put on jeans and a vintage sweater I'd found at
a thrift store, dark blue with a sequined dolphin on the front,
and a pair of gray ankle boots. I gathered my hair into a pony-
tail and put on berry-colored lipstick and no other makeup.

Pilar came out of her room. She'd toned everything down —
from her just-bought-in-Paris Burberry moccasins all the way
up to her hair, which lay in soft curls over her shoulders. She
moved hesitantly.

"Hey, you look great!" I said.

"Thanks." She relaxed. "I thought I'd try your style today —
it's so fast."

Hannah came out looking like her usual dressed-to-the-nines
and made-up-to-the-nines and flat-ironed-to-the-nines self. She
did a double take when she saw Pilar, and her head made an
unhappy little tilt to the side, but she didn't say anything.

Well. Ten points for the *duchesse*.

*　　*　　*

Our first destination was a place called the Catacombs. I
remembered Jules mentioning that Marie Antoinette's bones

could have been there, and it was all I could think of as our group waited at the Metro station for him to meet up with us.

"Don't look now, Colette," Hannah said quietly, "but I think that puppy you fed has followed you home."

I didn't understand what she meant until I turned to see Audrey standing a few feet away, watching me anxiously.

"See? That's the problem with getting buddy-buddy with people you don't really like," Hannah said, in the manner of a wise elder advising a pupil. "They think you're BFFs, when really you were just bored or whatever."

I nodded, a little distracted. Audrey seemed genuinely worried about something, and I kind of wanted to go ask her if everything was okay.

I didn't have to, though. Because a few seconds later, she was tapping me on the shoulder.

"Hey," I said.

"Hey," she said.

"Oh, hey," Hannah said. "What's up, Autumn? Love your sweater. Is that from Walmart?"

Audrey, who was wearing a perfectly serviceable black sweater, shot her a confused look and then looked back at me. "Do you have a minute?"

"We're actually kind of busy at the moment." Hannah gave her a sad little smile. "Maybe Colette can just check in with you later?"

Audrey's glance traveled to Hannah and stayed there. And as she stared, her expression went from one of worry to one of utter apathy.

"You know what?" she said. "Never mind."

Audrey spun on the wide rubber heel of her athletic sneaker and marched back to Brynn. She said something in a low voice, and Brynn's face scrunched up in disgust.

"I'm telling you, it's for the best," Hannah said to me. "People like us don't have time for people like that."

I didn't answer. Audrey always seemed to have time for me, when I needed her.

Hannah draped her arm around my shoulder. "Don't look so tragic. We're about to explore some dusty old French place — that's like your favorite pastime."

*   *   *

When we arrived at the Catacombs, we walked into the small building and Madame Mitchell herded us all into an even smaller room. I didn't really see what was happening until we were right on top of the next phase of the attraction — a spiral staircase.

A tiny one.

That went straight down into the ground.

I came to a full stop.

"Um," I said.

Madame Mitchell was already out of earshot.

"What?" Hannah said. "Go on."

"I can't."

Pilar went around me and started down the steps.

"Colette, go." Hannah's voice was insistent.

"What exactly is this place?" I looked around for some sort of poster or sign.

"It's the Catacombs."

"What's a catacomb?"

She wrinkled her nose with displeasure. "It's a place where we're about to go. What is your problem?"

"I don't . . . I don't like enclosed spaces."

"Oh," she said. "Well . . . I'm pretty sure once you get down there, it's like a big cave or something."

"Really?"

She nodded. "The Basilique was like a catacomb, I think."

I glanced at the stairs, uncertain.

"You're really scared, Colette," Hannah said, her voice rising in surprise. "I had no idea. Is this why you won't take the elevator?"

I nodded, and then the most extraordinary thing happened: Hannah hugged me.

"It's going to be fine," she said. "I'll help you. We'll do it together."

I could hardly refuse now. Besides, the people lined up behind us were getting pretty grumbly. Hannah gestured for me to start down the steps, so I did. One at a time.

When I say these were tiny stairs, I mean they were minuscule. And they went around and around and around in an endless downward spiral. About thirty seconds into our descent, my fingers started to feel numb.

Hannah put her hand on my shoulder. "Breathe," she said. "You're fine. It's not much farther."

I took a deep breath. It did seem to help. And the fact that she was being so insanely nice to me was a terrific distraction.

So I kept going. Hannah cheered me on and made jokes and sang little songs, and before I knew it, we'd reached the bottom.

I expected the next doorway we went through to be the wide-open space — the underground cavern Hannah had promised me — but it wasn't.

It was a tunnel.

A very small, very dark tunnel.

In a slight panic, I turned to the nearest person — who didn't happen to be Hannah. It was an older woman holding a tour book.

"Is this the Catacombs?" I asked.

"No, this gets you there," she said. "It's just a little walk."

Hannah watched me quizzically. "Okay? Come on. You can do it."

I wasn't so sure. Now my whole body was buzzing. "I don't think I can, actually."

For a moment, I saw a sliver of impatience beneath Hannah's sweet exterior, but it was gone as quickly as it came on.

"You heard the lady — it's just a short walk." She gave my arm a gentle tug. "Let's go."

"It's so small," I said.

"Don't think about that. Think about something that makes you happy."

Something that makes me happy . . .

Jules's face popped into my head.

We made our way through the tunnel, and I survived by pretending to be somewhere else. My feet carried my body along, but my mind was at the Martins' apartment, having dinner and laughing and hanging out.

"You're doing great," Hannah said. "Now, look, here we go . . ."

I blinked back to the present. We turned a corner, and I waited for the relief of soaring ceilings and far-off walls.

"Oh," Hannah said.

"What . . ." I couldn't form words. "What . . ."

In point of fact, the Catacombs weren't like the Basilique at all. They weren't cavernous.

They were basically dark, dripping, cold tunnels, much like the one we'd just come through . . .

Except the walls were lined with bones.

Millions and millions of bones.

"Well, this isn't what I expected at *all*," Hannah said.

I couldn't speak. I couldn't move. I could only stare at the walls of bones stacked like logs in an endless woodpile. Arranged among them in decorative ways — stripes, crosses, even hearts — were skulls. Thousands of skulls. Brown with age, chipped and cracked, with gaping, eyeless sockets and sharp, hollow spaces where people's noses had been. They seemed to sneer with the jagged lines of their missing teeth.

"Okay, I'm going to die now," I said.

Hannah's saintly expression was gone, replaced by one of distinct irritation. "It's not my fault, Colette. How was I supposed to know?"

I didn't blame her. I blamed myself for being so clueless that I'd allowed myself to be led down into this horrible place.

Not that my mind was working well enough to focus on hating myself. Or on reassuring Hannah that I didn't consider this catastrophic, sanity-ending situation to be her fault.

"You're making a scene." Hannah pushed me farther into the maze of bones.

The light fell in dim orange pools on the floors, leaving the edges of the passage shrouded in dingy darkness. People around us stopped to pose for pictures, smiling and laughing and joking.

How could you joke or laugh in a place like this? How could you do anything but expect to have a heart attack and die?

I stood ramrod straight, my eyes focused on the floor, stepping along in time to the drumming of my heart. My hands were slick with sweat, but the rest of me was freezing.

"Where did our class go? Pilar should have waited for us." Hannah was apparently bored with her humanitarian efforts. At one point my foot slipped on the wet ground, and I managed to catch myself, but not before noticing the dirty look she cast in my direction.

I kept walking, because the only other option would have been to drop to the ground and curl into a ball and hyperventilate until I passed out, then hope someone came along and dragged me back up to the street.

Every so often there would be a piece of flat stone with a quote carved into it — and the word *MORT* seemed to feature in every single one of them.

My French might not be great, but I knew the word *mort*. It meant *dead*.

So just in case being down there didn't make me feel enough like I was dying, I was surrounded by quotes about dying and death . . . all spoken or written by people who were themselves now dead.

The only pinhole of light at the end of the tunnel (metaphorically, of course . . . this tunnel didn't seem to have an end) was that I knew, in some deep pocket of my mind, that it couldn't last forever. It might seem like forever, but it would end eventually.

I couldn't say this to Hannah, of course, because I could hardly feel my mouth. Forming an intelligent sentence was far beyond my capabilities.

"Wait, Colette," Hannah said.

I stopped and turned to her.

She was looking to our right, at a little grotto off the side of the main path. Two large concrete pillars ran from the floor to the ceiling, and between them was a shorter pillar, with a stone bowl balanced on it.

"I think this is it," she said. "It looks like the place he described. . . ."

"What?" I managed to ask. "The place who described?"

"Armand was supposed to be here," she said. "He said to go to the Crypt of the Sepulchral Lamp. That's what this is, right?"

"You're having a secret romantic interlude here?" My appalledness cut through the fear like a hot knife through an ice cream cake. "*Here?* In this tomb? Surrounded by *dead people?*"

She scowled. "I didn't know it was this dark . . . or dirty . . . but that doesn't matter. If he wanted to talk to us —"

"Wait," I said. "Us?"

If Hannah was ever sheepish about anything in her entire life, I would eat my eighteen-dollar faux-leather ankle boot. But in that moment, she came pretty close.

"He wanted to talk to me about being a duke," she said, "and he said I might as well have you here, too . . . but where is he?"

So that was why she'd been so supportive. She knew Armand was expecting me to be there, and she didn't want to risk his displeasure by showing up without me.

"I'm sure he'll be here in a minute." She reached up and twisted a section of her hair, glancing down the path behind us.

"Well, I won't be," I said. "I can't stop now. I have to keep going."

"Are you serious?" Her lower lip pooched out in a pout. "But I stayed with you. . . ."

Why should she care? She was getting her chance to meet Armand, with or without me. I actually figured she'd prefer that it be the latter.

"I'm serious, Hannah. . . ." I shifted uncomfortably and hugged myself.

Her green eyes fixed on me in the darkness. "I can't *believe* you, Colette! I hung back with you out of the total goodness of my heart. Is it too much to ask that you do something for me?"

That's not how the goodness of your heart is supposed to work, I wanted to say, but some grabby little feeling nagged at me, like a memory. And then I thought of what my brother had said when he came down to help me with the suitcase: *You just do nice things to be nice.*

I looked around helplessly. It was almost surreal, to be trapped underground in such an awful place and to have a person who was supposedly one of my closest friends urging me to stick around even though it made me feel like I couldn't breathe.

"You're fine right now, aren't you?" she asked pointedly.

"No," I said, and frustration grated on my nerves like sandpaper. "I'm not fine, Hannah — I'm about to lose my mind! I need to keep going before I freak out."

An edge crept into my voice, and I saw in her eyes that she was beginning to believe me.

"Fine," she said, crossing her arms. "Go. See if I care."

I looked nervously at the path ahead.

"Just leave, Colette. Enjoy the walk. Alone."

Part of me — a big part of me — wanted to stay. I'd made it that far, and to leave Hannah now might be the undoing of so much work I'd done over the school year, trying to cement myself in her inner circle.

But the comforting numbness was starting to wear off, and without the mechanics of moving ahead to keep me calm, I was beginning to feel shaky and weak. My chest was growing tight, and my feet seemed heavier. If I tried to stay much longer, I would melt down, and Hannah would be furious anyway.

So I said, "I have to, Hannah." I almost added *I'm sorry*, but something stopped me. Maybe it was my last sliver of self-respect.

I started walking.

I ignored the bones and the skulls and looked at the floor — a slippery, uneven surface. I walked doggedly past tourists who

had paused to admire some new horrible death quote or grue-
some arrangement of femurs.

Go, go, go, said the voice in my head. And I went, went, went.

At one point, the path forked off in two directions. I stopped
for a moment to consider which one was shorter.

Then something caught my attention, at the corner of my eye —
movement. A flash of pale colors moving in the shadows.

I spun around.

There was no one there.

But then another flash, almost behind me, made me turn
again —

And again, nothing.

Off to my right, this time — but instead of turning, I stayed
perfectly still, moving only my eyes.

She was there. The ghost. The width of her skirt blocked the
path in front of me completely. In the low light, it was obvious
that she gave off a faint silvery-blue glow of her own, a light that
seemed to undulate through her.

Without thinking, I spun around to go back, toward
Hannah —

But when I turned, the ghost was in my way.

"Go away!" I said, as if she were a stray cat. "Go! Leave me
alone!"

A ripple seemed to move through her form, causing her glow
to sputter and spark. I got the distinct impression that I'd made
her angry.

"Please," I said. "Please move. Let me go."

Finally, she moved —

Toward me.

I tried to back away, but she kept coming, closer and closer. Finally, I was backed into a corner, where two walls of bones met.

And she kept coming.

I couldn't believe what I was about to do — but I took a deep breath and plunged forward. She was a ghost, right? So I should be able to go right through her.

Wrong. A shock wave passed through me as if I'd run head-long into an electrified brick wall, and I bounced back, slamming into the wall of bones behind me. I felt some of them crunch under the impact of my weight, and heard the dry smattering of dust and broken bits of skull hitting the ground around my feet.

My vision was filled with what looked like bright-blue flashes of lightning. I yelped and curled forward, away from the wall, trying to make out the ghost through my momentary blindness. She stood above me, cold and imperious, looking down.

She opened her mouth to speak. Her voice was like the hiss of a snake. *"Véronique . . ."*

I felt something in my throat give way, and everything went black.

CHAPTER 14

"COLETTE," SAID A soft voice.

Gentle fingertips rubbed my cheek, and I opened my eyes to see Jules kneeling over me. Behind him were about fifteen tourists. One guy lifted his camera and took a picture, which made Jules turn around and snap at him in French.

When Jules turned back to me, his eyes were bright with concern. "Are you all right?"

"I don't know," I said. I scanned the gathering of people, but the ghost was nowhere in sight. That didn't mean she wasn't lurking around some corner, of course, but the relief of her absence was overwhelming.

I realized I was lying on the ground and tried to push myself up.

"Hold on," Jules said. "You fainted. Do you want some water?"

"No, I'm okay."

He helped me to my feet. "You're shivering."

"Really, I'm fine —" But he had already draped his red hoodie over my shoulders, and the warmth radiating from it — his warmth — sank into my whole body. It felt so nice that I stopped protesting.

As we moved, I couldn't stop glancing from side to side like a hunted animal. But with Jules's hoodie around my shoulders and his hand on my arm, I could put one foot in front of the other and plod forward.

"What happened?" he asked.

I told him the truth — part of it, anyway. "I couldn't figure out which way to go. I got disoriented."

"I'm so sorry," he said. "I didn't notice you had fallen behind until Audrey pointed out that you were not with us. I turned around and came looking for you."

"It's fine," I said. Of course, it wasn't fine — there was a terrifying ghost following me — but none of that was Jules's problem.

As a remote semblance of normalcy returned, I finally had time to ask myself the question . . .

Who was Véronique?

* * *

I wouldn't say our trek to the end of the Catacombs was the happiest fifteen minutes of my life or anything, but it could have been worse. Jules's presence made me feel safe, and the question of Véronique distracted me from the sight of all the bones.

Finally, we stopped in a small, square room with stairs leading upward.

"Will you be okay?" Jules asked. "It's a lot of steps."

"Are you kidding?" I asked. "These stairs are the most beautiful thing I've ever seen."

He cleared his throat. "I'll be behind you, if you start to feel weak or need anything."

I took a deep breath and looked back at the doorway through which we'd just passed. Then I looked at Jules.

"This has been horrible," I said.

"I'm sorry to hear that."

"And I never want to do it again," I said. "Let's be clear about that. But . . . I did it. I can't believe I did it."

"Yes, you did." The outside corners of his lips turned up in a smile. "And you fainted only one time."

"Ha ha." I stepped onto the first stair. "That wasn't because of the claustrophobia."

And then we were both going up — not too fast, because the stairs were small and steep and I had to pause to catch my breath.

"What was it, then?" he asked.

Feeling reckless from the craziness of the past hour, I looked back at him. "I saw a ghost."

I paused, and he paused, and we both panted for a moment.

I kept a close eye on his expression. Finally, he squinted. "You are a funny girl."

Right. I turned and started climbing again.

When we reached the top, Pilar came running over to give me a hug. "I had no idea! Why didn't you say something? I feel so bad for leaving you behind! Where's Hannah?"

I didn't want to get Hannah in trouble.

"I'm not sure," I said. "We got separated."

"Well, there's only one way out," Madame Mitchell said, not sounding particularly worried.

Fifteen minutes later, Hannah appeared at the top of the stairs. Her cheeks were drawn in like she'd sucked on a lemon, and her brow was lowered.

Armand had stood her up.

No one could nurse a funk like Hannah. She stayed off by herself for the rest of the day, pouting through the Musée Rodin and all the way back to the hotel. When we stopped in the lobby, Hannah lurked on the fringes with her arms crossed in front of her.

I was about to start up the stairs when I felt a hand on my arm.

"Colette," Jules said, looking a little awkward.

"Hi," I said.

"I still feel very guilty about what happened earlier," he said.

"Don't worry about it."

"I'd like to make it up to you." He spoke in a rush, words pouring out of his mouth. "Let me take you to dinner. Madame Mitchell said it is all right . . . if you would like to go."

I stared at him in surprise. And then, to my even greater surprise, I heard myself saying, "I'd love to."

* * *

"What are your friends doing tonight?" Jules asked as we walked through Saint-Germain. The sidewalk was so narrow that whenever we passed someone going the opposite way, Jules had to jump down and walk in the street. The smells drifting from the small pâtisseries, warm and sweet, filled my nose.

"I don't know," I said. "But maybe we don't have to talk about them."

"That works for me," he said. He glanced at my outfit — the white dress/black blazer/cowboy boot combo I'd wanted to wear the medallion with. "You look really nice this evening."

"Thanks," I said, looking at his blue shirt, which brought out the soft blue of his eyes. "So do you." I felt myself blushing, so I tried to change the subject. "So . . . what do people in Paris talk about?"

"Anything," he said. "Everything."

"Okay." A pair of old ladies were approaching, so I followed Jules into the street, then hopped back up to the sidewalk. "Tell me something no one else knows about you."

He rubbed his neck with his hand. "No one? At all?"

"Yeah," I said. "No one. It doesn't have to be a horrible secret, but it has to be interesting. Or, no. It just has to be true."

He smiled, showing a dimple in his right cheek. "Good, because I'm not very interesting."

"How can you say that?" I asked. "You know so much about everything."

"Ah, but that's not me. That's France. Perhaps that's why I want to be a historian — so that I can become more interesting by knowing things about the past."

"You're not answering the question," I said.

He was quiet for a moment as we veered onto a narrow, one-way street. Every so often, a car drove by, but they were few and far between. So we, like everyone else, walked right down the center of the road.

"Something about me that no one knows," he said. "Okay. When I was fourteen, I wrote a poem and emailed it to my favorite singer."

"A love poem?" I asked.

He shrugged. "The words were not a love poem, but I think that was why I wrote it. From love."

And now for the million-euro question. "So who was it? Who's your favorite singer?"

"Ah, I can't tell you. But I can tell you that she replied and said thank you and that I should write more poetry."

"So did you? Write more poetry?"

He laughed. "Not a single line since then. I felt quite stupid, in fact. I regretted it, even though she was very nice."

"You shouldn't regret that," I said. "I'll bet she thought it was really great."

"She probably gets a thousand emails like mine every day."

"I doubt it," I said. "Not poems. Not written from the heart."

He shrugged.

"What made you decide to write it?" I asked.

"I think . . . I wanted to thank her, in a way? For saying in her songs what I kept thinking and feeling but couldn't say. It was just a few dumb lines about, I don't know, darkness and pieces of light and . . . something about a cat, I think. But of course that was only a symbol."

"Of course," I agreed. I pictured fourteen-year-old Jules sitting in his tiny room, at his tiny desk, composing poetry.

Seriously adorable.

"That's amazing," I said.

He blushed and tilted his head. "Oh, it's no great story. But it's true, and no one else knows about it."

"And it's interesting," I said. "Ten points."

"How about you?" he asked.

I laughed. "You already know all my secrets."

"Those are things about your family. What about you?"

Headlights approached up ahead, and Jules gently wrapped his hand around my elbow and guided me to the edge of the street to let the car pass.

"I don't have secrets of my own, I guess." Except for the latest revelation that I was possibly a duchess. But somehow I sensed that wouldn't impress Jules — especially since it had so much to do with Armand.

I could mention the ghost again . . .

Or you could get a marker and write JE SUIS TRÈS CRAZEBALLS on your forehead.

"What about . . ." Jules spoke more slowly. "Perhaps this is too personal."

"What?" I asked.

"You don't have to say. But I wonder . . . why you're claustrophobic. Did some specific incident cause it?"

I walked along for a while without responding. Jules didn't press.

"Please don't answer if you don't want to," he finally said.

"No, I — I want to. It's just that it sounds so stupid. I'm afraid you'll think I'm faking it or something."

He came to a complete stop and turned toward me, shaking his head. "You are not stupid, Colette."

Had I done anything to make him think otherwise? But something about Jules was disarming. So I began to speak.

"When I was seven, during the summer, I spent a week with my grandmother — Grandma Lucille; she was born in France. My dad came to pick me up, and I told him I didn't want to go. So I hid in the storm cellar. Except Grandma thought I went home with my dad, and my dad thought Grandma said it was okay for me to stay. And they both left. And the door latch got stuck."

I could remember the sudden, shocking feeling of the trapdoor overhead not lifting when I pressed on it.

Jules held my gaze. "That must have been very scary."

"Pretty much," I said. "I know it doesn't sound that bad, but . . ."

I could still smell the scent of the raw dirt, feel the humidity on my skin. The sick "they forgot about me" sensation that started in my stomach and then wrapped around my heart like a snake, squeezing until I thought I would stop breathing and die.

Eventually, tired of banging on the door, I retreated to the corner of the room. I found a flashlight, but its beam died after about three minutes. In a way, the light made things worse, because now I knew exactly how tiny and closed-in my surroundings were.

Hours later, I was covered in sweat, so thirsty my throat felt raw, and had to pee so badly I could hardly move. I had no idea where my grandmother might have gone, but I knew vaguely in the back of my head that she had a friend named Patricia who lived in Cleveland and that sometimes she went there to visit for days at a time.

I thought there was a very real possibility that I would starve to death or die of thirst before anyone could find me.

Which is a really, really sucky thing to think about when you're seven years old.

So I cried. And I peed my pants. And then I cried some more.

I kept thinking of all the creepy-crawlies that might be hiding around me and imagined them inching across my skin, up the wet legs of my shorts, through my hair . . .

Finally, I managed to cry myself to sleep. When I awoke, it was to the sound of the door above me being jerked open, and my mother's worried voice calling, *"Colette?!?"*

I mewled in response, still too frightened to move, and she barreled down the ladder toward me.

"Oh, Colette!" she cried, picking me up off the floor and hugging me tightly. My grandmother and father peered down into the darkness. They were arguing, sniping at each other, but I didn't pay attention to them. I was focused on being in my mother's arms, safe and loved and not dead.

Dad hauled me out and set me down in the hallway as Mom climbed back up.

Grandma looked down at me — and if I live to be a hundred and fifty years old, I'll never forget what she said: "Get her off the rug, Leo — she's covered in urine!"

Mom must have said something to her (and knowing Mom, it was a doozy of a something), because the next thing I remember is being home, and being plunked into a warm tub, and then given one of my dad's oldest, softest T-shirts to sleep in.

And being tucked into bed and kissed good night and the door closing gently behind my mother . . .

Then screaming my lungs out.

I woke up Charlie, who cried because he thought we were all being murdered. He'd accidentally seen a TV show about someone who got murdered and he was going through a stage where he thought murder happened to everyone, like it was inevitable. He'd heard the phrase *screaming bloody murder* and ended up actually screeching the words, *"BLOODY MURDER! BLOODY MURDER!"* so loud that our neighbors woke up and called my parents to make sure we weren't all being, you know, bloodily murdered.

I ended up sleeping with my lights on . . . until I was ten years old.

So, yeah, I was a foolish kid who did something foolish and then drew a lot of foolish conclusions about what had happened to me. I wouldn't have died. It wasn't like the story about the bride who gets locked in her hope chest and isn't found until she's just an old skeleton. The storm cellar was the first place they looked when they realized I was missing.

But still.

I gave Jules the broader strokes, leaving out the pants-peeing but leaving in the part about Charlie and the murder, since I thought it would be nice to end on a lighter note. Then, of course, I had to explain the phrase *screaming bloody murder*.

"Your grandmother must have been so sorry," he said.

"Well . . . kind of." I tried to remember any sorriness. Mostly she'd been angry about her hall rug.

Not that I blamed her. Grandma had other things going on in her world besides me . . . besides all of us, really. There were her cruises, her weekends in Miami or Saint Thomas. Her golf league, her charity groups. From the time I was old enough to know my grandma, I was old enough to know that we, her family, were somehow not enough for her.

Mom's mother, Grandma Carol, can't get enough of knitting and cooking turkeys and mailing us care packages.

But Grandma Lucille just never quite embraced that side of grandmotherhood.

In a way, that took away the biggest part of the hurt when Dad left. After all, how could he help it? Look who he'd had as an example.

Maybe, in discovering our heritage, I'd finally found the explanation for why people in my dad's family had always been so concerned with outward appearances and material possessions. The Iselins were nobility. We were used to getting our own way and being surrounded by sumptuous settings. It was just in our blood.

"I think you must have been a brave little girl," Jules said.

"I don't know if I'd go that far," I said.

Another car came toward us. Jules took my hand and once again led me up onto the sidewalk, then back down again.

And then he didn't let go of my hand.

* * *

We ate dinner at a little hole-in-the-wall that served incredible *steak frites* — just grilled steak with a pile of fries, but somehow it felt fancier here. We finished with the world's most unbelievably delicious crème brûlée. Jules paid for everything, despite my protestations, and then we went for a walk along the Seine, where the breeze blew a steady stream of cold air that made us unintentionally huddle closer. After a few minutes of walking, Jules reached for my hand again, and I let him take it.

I couldn't believe I'd ever thought he was plain-looking. His face wasn't hollow-cheeked or angsty, but it was square-jawed and open and strong. His eyes may not have gleamed like Armand's did, but they had a depth to them that Armand could never hope to achieve. Armand was all show — and Jules was all substance. I never felt like Armand was really seeing me for me — even when he stared directly into my eyes.

With Jules, I felt like he was seeing me even when we weren't looking at each other.

"Hey," I said, trying to sound casual. "Have you ever heard of someone named Véronique?"

He gave me a sideways look. "Ah . . . a lot of people are called that."

"No, I mean, someone famous. A historical figure."

His eyebrows went up. "Is it someone you're related to?"

"I don't know," I said. "Maybe?"

Jules pursed his lips, and I was afraid I was going to drive him off with my crazy talk. So I changed the subject.

"What's your favorite part of Paris?" I asked instead. "You've been everywhere, right? Is there someplace you never get tired of?"

He smiled at me, a dimple appearing just left of his mouth. "What time do you have to be back?"

"Ten," I said.

He checked his watch. "We have time."

"Time for what?" I asked, but he was already hailing a cab.

"Come on, and I'll show you!" he said, pulling me inside.

A few minutes later, the taxi pulled to a stop in front of a narrow strip of lawn that ended in the brilliantly illuminated Eiffel Tower. I stared at it, shining against the dark sky, about four times bigger than I'd imagined it would be.

"Won't we be coming here with the class?" I asked.

"Not at night," he said.

"It doesn't even look real." I tried to gaze up at the top but couldn't keep my balance.

"Here," Jules said, standing behind me, his hands on my arms. "Now you can look."

I leaned back until I could see the tip-top of the tower. I was so engrossed in the sight that it took me a second to realize that I was leaning back against Jules's chest.

One of our hearts was pounding, but I couldn't tell if it was his or mine.

I leaned back a little further and looked up at his face. "*Bonjour*," I said.

"*Bonsoir*," he said, his eyes twinkling down at me.

I stood up and turned around. "Can we go up?"

"To the top? You are not afraid of height?"

"Not at all," I said. "Height is the opposite of what I'm afraid of."

"Then, yes, of course," he said. "As long as the line's not too long."

It was rather chilly, so the line was manageable, and within thirty minutes we found ourselves at the top.

I'd never been so high in the air before, except on planes. I looked at the cityscape below us, the way the warm, amber-tinted streetlights mixed with the whiter lights of the buildings on the meandering streets. The river curved gently away, criss-crossed by glowing bridges.

The breeze made me shiver, and then I was wrapped in Jules's arms.

"I don't get it," I said.

"What?" he asked.

I didn't get . . . what he liked about me.

To be honest, my week in Paris was making me wonder whether there really was a *me*. Who was I? Did Colette exist as a human, or was she just a pathetic mash-up of other people's expectations?

Maybe Colette is the person who asks these questions, I thought. *Even if she doesn't have the answers.*

Too hard to explain. I shook my head. "Never mind. Say something in French."

He said something, his voice sliding over the words in a way that made me feel kind of melty inside.

"What did that mean?" I asked.

"It was a question," he said, a dimple appearing in his cheek. "I asked if . . . if you mind if I kissed you."

"How do you say no in French?" I said.

"*Non?*" he said, mildly surprised. His expression was miserable. "I'm sorry, Colette, I —"

"*Non,*" I said, putting my hand on his cheek. "*Non,* I don't mind."

So he kissed me.

As we pulled apart — but not too far apart — I stared up into his eyes, warm and blue and earnest.

I'm in Paris, and I met a boy, and he really likes me, and I kissed him. At the top of the Eiffel Tower.

Maybe things were a mess back home. Maybe I was losing my mind and/or being stalked by an evil ghost. Maybe when I got back to the hotel Hannah would kill me for abandoning her in the Catacombs. Maybe I only had three days left in Paris with Jules.

But just for now . . . just for this moment . . . life was good.

IV

AT ELEVEN O'CLOCK *Friday morning, Armand sat at his desk, his notes in front of him. His files were immaculately maintained — he had learned that from his father, who was an excellent businessman.*

He thumbed through them to the letter I, *for* Iselin, *and pulled out the page he'd been creating for the American girl. Silly fool! She represented one of the most powerful and prestigious families in France, and even with the full knowledge in front of her, laid out like a banquet, she didn't know what to do with it.*

Not to worry. Armand could advise her. He pictured them attending formal functions together, being introduced as a duc *and* duchesse — *the hot couple in the magazines. Sure, she needed some instruction to be able to present herself in the proper manner, but it wasn't her outside that mattered — it was her blood. Her noble lineage.*

Most of Armand's friends were completely uninterested in marriage, but Armand wanted to marry young — provided he found the right girl. And as he stared at Colette's biography, pieced together from bits of information he'd collected from the internet, he felt fairly confident that he'd found her. Of course, she was only sixteen, but he could wait two or three years, until she was an adult.

And then think how powerful their families would be — united.

Think first of your legacy, his father often told him. Armand followed this advice as well as he could. He'd seen it work for his father — the way he'd found the most beautiful woman to marry and have his children, though there was no love in their marriage. What was love compared to honor, nobility, the respect of millions of people? Armand certainly didn't love Colette and in fact he doubted he ever could; there was something about her that made him impatient and irritated. Their marriage might not be a happy one — but it would be an important one.

And Armand was desperate to be important.

He thought over his plans for the next day. He would go to the hotel, tell Colette he needed to see her alone, and declare his intentions of uniting their families when she reached eighteen or nineteen years old. She would protest — she was always protesting about something — but then he would kiss her.

And Armand knew how to kiss a girl in a way that would change her mind about pretty much anything.

As for Hannah, she'd been a useful tool to get to Colette, but she was growing tiresome. Her latest idea was to transfer to a French school so she could be near him! He almost relished the idea of telling her he'd never really been interested in her. As if he would have anything to do with such a vulgar fool — as if mere money could buy her the kind of pedigree he demanded from the girl who would be his wife.

No, there was only one choice. And he was going to break the news to Colette very soon.

She might not be happy about it, but given enough time, he could wear her down. He was sure of it. After all, he had to think of his legacy.

There had been one small obstacle — that loser Jules. According to Hannah, Colette had gone out to dinner with him the night before. But Armand had spoken to Jules first thing this morning and let him know that Colette was off-limits. And Jules was too much of a goody-goody to put up a fight for some silly American girl.

Carefully refiling the page, Armand placed the folder in its hanging file and surveyed his desk to be sure it was spotless. He wondered for a moment if Colette kept her things clean.

Well, she would learn to, if she was to be his wife.

He glanced down as his cell phone lit up with yet another text message from Hannah. His nostrils flared in distaste. How desperate! At least Colette had this much going for her — she had dignity and didn't act like a lovesick child.

Spritzing cologne on his wrists, he took one last look at himself in the mirror and then opened the door that led from his bedroom to the living room.

Then he stopped.

He wasn't alone.

CHAPTER 15

WE SPENT THE morning at the Musée d'Orsay. I tried to appreciate the works of the famous painters on display there — Monet, Degas, Renoir, Picasso . . . but in truth, I couldn't focus very well on the art.

Half of me kept expecting to see the swish of a massive skirt out of the corner of my eye, and the other half of me kept stealing glances at Jules, who was leading the group as usual, playing it cool.

Not wanting to seem needy, I waited until we were breaking for lunch before I approached him.

"*Bonjour*," I said, standing a little closer than normal. I couldn't keep a little smile from creeping onto my lips.

"*Bonjour*," he said, not looking at me.

"How are you this morning?"

"Very well, thank you." He was leafing through his notebook, so I stopped talking for a moment to give him a chance to find whatever he was looking for. But he didn't seem to find anything. He just kept leafing. Finally, he glanced up. "Can I help you?"

I stared at him, not comprehending his coldness. "I . . . I just wanted to say hi."

He gave me a quick, fake smile. "Hi," he said, and then the smile disappeared.

Okay, correct me if I'm wrong, but this was not the way you treat someone after you've kissed her at the top of the Eiffel Tower on the most romantic night of her entire life.

"What's wrong?" I asked, hating the breathlessness of my voice.

"Nothing is wrong with me, Colette," he said, not looking at me. "Is something wrong with you?"

"I don't know," I said. "Maybe. I don't understand what you're . . . why you're . . ."

He didn't raise his eyes, but he finally stopped flipping pages, so I knew I had his attention.

The horror of the situation was sinking into my skin like rain through your clothes when you're caught in a downpour. "Or . . . or maybe last night didn't mean . . ." *What I thought it meant.*

It was too humiliating to come out and say it, so I stopped.

To my surprise, he closed the notebook with a loud snap and glared at me. "It did mean something. To me, anyway. But maybe American girls like to do things differently . . . to play with people's emotions."

"Wait," I said. "I played with someone's emotions — with yours?"

He shrugged.

"No I didn't," I said, my voice rising. "How can you say that?"

"Please keep your voice down," he said softly.

"I didn't play with your emotions," I said. "I don't even know what you're talking about."

"Well." His voice was clipped. "Maybe you should discuss it with Armand Janvier."

"Armand?" I repeated, really loudly. Then I had to look around to see if Hannah had heard me say his name. Luckily, she was nowhere in sight.

"*Oui*, Armand." The look in his eyes told me exactly how he felt about Armand — and we're not talking warm fuzzies. "He called me early this morning and told me to stay away from you."

My jaw dropped. "He had no right to say that!"

"He told me that you two were . . . how did he put it? 'Connected.' And that I should leave you alone because you are too far above me." He shook his head. "He's not a good person, Colette."

"I know that," I said. "*I'm* not the one who likes him —"

"What did he mean when he said 'connected'?"

Telling Jules that I might be a secret duchess seemed embarrassing, like I was a little girl trying to play princess and taking the game too far. "It's hard to explain. It's something to do with our families."

His eyebrows pressed downward in confusion. "I don't think you should see him. You are too young to —"

"Too young?" I asked, bristling. "You think I'm too young? You didn't think so last night, when we were kissing."

His cheeks turned red. "That is not what I am saying. You have not dealt with people like Armand before. He has spent his whole life watching his father, who is one of the greatest financial criminals in France."

"So he's trying to steal my money?" I asked. "Ha ha — too bad for him."

"No." Jules sighed. "It is about his philosophy that I am warning you. He sees people as objects to be used and manipulated for his own profit."

I wanted to shout, *I'm a freaking duchess; I can handle myself!*

The thing was, I knew Armand was just using me. But if he was using me for something that benefited me as well as himself, didn't that sort of make it okay?

"There's nothing going on between me and Armand," I said. "I swear."

"Of course I believe you." Jules turned to me, his expression less severe. "I just need you to promise me you'll stay away from him."

I took a step back. "Why are you telling me what to do?"

"For your own good."

"I can decide what's good for me or not," I said. "But thanks anyway."

His mouth made a pinched-looking frown. "You obviously can't, Colette."

"What does that mean?"

"Just look at your friends," he said. "They're wrong for you, yet you cling to them."

Okay, now I was getting mad. To warn me about Armand was one thing — but to get angry at me for even knowing him? Then to order me to stay away from him? And *then* to criticize my friends?

"I don't feel the need to continue this conversation," I said. "So I'm going to just . . . go away now."

Way to zing him, Colette, Hannah would have said.

Except I didn't want to zing him. I just wanted things to be the way they were before. I wanted life to have a rewind button. I wanted Armand to mind his own stupid onions.

"All right." Jules sounded tired and disappointed.

I wandered away in a fog.

I'd been avoiding Hannah and Pilar as much as I could, pretending to be really drawn to the art and listening to what Jules was saying . . . but now that we were finishing up at the museum, there was nothing left to pretend about. We were all going to lunch, and then to the Eiffel Tower. The thought of going there now, a glaring reminder of how perfect the previous night had been and how messed up everything had become, made me feel ill.

But unless I could find an excuse to get out of it, I was stuck.

"Colette, hang on a sec." Audrey touched my sleeve as I started to walk past her. Her voice shook, like she was about to cry. "I'm so sorry about yesterday. I feel terrible."

"What?" I said. "You didn't do anything."

"Exactly." She turned her wide, miserable eyes down to stare at her shoes. "I should have warned you about the Catacombs. I was going to — but then I didn't."

"Well, Hannah didn't exactly make it easy for you. She was pretty rude. I think you were justified in staying away."

"I hope I never start judging my actions by Hannah Norstedt's standards," Audrey said. "Anyway, I had to apologize. I know we're not really friends, but . . . I'm scared of heights, and the thought of someone knowing that and letting me go to the top of the Eiffel Tower anyway . . ."

I stared at her, remembering how she'd gone out of her way to show me the key symbol. And how she and Brynn had helped me in the Conciergerie.

"Wait," I said, "so you don't want to go to the Eiffel Tower? Do you have other plans for this afternoon?"

"No," Audrey said. "Why, do you?"

"I was thinking about walking and looking at that cemetery, and I'm positive Hannah and Peely won't want to go with me. Want to come?"

"Which cemetery?" she asked.

"The one that Jules said doesn't exist anymore."

She looked confused. "Tell me the truth, Colette . . . are you just inviting me because you can't go without a buddy?"

For a second, I was speechless. Even a little offended. Then I realized that I'd never done or said anything to earn Audrey's trust or to show her that I wasn't just using her.

"I promise," I said. "I do need a buddy, but I think it would be kind of fun. Is that . . . is that weird?"

She smiled. "No, it's not. I just had to be sure. Do you know how to get there?"

Um, nope.

"Are you going to check with Jules?" she asked.

I hesitated and inspected the sleeve of my cardigan. "Could . . . uh . . . is there any chance you could ask him? I would, but . . . it's a long story."

Her right eyebrow went up, but she didn't say anything else. She disappeared for a minute and returned with a half sheet of paper covered in notes. "It's called Errancis. . . . It was located in the block between boulevard de Courcelles, rue du Rocher, rue de Monceau, and rue de Miromesnil. It's not far from here. But you know it's not a cemetery anymore, right? He said the only thing left is a marker on one of the walls."

"I know," I said. "But I want to find it anyway."

I basically ran past Hannah and Pilar, calling out that I was going somewhere to see something boring and that they should have fun without me. While I did that, Audrey was clearing our expedition with Madame Mitchell. No teacher has ever been able to say no to Audrey — and besides that, Madame Mitchell was eager to avoid two fainting episodes on a single trip.

And then we were on our way.

CHAPTER 16

"WE'RE HERE," AUDREY said, looking up at a sign on the corner of a building that read RUE DE MIROMESNIL.

We slowly circled the block. But aside from some little shops and a lot of apartment buildings, we didn't see anything.

"Wait," Audrey said. "Look!"

We were near the corner of Monceau and Rocher, and she was looking up at a small plaque on the wall. "Eleven hundred and nineteen people guillotined during the Revolution were buried here," she translated.

"But . . . where?" I looked around. There was absolutely no sign — besides the actual sign — that the area had ever held a thousand-plus dead bodies.

"Just . . . here, I guess." Audrey peered around us. "Wow. Do you think any of those people have ever seen this?"

She was looking two doors down the block at a preschool, outside of which waited a couple dozen mothers.

"Fair question," I said. "Maybe French people aren't afraid of death."

"Or they're not afraid of plaques."

I laughed a little. "Yeah, or that."

Personally, I wasn't sure if I would be comfortable dropping my four-year-old off on the site of a grisly burial ground, but who was I to judge? Even if, as Jules had said, the remains had been moved down to the Catacombs. They couldn't have possibly gotten them *all*.

I took a picture of the plaque and then we kept walking, circling the block. Once again, I expected to see the ghost pop up, but there was no sign of her. Maybe she'd grown bored with me.

"I guess we'd better get back," Audrey said. "We could find someplace to grab a baguette along the way."

"I'd rather not," I said.

She didn't answer, but I was starting to recognize the way she smiled into the distance when her feelings were hurt.

"I mean, I need to eat at the hotel," I said. "I'm . . . I just . . ."

Why couldn't I come out and say I didn't have any money?

"Oh, right!" she said. "I wasn't thinking. Free food always tastes better anyway."

We turned the corner onto rue du Rocher and stopped.

The sidewalk ahead of us was blocked off.

The street was completely torn open. The roadwork was enclosed by orange mesh walls, but as we got closer, I could see excavators and trucks moving around inside, digging roughly at the ground. Piles of rubble surrounded the work site. Nothing about the way the men worked seemed to show that this was a place where a thousand bodies had been buried in a mass grave.

Again I wondered if there was a chance that something of the remains had been left behind. If so, it would be entirely feasible that those remains might have been unearthed by the construction —

And not just any remains — the queen's.

There seemed to be a chill in the air that I hadn't felt that morning.

A man walked by carrying a clipboard and wearing a hard hat. *"Pardon, monsieur,"* I said.

He stopped, and I realized that I had absolutely no way to ask what I wanted to ask.

"Parlez anglais?" I asked.

He shook his head.

"Um," I said, trying but failing to come up with the correct French words. "Ah . . ."

Audrey looked at me oddly. "What are you trying to say?"

"I just want to know how long they've been working here," I said.

"Combien . . ." she said to him, *"Combien de jours . . . travaillez-vous ici?"*

The man looked confused, but seemed to decide that there was no harm in answering. He spoke in slow French to Audrey, ignoring me completely. Then he gave us a quick, unfriendly smile and walked away.

"A week," she said to me. "They started on the twenty-fourth. The day before we got here. Why do you ask?"

"No reason," I said. "Just curious."

The evening was growing chilly, so we decided to take the Metro instead of walking. The route maps might as well have been the technical specs for a rocket ship, for all the sense they made to me, but Audrey knew exactly which train we should take and where we should change, too.

"I don't know how you can tell what goes where," I said.

She shrugged. "It's a lot like the subways in New York City. Once you learn to read the map, you can get anywhere."

A flutter of excitement traveled through me as I pictured myself riding the subways around New York over the summer. Next time we were in a Metro station, I would pay careful attention, to prepare myself. I imagined my father's surprise the first time I'd say, *I can just take the subway, no big deal.*

As we emerged from the Saint-Michel Metro station and began the short walk to the hotel, Audrey cleared her throat. "So, uh . . . what's going on with you and Jules?"

"Nothing," I said automatically.

"Are you sure?" There was a gentle, teasing tone to her voice.

"I don't want to talk about it." I felt my cheeks redden, and the memory of the painful exchange Jules and I had had earlier echoed miserably in my mind.

"Okay," she said, sounding taken aback. "I just wondered if —"

"Look, Audrey," I said, stopping and turning to her. "I know we keep doing stuff together, but that doesn't mean we're BFFs or anything."

"Oh." She adjusted her glasses and looked away.

"We've had fun, but we're just too different. I mean, you're really nice, and I'm sure —"

"I get it, Colette." There was none of the usual lightness in her voice. She sounded tired. "I'm sorry I expected you to treat me like a human being. I should have known better."

I didn't know what to say to that. So I didn't say anything.

Neither of us spoke, all the way back to the hotel.

I felt awful. And I was on the verge of apologizing, but as we stepped into the lobby, someone called out, "Colette!"

Jules was waiting for me.

I was caught off guard. "Oh — hi."

Audrey took the opportunity to slip away.

Jules didn't smile. "We have to talk."

"Okay. Can I just —"

"Right now," he said. "I need to speak to you right now."

Something prickled at the back of my neck. "Why? What's going on? If this is about before —"

"It's not," he said.

Jules took hold of my elbow and led me to the small sitting area where I'd talked with Armand a couple of nights earlier. My throat went dry.

"What happened?" I asked. "Please tell me."

He waited until I was sitting, and then he sat down. He reached over and took my hand, then let it go — then grabbed it again.

"Please," I said, beginning to feel light-headed with worry. "Just say it."

Jules took a deep breath. "I don't know if you are aware, but there has been talk of a serial killer on the loose in Paris. There have been many murders, all committed the same way —"

"Yes, yes," I cut him off. I knew all about the murders — you could hardly walk down the street without passing blaring headlines and photos of the glamorous victims. And it went beyond that, in a way — I felt as if the news of the murders was somehow following me.

"There has been another death. . . ." Jules swallowed. "Colette, it was Armand."

"What?" I said, my voice echoing through the lobby. *"What?"*

"He was murdered in his flat early this morning. I'm so sorry. I know you and he were . . ." Jules spun his hands, looking for the right words. "You were . . ."

"I keep trying to tell you, we weren't anything." Even though I was stunned, I could say that much.

Jules exhaled for what felt like ten seconds.

I felt itchy, like my whole body was being bitten by ants. "Are you serious, Jules? He's dead?"

"He was found this afternoon by his housekeeper." Jules tapped on the screen of his phone and handed it to me. I couldn't read the headline on the French news website, but it was clear enough — I saw Armand's name. And his picture.

My hands were shaking so badly I was afraid I'd drop the phone, so I gave it back to Jules. "And how did it . . . I mean, what was . . ."

"Like the others." He glanced away. "His head . . ."

The head. She is cut off.

"No way," I said. "Oh my God. *Oh my God*, does Hannah know?"

Jules blinked at me. "I'm not sure."

"How am I going to tell her? She was the one who really liked him." It would destroy her. Or it would turn her into a raging beast who, desperate with grief, destroyed everything around her. . . .

Either way, destruction was imminent.

"Could Pilar help you?"

"I don't know," I said. "I don't think so."

"Or your teacher?"

I shook my head. "She doesn't know we sneaked out and met a French boy."

Jules looked uncomfortable. He put his hands in his pockets. "I suppose I could go with you."

I appreciated the offer, but I sincerely believed that his presence would make things worse. God forbid Hannah start wailing about how it should have been Jules.

"No," I said, standing up before I lost my nerve. "I have to do it."

"Do you want me to wait for you?" He stood up, too.

"You'd better not," I said. "This could take a while."

V

STÉPHANIE VOCLAIN COCHER *leaned out the fourth-floor window, cradling her camera in her hands, and held her breath. She snapped off a few exposures and then reviewed the pictures.*

Good — the second one was in focus. It would be a great "don't" picture for her street-fashion blog — demonstrating the ugliness of too-short pants.

From the time she was a child, shopping with her mother at Le Bon Marché, Stéphanie had known she had an eye for fashion. It wasn't that she was particularly careful of what she wore — mostly she stuck to jeans and simple sweaters, with a pair of flats — but she always seemed to be able to spot the fashion missteps of the people around her. That, combined with her ability to make razor-sharp comments deriding those missteps, had made her the leading authority on fashion among the students at her school, and now brought readers thronging to her blog.

Being able to come up with the precise statement to express the contemptible cluelessness of other people was a true gift.

Stéphanie checked her watch. Her friends were supposed to be arriving soon so they could all get lunch together. She sat down at her computer and started typing, hoping that she might have time to finish a blog post before they showed up.

Next to the keyboard, her cell phone buzzed with an incoming text: FIVE MINUTES LATE.

She was relieved. Now she would have time to get the short-pants post up on the blog. She rubbed at a smudge on her arm — likely from leaning against the window frame — and turned back to the computer.

What should she say? Perhaps something like, Where's the flood? *Or maybe,* You know the economy is in trouble when they start selling pants by the centimeter?

There was a sound behind her, but she ignored it, thinking it was the cat.

Another sound. Still, she focused on the screen in front of her.

And yet another noise —

"Va-t'en, chat!" she shouted, turning around in her chair.

Stéphanie sat frozen, looking at the woman in her bedroom. She wore an exquisite ball gown, a powdered wig, and a scornful expression. How had she gotten in?

"Ah . . ." Stéphanie blinked. "Bonjour?"

The woman moved closer.

Stéphanie stood up and backed toward the window.

"La fille de la famille Voclain," *the woman whispered, her face a ghostly gray color.*

Above Stéphanie's bed was a samurai sword that her father had smuggled into the country from Japan. The priceless object was mounted on a polished piece of wood, its sheath below it.

As Stéphanie tried to get as far from the woman as possible, she heard rattling — the sword was coming loose from its mount.

The woman glared at her through eyes of icy-blue hatred.

Without stopping to think, Stéphanie ran for the window and threw herself out of it, crashing down to the street three stories below.

CHAPTER 17

I KNOCKED ON the door of the suite, and Pilar came and opened it, eating from a tiny bag of cookies she'd bought from the minibar.

"You look like you just ran a marathon," she said.

"I took the stairs." I leaned against the wall near the door to catch my breath.

"Hannah's in a terrible mood," Peely whispered. "Armand hasn't texted her back. And she's been texting him all day."

I nodded, gathered my courage, and rounded the corner.

Hannah sat with her knees pulled up to her chest in the middle of the couch. The television was off and the room was silent. Poor Peely had probably been stuck here like this since they got back from the Eiffel Tower.

Bored and quiet.

"Hey," I said.

"You've been a busy little bunny today." Hannah sniffed, but didn't look up at me.

She was searching for something on her phone. "Did you have fun with the Loser Brigade?"

"Hannah, I —"

"Don't apologize," she said. "Just be careful. You know what they say — if you roll in dog poo, when you get up, you're covered in dog poo."

I wasn't sure I'd ever heard those particular words of wisdom.

I sat down on the side chair. "I have to tell you something."

My hands were sweating, and my heart *thump-thump-thump*ed in my chest. I began to suspect that the news of Armand's death hadn't really sunk in for me yet . . . and if I didn't spit it out, I'd miss my chance to say it with any composure.

Hannah peered at me, suspicious. "I don't know why you even want to —"

"Armand's dead," I said.

Hannah closed her mouth.

Pilar wandered over and sat on the arm of the couch until Hannah turned to her and snapped, "Were you raised in a barn?"

Peely popped up as if the couch were on fire.

I pressed on. "I don't know many of the details, except —"

"You are *so not funny*, Colette." Hannah's eyes burned as she looked at me. "This is so not funny."

"I know," I said. "It's not a joke."

Even as I spoke, she was typing his name into her phone's web browser.

I took a deep breath. "I guess his housekeeper —"

Hannah's scream cut me off. Pilar and I exchanged alarmed looks and converged on the couch. But Hannah was up in a heartbeat, yelling and screeching and swearing. She knocked a lamp off an end table and threw the bowl of chocolates at the wall. She upset the umbrella stand and then started kicking the back of the side chair. There was a huge ripping sound as the fabric gave way, and finally Pilar pulled her away and back onto the couch.

"I'll get some water," I said, standing and going to the minifridge.

Hannah curled into a ball, sobbing. Pilar took the bottle of water from me.

"Here you go," she said, lightly rubbing Hannah's back. "Have a sip."

"*No!*" Hannah yelled, jumping up again. But instead of racing around trying to pull the room apart, she zeroed in on me. "How did you know? *How did you know before me?*"

"Jules told me," I said. "I saw him in the lobby."

"He couldn't come here and tell me himself?" she cried. "He couldn't be a man? He's such a boy! Such a stupid little boy!"

Then she collapsed, bawling her eyes out.

Pilar and I spent the rest of the evening being battered and abused like a pair of flags left out in a blizzard. When Hannah finally cried herself to sleep on the couch, we were so exhausted that we didn't even change into our pajamas. We just flopped onto Peely's bed. Pilar dozed off almost immediately, but even in my bleary-eyed, bleary-brained haze, there was a spark of alertness that kept me awake for hours, until I finally passed out.

* * *

THE WOMAN ON the settee looks up when she senses me approaching, and her smile is genuine. The man at her side stands to give me his seat, and I look into his golden eyes and feel a thrill of dread.

"Duchesse," he murmurs, before bowing and backing away, to leave us alone.

"Ah, ma très chère amie," the woman says, extending her arm. Her fingers uncurl gracefully, and I kiss her hand and curtsy. She slides over and makes room for me on the sofa.

It's hard to get comfortable. And it's hard to relax, knowing every move we make is being studied. There's no getting away from it, though. People will always be watching her. And tonight, many of them are watching me, as well.

She takes a moment to sit up even straighter, to toss her hair haughtily over her shoulder. She, at least, will not show that she is afraid.

But she should be afraid.

I lean closer.

I want to get away from here and take the woman with me. There is something I'm desperate to tell her . . .

But when I look around the room, I see eyes on me — steely, burning gazes, heavy with meaning . . . and warning. The faces that watch me are faces I know as well as I know my own — Thérèse with her red curls, Laurent with his chiseled jaw and jet-black hair. They are like brothers and sisters to me — but I have never seen them look at me like this before.

I sit back once again, the weight of my unspoken words crushing my chest like a vise.

My friend turns to look at me. "Nous n'avons pas beaucoup de temps," she whispers. She takes my hand and squeezes it. The gesture is full of love and trust . . . and despair. "Ah, Véronique, ma chère . . . que faisons-nous?"

CHAPTER 18

"ARE YOU AWAKE?"

Hannah's voice, stuffy and hoarse, woke me.

She stood in the doorway of Pilar's room, freshly showered, her hair wet and combed out. Her face was pink and puffy, and her pale eyes looked vividly bright beneath her swollen eyelids.

I propped up on one elbow, confused. The name *Véronique* echoed in my head, and I needed to stop and think before I forgot what it meant. Already, I was forgetting. "Um . . . what time is it?"

"I don't know."

I glanced at the clock. It was 6:45 a.m. Pilar lay next to me, arms over her face, snoring lightly.

"I'm hungry," Hannah said. "I was going to order room service but I thought it might be better to get some fresh air."

"Peely's asleep," I said. "But I'll come."

I washed my face, brushed my teeth, and pulled my hair back into a sloppy bun. Hannah was wearing a simple white T-shirt and a pair of jeans, with a six-hundred-dollar blue wool pea-coat. She pulled on a hat knit from thick white yarn and a matching scarf. I was still wearing the clothes I'd slept in, but I grabbed my coat, scarf, and hat, and we descended the stairs together.

"You always take the stairs, everywhere?" she asked.

"Yeah," I said.

"I can't believe I've never noticed." She was silent for a few seconds, contemplating this.

I was only half paying attention to her. In my mind, I was thinking, *Véronique . . .* And there was a question. Some question. I reached for it the way you reach for an itch in the center of your back.

Véronique . . . ma chère . . .

"What are we to do?" I said suddenly, the words slipping out of my mouth.

Hannah thought I was talking to her. She tugged on my sleeve. "I don't want to go to the hotel café. Is that all right?"

The shock of finding the phrase in my memory left me momentarily speechless. "Yeah, sure."

"We can probably find something good to eat in one of the places around here."

"Definitely."

She walked out ahead of me — not quite holding the door open behind her, but careful not to let it shut in my face. The shock of the cold morning stole the breath from my mouth for a moment.

Hannah didn't react. She was in her own little universe. "Which way?"

I shrugged and pointed to the left, toward the small hub of streets lined with tiny shops and restaurants. The cafés were all open, the buttery scent of pastries wafting out their doorways. Hannah stopped in front of one at random and gestured for me to go inside.

Véronique, my dearest one . . . what are we to do?

We got in line and ordered croissants. Hannah ordered a coffee and I ordered a *chocolat chaud*, a steaming hot chocolate that came in a little pitcher along with an empty coffee cup. We sat at a table just outside of the door, and I poured the chocolate into the cup. Then we wrapped our cold hands around our warm drinks and watched the Parisians walk by. I nibbled on my croissant, which was hot and flaky.

"I can't believe he's really gone," Hannah said.

I didn't know what to say. I couldn't really believe it, either, except that it was a fact.

"Do you think he —" She cut herself off. Her pale skin had gone white. "I mean, I hope he wasn't too scared."

That hadn't occurred to me. I guess I'd never thought of Armand as a person who could be scared — he was too cool, too smooth. But was there a moment when he knew he was doomed? I thought of his golden eyes wild with fear and my heart skipped a beat. The realization that he was really, truly dead seeped a bit farther under my skin and made the sun seem one shade brighter.

"I wonder if he thought of me," Hannah said, setting her coffee cup on the table and covering her face with her hands. "I would have been thinking about him."

That was when I started to think that what Hannah had felt for Armand was something real.

Maybe she was controlling. Maybe she could be snooty and snappy and snarly. But she was a human being with real feelings, and she was in pain.

I didn't want to think ill of the dead, but it made the way Armand toyed with her even more offensive. And all for what? Just so he could tell his friends he'd made some American teenager fall in love with him — and the whole time, he'd been pursuing someone else? Impossibly, that someone else was me. And though our relationship had been mostly based on the Order of the Key and Armand's crazy plan to restore us to our noble places in society, there was no point lying to myself — there had been something else behind his interest. Even if he'd mostly been interested in persuading me to help him, he'd still been intrigued by me.

So then why play with Hannah?

The answer hit me like a brick to the head:

Because Hannah could control me.

Because when I went back to Ohio, Hannah would be right there, urging me to pursue my rightful title as a duchess. If she let it slide, I would have let it slide, too. It would have been a cool little blip in my life, something I'd eventually tell my grandchildren. But with Hannah's influence, I couldn't let it go, not without massively angering her and losing my social footing.

I was the puppet. Hannah was the strings.

And Armand had been making us dance.

*   *   *

When we got back to the penthouse, Pilar was sitting on the sofa and watching an English-language news channel.

The anchorwoman sat up straight and put on her "serious" face.

"Shocking new developments in the Parisian serial killings . . . Authorities have confirmed that a woman who survived a murder attempt appears to have been targeted by the same killer responsible for several other deaths in the city this week."

I looked up. And Hannah was staring at the screen, too.

Next to her, a graphic popped up — the photograph of a college-aged girl.

"The young woman, a third-year student at the International Fashion Institute in Paris, is in stable condition at Saint Marina Hospital after being attacked by an unknown assailant in her apartment. She reported to police that the assailant was waiting for her in her home, and only by jumping six meters to the ground from an open window was she able to avoid the terrible fate experienced by the other victims. Police say the girl is very fortunate not to have suffered any serious injuries, though she is being kept under observation due to severe shock."

They cut to a shaky phone video of a girl being loaded into an ambulance. She was young and very pretty, but what drew my eye was her forearm. On the skin between her elbow and wrist, I could clearly see a dark, elongated smudge . . .

Just like the one on Armand's arm. The one that, because I could see it, meant we were "connected."

"The victim has been identified as Stéphanie Voclain Cocher," the newscaster said.

I sat back.

Voclain. The name was familiar — because it had been on the list, the one I'd seen on the plaque.

It was completely, totally *not* okay for not one but two of the murder victims to be associated with a 230-year-old club of which I was apparently a member.

When the report was done, Hannah looked disgusted. "They didn't even mention him! And he was the most important one!"

I looked at the clock. It was almost time to meet our group in the lobby, but I had other plans. "Are you going out with the class today?" I asked.

Hannah gave me an "are you serious?" glare.

"I think I will," I said. "Is that all right?"

I knew she'd never come right out and say it wasn't, so after she nodded stiffly at me, I hurried through my shower and threw on a simple outfit — plaid wide-leg pants and a white sweater. I tied a scarf around my wet hair and grabbed my bag.

"So we're skipping the party tonight, too?" I asked.

Hannah looked straight at me. "Of course not," she said. "Armand would have wanted me to go."

"Oh," I said. "Okay."

"The car's coming at six thirty," she said. "We're picking up our dresses at three. But what are you going to wear? You never went back to the rental shop. You really need to have a costume."

"I'll find something."

"I mean it."

"Me, too," I said, my voice rising in annoyance.

Hannah looked at me darkly.

"Well, I guess I'll see you guys later," I said. "I'll tell Madame Mitchell you're not coming, if you want me to."

"That would be good," Peely said, staring glumly at the TV. Hannah didn't even toss me a tiny scrap of attention.

I was on thin ice, and I knew it, but I left anyway.

I called Madame Mitchell from the lobby phone and told her the three of us weren't feeling well. She must have thought I was the dumbest person alive, thinking she'd fall for it, but as I suspected, she didn't really care. Plus, she probably figured that if I was going to sneak around behind her back, I'd be trying to sneak around with Jules, who would be approximately fifteen feet from her all day.

* * *

About a half mile from the hotel, I found an internet café and sat down at an open station to search for information on the murder victims.

The whole time I'd been in Paris, I'd figured that a bunch of dead people had nothing to do with me. Now it was starting to look like my week in France was all about dead people.

News of the killings had made worldwide headlines, so it was easy to find articles in English. And as I read, the blood in my veins turned iced-tea-on-a-hot-August-day freezing.

Gabrielle Roux. Pierre Beauclerc. Rochelle DuBois. Armand Janvier.

And Stéphanie's middle name was Voclain.

Every last name was from *L'Ordre de la Clé*.

Each victim was young and glamorous — Gabrielle had been a model. Pierre's photo was taken from a movie premiere, where he had his arm draped around an American starlet. Stéphanie was beautiful, too, in the photo of her that the news website had found from her street-fashion blog.

And, of course, there was Armand — the most striking boy I'd ever seen.

They were all the kind of people that, from a distance, look sparkling and fascinating and worthy of being envied and emulated.

But up closer, I wondered if the shiny exteriors were just that — shiny shells, concealing not-so-awesome personalities. Pierre Beauclerc seemed to have spent the past few years narrowly avoiding facing charges for crimes ranging from drug possession to beating up a bartender. During the last few years of his life, the French tabloids had gleefully followed his exploits, plastering words like *MALFAISANT!* over his photos in gleeful red type.

Stéphanie was your classic label-obsessed mean girl — her fashion blog featured three times as many snarky examples of hapless fashion *don't*s as inspirational *do*s. Gabrielle Roux had achieved a small degree of notoriety for throwing a screaming fit in the middle of a nightclub.

As for Armand . . .

My heart hurt as I searched for news articles about him. I didn't want to find accounts of his bad-boy exploits, tossing innocent deckhands off yachts, yelling at old ladies — or whatever being brought up rich and overindulged made you do.

Fortunately, all I found was a website for a movie he was trying to produce, a documentary about France's *noblesse ancienne*.

Finally, I forced myself to stop searching for information on the victims.

All I was doing was distracting myself from the fact that these murders had something to do with the Order of the Key . . . and that meant they had something to do with me.

* * *

I looked up the address of the Hôpital Sainte-Marina and then found my way there, first taking the Metro and then cutting through a manicured city park to get to the brick-and-glass building. Buoyed by the fact that I'd successfully navigated the subway, I walked with confidence past the reception desk, pausing in front of the elevator to look at the directory. On the third floor was a department called *Traumatologie*, which sounded like *trauma*, which seemed like a pretty good fit for what Stéphanie had been through.

There was only one problem: the stairwell was off-limits. I'd come across enough ALARM WILL SOUND IF DOOR IS OPENED signs in my life to know one when I saw it, even in French.

I turned back to the elevator.

The doors opened and a bunch of people poured out. None of them seemed freaked out, as if there had been strange noises or unexplainable shaking or anything else that might indicate that getting on the elevator would actually physically kill me . . . which was what my gut was telling me would happen.

Three times I watched the doors open and the exchange of people happen, and three times I let the doors close again.

You have to do this.

When the doors parted for the fourth time, I held my breath and rushed in.

In the almost ten years since I'd been inside an elevator, I'd forgotten basic elevator etiquette, such as — which direction was I supposed to face, toward the door or away from the door? And was I supposed to press the number myself or ask the person closest to the numbers to press it for me?

Luckily, one of the other people hit the 3 button without being asked. And I faced the door, like everybody else.

It was a pretty large elevator, as they go — big enough to roll a bed into if you needed to get a patient to another floor. But still, the saliva evaporated out of my mouth and the tears dried out of my tear ducts, leaving me gasping slightly and completely scratchy-eyed. When the doors opened on the third floor, I waited my turn, fighting the urge to push past a pair of elderly nuns and run out.

It was easy to find Stéphanie once I was on her floor. There was a policeman stationed outside a closed door, as well as a cluster of people I guessed were reporters. I didn't know what else to do, so I pretended to know exactly where I was going and walked into the center of it all.

"Mademoiselle," one of the police officers said, putting a hand on my shoulder. Then he said something in rapid French.

I put on my best "innocent" face. *"Je suis une amie de Stéphanie."*

He didn't answer; he just stared. But the idea was pretty clear: no way, no how was I going to be allowed to see Mademoiselle Cocher.

I held my hands to my heart. *"Très, très bonnes amies."*

He frowned.

"S'il vous plaît," I said. *"C'est très important. C'est de la clé."*

"The key?" His eyes narrowed. "What about a key?"

"Oh," I said. "You speak English?"

"I never said I did not," he said. "What is this about a key?"

Whoops. Naturally, if the police were looking for an intruder who seemed to be able to pass easily through locked doors, information about a key would be interesting to them. Time to backtrack. "It's not a real key," I said. "But she'll know what I mean. Please, just ask her."

He opened the door and went inside. A moment later, he was back. There was a new, different expression on his face. Where there had been contempt, there was now curiosity.

His eyes studied me. "She will see you."

He held the door open, and I went in.

Stéphanie was propped up against the raised back of the bed and a few pillows. Her right leg was in a giant cast, and she had a bandage on her cheek. I instantly recognized her from the photos I'd seen online. She was quite lovely, with a sandy-colored pixie-style haircut and delicate features to match — wide brown eyes, small lips, and chiseled cheekbones. Even her ears were petite.

She stared at me, trembling uncontrollably. One hand grabbed the bar on the far side of the bed, as if she was trying to hold herself still, but it wasn't working.

There was an older woman sitting in a chair in the corner, crocheting. Stéphanie spoke to her in French, and the woman got up and left without a word.

Then Stéphanie turned to me. "Who are you? How do you know about the key?"

"My name is Colette Iselin." I started to step closer, and she flinched. So I stayed where I was and pointed to the dark smudge on her arm. "I can see it."

"You can? Truly? No one else can." She held the arm close, as if hiding it from me. "What does it mean?"

She seemed so fragile — I was afraid that explaining my suspicions about *La Clé* might send her over the edge. So I decided to start asking questions.

"Can you tell me about the person who attacked you?" I said. "What did they want?"

"They wanted nothing," she said. "Only to kill, to destroy."

"Who was it?" I asked.

She closed her eyes and moved her head quickly back and forth, back and forth. "I can't say. You will not believe me."

"I will," I said. "I promise."

"No, no, no." Stéphanie buried her face in her hands.

I decided to share what I knew. "Back in the time of Marie Antoinette, our families were a part of a secret society. It was called the Order of the Key, *L'Ordre de la Clé*. Everyone who's been . . . attacked — has been from one of the families. I think whoever's doing this is trying to kill us off because we didn't die during the Revolution."

Stéphanie stared at me. "*Oui*," she whispered. "You're right. She is trying to kill us."

"*She?*" I asked. "It was a woman? Do you know who it is? We need to tell the police!"

"The police? They can't help us. No one can help us." Now her eyes glinted. She knew something I didn't, and because she was so frightened, she wanted to frighten me, too. "Yes, she is a woman. She came for me, and she will come for you, too. She will wait until you are alone — and she will wait until you are awake — because she wants to taste your fear. And then she will attack you, and you will not be able to escape."

"Who?" My stomach turned sour. "Who is she?"

Stéphanie let out a crazed, high-pitched laugh, a cross between a giggle and a cackle, and sat up straighter in her bed. "You know who I mean," she said softly, staring at me.

I did.

"*Un fantôme*," she whispered. "Of course you know. If you can see this mark, then you know . . . and you also know that she will be coming for *you* soon enough."

CHAPTER 19

I LEFT THE room with the cold, crazed sound of Stéphanie's mindless laughter bouncing around inside my head. The rest of me felt like a shell, hollowed out and still and silent. I got on the elevator without thinking and rode it to the first floor.

She couldn't really mean . . .

That the killer was a ghost?

Marie Antoinette's ghost?

It made sense, in a twisted way. Marie Antoinette herself had been beheaded. Now she was bringing that same fate to people today. But why? How?

She always waits until you are alone.

Alone how? Alone in a crowd — the way I was alone now, while I walked back across the park? Alone on the Metro platform, waiting for the train? If I, say, stopped to use the restroom somewhere, would she pop into view and chop off my head?

At the image of the two of us squeezed into a tiny bathroom stall, I let out a burbling, high-pitched laugh that made a guy with a Mohawk give me an uneasy glance and move to another seat in the train car.

But hadn't the queen already found me alone? In Le Hameau? And in the Catacombs? She hadn't killed me — she'd only called me Véronique.

Véronique, my dearest one, what are we to do?

Maybe she wasn't trying to kill me. Maybe I was exempt somehow.

By the time I got back to the hotel, I was utterly at a loss. I had no idea where to turn, what to do.

There was the possibility that Stéphanie was crazy — that she had always been crazy, even before someone tried to kill her. Except craziness didn't explain away my dreams. Or the fact that Stéphanie claimed to have been attacked by the very same ghost I'd been seeing all week.

Come to think of it, I'd never even said I'd seen a ghost. Stéphanie had brought that part up on her own — more proof that she was telling the truth.

Back at the hotel, I went to the penthouse and inserted my keycard.

The room was empty and quiet. I took about three steps in, and the door closed behind me with a click that made me jump out of my skin.

Calm down, Colette.

There was a note on the coffee table in Peely's bubbly handwriting:

Gone to pick up dresses. Leaving for Versailles at 6:30!

Hannah says be ready!

Ready was underlined about four times. The note was signed with a letter *P* that had a happy face drawn in its loop.

Versailles? Yeah, right. Maybe in about a million years, I'd set foot at Versailles again. Even if I had a dress, which I didn't, I couldn't think of anything on earth that would persuade me to step foot onto the grounds of what had once been the queen's home.

But how would I get out of it? Hannah would be furious.

There's a psychopathic ghost stalking you. Why are you worried about Hannah?

What I needed to do was get out of Paris. Get on a plane and go home to Ohio, where the closest thing I'd ever seen to a ghost was Charlie in the Halloween costume he made by cutting eyeholes in the expensive sheets, much to Dad's dismay.

The only problem was, we were scheduled to fly out the following night. Mom would tell me to wait it out. After all, it was only one day. What could happen in one day? Logistically speaking, I might not even be able to get on a flight any faster than the one I was already booked on.

It was okay. I would be fine.

I didn't *really* believe the ghost was trying to kill me, because if that was what she wanted, she'd had her chance. And besides, I didn't have the mark on my arm. I'd checked four times on my way back from the hotel. There had to be some other explanation for why she was following me.

Still, I was *not* going to go to Versailles. Hannah would just have to deal with it.

I stepped into the bathroom to wash my hands. I was lost in thought, picturing Hannah's inevitable hissy fit and imagining what she'd say to me.

I dried my hands and turned back toward the mirror.

And then I froze.

She was back, in the mirror, watching me. She wore a simple black dress, her hair in gray-powdered ringlets.

The woman from the postcard. *La duchesse.*

And this time I knew exactly who she was.

"Véronique," I whispered.

She gazed at me without answering.

"What does she want?" I whispered again, taking a chance. "How do I stop her?"

Her eyes turned to the floor for a long, thoughtful moment. Then she glanced up at me and spoke.

"Ce n'est pas seulement le cou — elle veut briser le coeur."

Oh, crud.

"I don't really speak very much French," I said.

She repeated the phrase once more, and then her image melted away, leaving me staring open-mouthed at my own reflection.

I ran out of the bathroom, trying to speak the words as she'd spoken them. I managed to jot the phrase down on a piece of paper, though I was sure I was getting it wrong.

All I had was questions. It was time to start finding answers.

And that meant it was time to get help.

* * *

Audrey answered the door of room 304 on the first knock.

"Oh," she said. "Hi."

"Can we talk for a minute?" I asked.

She nodded slowly. Behind her in the room, Brynn glanced up from the book she was reading.

"Out in the hall, maybe?" I added.

When we were alone, I took a deep breath. I'd worked out what I was going to say on the walk down there, and even if it wasn't the best plan, it was the only plan I had.

"So, first of all, I'm really sorry about yesterday. I shouldn't have snapped at you. I was a little stressed out, and I —"

"You totally mean-girled me," she said. "But whatever. I don't know what I expected. I guess I forgot you've been taking Hannah lessons for a year."

"I didn't mean to hurt your feelings," I said. "Jules and I had an argument and I was pretty upset about it."

"You couldn't have just said that?" She stuck her hands in her pockets. "So . . . are we done?"

"The reason I came here . . ." I took a deep breath. "I have an idea. You know how I said we weren't really friends? Well, what if we *were* friends?"

She made a confused face.

"If you come hang out with me for a while, maybe we can, like, bond. And then when we get back home, I'll totally be your friend. We're already going shopping, remember?"

A smile spread across her lips, and instantly, I felt relief.

But she just laughed.

"Colette, that's the most ridiculous thing I've ever heard. Why would I want to hang out with someone who treats me like dirt? So I can make people think I'm 'cool'?" She punctuated the word with air quotes and started to turn away, shaking her head. "I think spending so much time with Hannah has actually made you crazy."

"Wait!" I cried. "Don't you wish you could improve your social status? This is your chance."

Her expression didn't change. "Not everyone is obsessed with what other people think about them."

Then she reached for the door, and I felt my options slipping away.

"Audrey, please!" My voice caught. It was close enough to being a sob that Audrey turned back to look at me.

The look on her face made it clear that she really did think I was nuts.

Might as well go ahead and reinforce that.

"I lied," I said. "I wouldn't be doing it as a favor to you. It would be a favor for me."

"If . . . I come hang out with you?"

"Yes." I thought about what Jules had said, about Audrey being a better friend than Hannah and Peely. Then I spat the truth out in one go. "I need your help with something. But it's . . . it's weird."

Audrey took a moment before she replied. "Weird how?"

"Weird, like really weird." I shifted my weight from one foot to the other. "Weird, like you're the only person in the world I can turn to."

She stared at me.

Oh, forget it. I dropped my eyes to the floor. I didn't blame her.

"All right," she said simply. "Let me tell Brynn."

It was like a chorus of angels began to sing. "Seriously?"

"Yeah," she said. "If you need help . . ."

"You have no idea," I said. "You have no idea how much this means to me."

I almost said *I owe you one*. The words made it all the way to the end of my tongue. But suddenly I knew that wasn't what Audrey would want to hear. It wasn't about owing and being owed. For the first time, that was really clear to me.

So instead, I just said, "Thank you."

* * *

By the time we got back to the penthouse, I'd changed my mind. The words I'd been planning to say sounded completely nuts. There was just no way Audrey would help me, even if I appealed to her charitable side.

"So, what's up?" she asked, after taking a second to look around the room. "What's going on?"

I was searching for a way to tell her that I was sorry, that I was wrong, that I didn't need her help, when the events of the week snowballed and rolled right over me. I broke down crying.

"Oh, no, Colette." Audrey's dark eyes searched my face anxiously. "What happened? Please tell me what's wrong."

For a minute, I couldn't answer. She looked around a little awkwardly, and then she stopped in front of the coffee table and picked up the paper where I'd tried to record Véronique's words.

"What's this?" she asked. She read over the words silently, then translated them out loud. "It's not just your neck — she wants to break your heart . . . ?"

I sat up straight. "Is that what that says?"

"Well, kind of," she said. "The spelling's pretty bad, but I think that's the general idea. What does it mean?"

It meant that the queen hadn't killed me when she had the chance because she was planning something else . . . something worse.

"Audrey." I said her name to test my voice, and then I looked into her eyes. "Do you believe in ghosts?"

CHAPTER 20

AUDREY SAT IN the desk chair, staring at her hands.

"It sounds crazy, right?" I said.

She nodded. "Yup."

"But I swear it's all true."

She still didn't look up at me. She seemed to be thinking things through, murmuring to herself. "It can't be a coincidence, can it? The names? I mean, it's every family from the list. . . ."

I didn't talk. I'd done plenty of talking, and now I needed to let her decide whether she believed me.

If she believed me, I would have a powerful ally. If she didn't . . .

Finally, she looked up at me.

"I don't believe in ghosts," she said. "But . . . I don't *not* believe in ghosts, either, you know?"

I gave a tiny nod.

"I've never seen any evidence of that kind of thing. But I suppose it's . . . possible." She looked right into my eyes. "Swear to God, Colette, you're not just doing this as some sort of huge prank."

My stomach was in my throat. "I swear."

"What are you going to do about it?" she asked. "I guess that's the first question. You haven't mentioned it to Jules, have you?"

I shook my head.

"Well . . . maybe don't tell him about the ghost part. But we should ask him if he can find out anything else about the Order of the Key. He must have access to some restricted materials."

"Do you think he would?" I asked.

She raised one eyebrow. "He's totally infatuated with you, Colette. I think you could ask him to steal you a puppy or something and he would do it."

I managed to laugh — but then I remembered the argument Jules and I had had the day before. Not exactly a puppy-stealing moment.

"You need to call him," she said. "Right now."

"What could he possibly learn?" I asked.

"He's a historian. Maybe he can dig up some clue that would show us how to stop her. Or why she's doing it. Doesn't it seem strange that she's killing the people who were supposedly her best friends? Anything he can find out about the order could be helpful. So call him."

"Right now? But he has the afternoon off," I said lamely.

"Even better," she said. "Call him."

"But what if he —"

"Colette," she said. *"Call him."*

So I took the folded-up piece of paper with Jules's phone number on it out of my purse, sat down at the phone, and called him.

There was no answer. I left a message asking him to call me at the hotel and hung up.

"So what now?" I asked.

"We're leaving tomorrow," Audrey said. "So the big question is, will the ghost follow you?"

"Follow me home?" I hadn't even thought about that. "She wouldn't hurt my mother or my brother, would she?"

Audrey was silent.

She wants to break your heart.

I thought of Mom and Charlie, alone and vulnerable in that little apartment.

"I need to call them," I said. "They could be in danger —"

"Your mother's not an Iselin by birth, though," she said. "It would be your dad, right?"

That's right.

I could call my father. It was early, but he would *want* to be woken up, when he heard he and Charlie and I could be in trouble.

I dug out my calling card and dialed Dad's cell phone number.

It seemed to take forever for the call to go through. Finally, it rang. And rang. And rang.

And went to voice mail.

"Dad, it's me. Please call me at the hotel in France. It's important."

I hung up.

Then I dialed again.

This time, it rang twice and then someone picked up. "Hello?"

"Dad?"

My father's voice was raspy and tired. "Colette? What time is it? I thought you were in France."

"I am," I said. "Listen, I'm sorry to wake you up, but this is important. There's something really weird going on and —"

"Have you called your mother about it?" he asked.

"No," I said. "I wanted to talk to you first."

"Look, sweetie. I'm really busy these days, and I think you should try your mom first."

It was like getting slapped in the face. "But, Dad . . ."

"I'm sure your mom can handle whatever it is you need. I'm just a little overbooked, you know? I'm flying out today for a job interview in San Diego and —"

San Diego? "What about New York?"

He was silent.

"I thought we were going to New York this summer."

"Well, honey, that's not going to happen. You know that was never set in stone."

Never set in stone? My father had taken me out to dinner and asked me how I'd like to spend the summer in Manhattan with him. He'd told me he would find a short-term lease on the

Upper West Side and I could get a part-time job and we would go see Broadway shows on the weekends.

I didn't answer.

Dad went on. "Anyway, Estelle found this opportunity for me in California, and we're thinking —"

"Who's Estelle?"

"She's the . . ." I heard a murmur in the background, a female voice. "She's my girlfriend, Colette."

"Oh." Suddenly, I felt exhausted.

"I just think maybe it would be better if you stayed in Toledo this summer. Maybe you can come see me in San Diego after graduation."

That was more than a year away.

"All right, Dad," I said.

"You understand, right? I'll owe you one."

My heart sank. "Sure."

He hung up.

I sat with the receiver in my hand until Audrey came and placed it back in the cradle. "You'll use all your calling card minutes," she said softly.

"He didn't even ask how I was," I said. "I could have been dying and he wouldn't have even known."

She sat on the edge of the sofa. "I'm sorry."

"And I was supposed to go to New York for the summer — I've told *everyone*. . . . I'm going to look so stupid."

"No one is going to care," she said. "No one who matters, anyway."

Hannah would care.

Then it hit me — all the members of the order were shallow jerks. And my dad was a shallow jerk.

And as long as we're being real, here . . .

I was a shallow jerk, too.

* * *

"Did you try . . . let's see . . . saying a prayer?" Audrey offered. She sat at the desk with the laptop we'd borrowed from Brynn. She was reading from ghost websites. "Or telling the ghost that her presence isn't welcome?"

"I don't think so. I guess I might have said 'Go away.' Is that what you're supposed to do?" I was lying on the sofa with my feet on the armrest. "I was too busy peeing my pants."

Audrey looked back at the screen. "It's what a bunch of people on this website are saying."

"And the internet is never wrong," I said. "Especially about ghosts."

She sighed and sat back. "Okay, next website."

We'd been searching for information on ghosts for an hour. Unfortunately, most of it was obviously made up by people who had no idea what they were talking about.

I glanced at the clock. It was four. Hannah and Pilar would be getting back from the rental shop with their gowns soon and starting to get ready. And I would have to come up with a good reason for not going.

"What about apologizing?" Audrey asked.

"For what?"

"I don't know," she said. "I mean, she was beheaded. . . . That has to be stressful."

"But those families were her friends."

Audrey turned around. "Why weren't any of them tried or executed during the Revolution?"

"I don't know," I said. "Maybe they got lucky."

"Or they didn't. What if —"

She was interrupted by a sharp knock at the door.

We glanced at each other.

"Ghosts don't knock, right?" she asked.

I got up and went to open it.

Jules was outside. "Let me in before someone sees me," he said. "I'm not supposed to come into your room."

I let him pass and shut the door behind him. "What are you doing here? I tried to call you —"

"You did?" He pulled out his phone and looked at the screen. "Oh, yes. I'm sorry. I didn't get your message. I was in the archives at the university library, and reception there is very poor."

I'd never seen him like this. He was agitated, pacing back and forth, clutching a notebook tightly in his hand.

"What's going on?" I asked.

He turned to me so quickly that it startled me.

"Don't think I am crazy," he said. "But I think you may be in danger."

"Oh, yeah, that," I said.

He blinked.

"What did you find, Jules?" Audrey asked.

He looked at her and then back at me. Then he seemed to collect himself and opened his notebook. "I remembered that you had

244

asked me about someone named Véronique, and I had a feeling it was related to your family. So I went into the rare books section and looked up Véronique Iselin — just to see if something would turn up. I found a group called *L'ordre de la Clé*. Initially, the group was formed to support the monarchy — especially the queen."

"'In eternal service of Her Majesty, the queen,'" I said.

"*Oui*, exactly," he said. "How do you know this?"

"I've been doing some research of my own," I said. "What else did you find?"

"Six families took a blood oath with one another to look after the interests of Marie Antoinette and her family."

A blood oath? I exchanged glances with Audrey.

"And then, when the Revolution came, they swore to help the king and queen escape. They coordinated efforts to get the royal family out of France. After the first effort failed and the family returned to Versailles, the order stayed close by, to protect her."

So she was paying them back by killing them off? Nice.

"There were even rumors that they built a secret room where the royal family could hide until their allies came to rescue them, should they ever find themselves in danger."

"Like a panic room?" Audrey said.

Jules nodded. Then he looked at me. "But as I researched the order, I realized — the last names — they are the same as the people being murdered now. Roux, Janvier, DuBois, Beauclerc —"

"Yes, I know," I said. "And Iselin is one of the names."

"Yes," he said. Then he stared at me. "And that is why I believe you are in danger. But then I asked myself, why would someone kill the members of a secret society from two hundred years ago?"

Not just any someone — the ghost of the woman they swore to protect.

"And I found the answer in the very last chapter of a book written by royalists in the 1830s. The Order of the Key was established to serve the queen, but in the end . . . they betrayed her."

I gasped. "They did?"

"Every single family," he said. "And they did it to save themselves."

Just thinking about it made my neck hurt.

"It was an elaborate plan," he said. "They made a deal with the Jacobins — the revolutionaries — who promised the families safe passage out of the country in exchange for making sure the king and queen did not leave Versailles until they could be taken prisoner."

I stared at the rug, feeling sick to my stomach.

So the queen was taking her revenge. And since the original members of the order were long dead, she was taking her rage out on the next-best thing — their descendants.

"What about Véronique?" I asked.

He set the notebook down. "Véronique Iselin was the *Duchesse de Broglie*. She was the queen's most trusted and beloved friend. Her betrayal was the worst of them all."

The room was quiet for a long moment, except the rustling of pages as Jules looked back over his notes.

"And I'm worried because she's the only one left," he said.

I stared at him, not understanding.

"A member of every other family has been attacked. *You*, Véronique's descendant, are the only one left. So whoever's doing this may be coming after you." He gathered his notebook. "We need to go to the police. I almost went directly there, but I decided to stop here first . . . to make sure you were safe."

"The police can't help," I said.

Jules furrowed his brow. "Of course they can help."

"They really can't," Audrey said.

"I don't understand why you would say such a thing," Jules said.

I flopped backward on the bed, my arm over my eyes. "I guess I just make sure never to be alone again in my whole life."

"Actually . . ." Audrey spoke up from the desk. "It may not be that bad."

I peered at her through the crook of my elbow.

"Look," she said, pulling up a map of Paris on-screen. "I marked the location of each murder. . . ."

There was a series of little pin graphics that formed a path from Versailles right to the center of the city.

"It's pretty consistent," she said. "I'm not sure what it means, but it seems like there's a pattern. And the pattern doesn't include Toledo, Ohio."

"Wait," Jules said, leaning down to look at it. "This is the path the royal family took from Versailles to the prison."

"So every victim happened to be along the route?" I said. "Isn't that a little —"

"Is it weirder than the fact that there's an evil ghost killing people?" Audrey asked. "And look — here's our hotel. So you're on the route, too."

She double-clicked, and one last pin fell into place on the map.

"Maybe you're all drawn to this route," she said. "It was a blood oath, after all. Maybe it's in your blood."

Maybe so. We were quiet.

Jules cleared his throat. "Excuse me," he said. "Did you say . . . a *ghost*?"

We both turned to him. I glanced at Audrey, who shrugged.

"Yes," I said. "A ghost."

He looked like a chicken who'd just realized he was hanging out in a fox den. "I don't understand. Whose ghost?"

I sighed. "Marie Antoinette's. I've been seeing her all week."

"Ah." He fidgeted for a moment, glancing at the door. I half-expected him to run for it. Then he wandered away, to stare out the window.

Audrey's eyes, full of sympathy, met mine, and I knew we were both thinking the same thing.

This was the end of my beautiful Paris romance.

"Well," Audrey said, "the good news is, maybe you just need to make sure you're not alone between now and tomorrow, and then . . ."

"And then never come back to Paris again." Ever. A sudden sense of loss settled over me.

Still, it beat dying.

"Maybe we should spend the rest of the night looking up other people who might be in danger and calling them," Audrey said.

"Who would believe us?" I asked. "Jules doesn't."

He looked at me. "I didn't say that."

"But you don't. It's obvious. You think I have terrible taste in friends and really awful judgment and now you think I'm a total idiot for believing in ghosts."

"I don't think that," he said. "I believe in ghosts."

Oh.

"You do?"

"Yes," he said. "We have one in our apartment building. We call him Henri. But I don't think he's ever tried to hurt anyone."

There was a moment when none of us said anything. And that was when the door to the room opened.

"Honey, we're home," Hannah called. She rounded the corner and stopped short.

"Hi," I said.

Hannah was dragging her enormous dress behind her. She draped it over a chair and looked from Jules to Audrey and then to me. "Having a party?"

I tried to smile.

There was something in her eyes that was dangerous. Her gaze poked into me like pinpricks.

"Colette, are you —" Pilar followed Hannah in, also carrying her dress. "Oh."

"So," Hannah said. "I guess maybe you've hidden your ball gown somewhere around here, right?"

"Hannah —" I began, but she cut me off.

"I knew you wouldn't get one," she said. "I don't know how I knew. But I knew you'd let me down."

"I'm sorry," I said.

"You're not sorry. If you cared enough to be sorry, you would have tried harder in the first place." Hannah gave Audrey and Jules a once-over. "You've chosen your friends, I guess. Pilar, let's go into my room and get ready. Thank God we only have one more night here."

Pilar gave me a stricken look but followed Hannah. I heard her say, in a low voice, "Can't she just wear a regular dress?"

The door slammed behind them before we could hear Hannah's response. But I had a pretty fair idea what it was.

They came out of the room a few minutes after six, both looking incredible in their ball gowns, with elbow-length gloves and beautiful necklaces and their hair piled up on their heads. But they didn't stop for our admiration. They sailed through the room, Pilar complaining that her gloves were itchy and Hannah fiercely shushing her and pulling the door closed behind them.

The air in the room settled in their wake.

"So what should we do tonight?" Audrey asked, picking up a purple feather that had fallen out of Pilar's little hat. "It's our last night in Paris."

I glanced at Jules, to see if the words seemed to have any effect on him. He was staring at the floor, looking like I felt — deflated. Defeated. Dejected. All the depressing *de-* words.

At least you're not de-ad.

"I don't know," I said. It seemed wrong to go around and act as if everything was fine when I knew it wasn't fine. But I couldn't stand the thought of leaving the city without . . . I don't know, saying good-bye. Not to mention that sitting around the

250

hotel room would just remind me that my two roommates might never speak to me again.

"We could go walk around a little," she suggested. "Jules, want to come?"

He shrugged. I didn't take it personally. It was hard to focus under the pall of a murderous ghost.

There was a knock at the door. Audrey ran to check the peephole. "It's just Brynn," she said, pulling it open.

"Hey," Brynn said. She came in and looked around, letting out a low whistle. "Wow. Nice room."

"What's up?" Audrey asked.

"Sorry to interrupt," she said. "But you have to see this. Hannah and Pilar came down to the lobby in their dresses and it was insane. They actually attracted a crowd of tourists in the street when they were getting into their car . . . then Hannah tripped and almost ate it on the cobblestone. Thank God she didn't see that I had my camera, but I totally got a picture."

She held it up, but none of us seemed particularly interested.

"Sorry," Audrey said. "We're a little distracted. Trying to figure something out."

Brynn looked a little hurt, so I reached for the camera to scroll through the pictures.

Yep, Hannah and Peely, looking exactly how they'd looked when they walked out on me.

Except — at some point between our room and the lobby, Pilar had taken off her uncomfortable gloves.

"Hey, Brynn," I said. "Can I zoom in on this picture?"

She showed me how, and I zoomed all the way in.

"This isn't the good one. What are you looking at?" she asked, studying the image.

Nothing she'd be able to see.

But suddenly Véronique's meaning was crystal clear: *she wants to break your heart.*

"Um, thanks, Brynn," I said. My whole body thrummed with tension as she took the camera back and then seemed to get that we were in the middle of something. She said an awkward good-bye and left.

"What did that mean?" Audrey asked. "What was in that photo?"

"I have to go to Versailles," I said.

"What?" Audrey sat up straight. "What are you talking about?"

I took a deep breath. "It's not enough just to kill me — the queen is going to make my punishment the worst one yet."

"How do you know this?" Jules asked.

I knew because I'd seen Pilar's forearm in Brynn's photograph.

And there was a dark key-shaped smudge on it.

The queen's mark — the one she reserved for the people she planned to kill.

"She's not just after my neck. She wants to break my heart." I began to shake. "She's going to try to murder Pilar at the party tonight."

"Can't you stop them from going there?" Jules asked.

"I can try," I said. I got out my calling card and tried Hannah's and Peely's phones. They both went straight to voice mail.

"We could try calling the security office," Audrey suggested.

"No," I said. "That won't work. Hannah wouldn't listen, and Pilar will do whatever Hannah tells her to. I have to go after them."

"Now, hold on," Audrey said. "Putting yourself in danger can't be the answer."

I thought of Pilar, cornered by an evil ghost in some dark, scary room. It was like picturing a kitten being cornered by a wolf. "I have to go."

I saw in her eyes that Audrey understood.

"They must be halfway there by now," Jules said. "And how will you get through security?"

Audrey leaned forward. "Were there tickets? Actual, physical tickets?"

"I don't think so — Hannah said we were on the list."

Audrey nodded. "Right. So she's just counting on the fact that you're not going — she's not going to go to the trouble to get you taken off the list."

Jules looked unconvinced. "Is there enough time?"

"I have to try, at least," I said. "Besides, it might take the ghost a while to get Pilar alone."

"You don't have a dress." Audrey's face fell.

I turned to look at Jules, who had already pulled his phone out and dialed. "Mathilde," he said. Then he spoke in French, his voiced hushed and urgent. She asked him questions, which he answered, and then he asked her questions. They seemed to agree on something and then he hung up.

Audrey and I waited breathlessly.

"Well," he said. "Luckily, the boy who has the key to the storage room is in love with her. She can call him and have him meet her there."

"How fast?" Audrey asked.

"Right now. She will be here in twenty minutes."

"All right." Audrey stood up. "Colette, do you need to do your hair or put on your eye shadow or . . . whatever? Sorry, I don't know much about that stuff."

With all the adrenaline rushing through my body, I wasn't sure I could actually manage to put on eye makeup without accidentally stabbing myself in the eye with the mascara wand. But I grabbed my makeup bag and went to the mirror over the dresser.

Audrey came over to me. "You don't have to do anything crazy, right? Just keep Pilar from going off by herself."

I nodded. "Right."

"And don't you go off by yourself, either. And don't get arrested or anything. If they try to make you leave, then just leave."

I paused mid-mascara-stroke and looked at her. "Without Pilar?"

"You can't exactly save her if you get beheaded, can you?"

Good point.

A few minutes later, there was a knock at the door, and when Jules pulled it open, Mathilde came in, dragging a gown.

"You, out!" she said to her brother. Then she looked at Audrey. "You, stay. We will need your help."

Jules backed out of the room, and Mathilde revealed the gown with a flourish.

Audrey gasped. "That's the most beautiful dress I've ever seen."

It was dark-gray silk, but the color was more than just a color — it had richness and depth, like it was made of shadows. It had a low, square-cut neckline, and the bodice was embroidered with silver thread in a delicate vine pattern. It fit my ribcage severely down to the waist and then hung to the floor in long, gathered vertical sections of fabric. The sleeves were elbow-length and fitted.

When they finally got me buttoned into the dress, Mathilde helped me finish my makeup and teased my hair into a voluminous puff that surrounded my head like a halo. I handed her my hair spray, and she used nearly the whole can.

Mathilde stepped back. *"Magnifique,"* she said.

Audrey was wide-eyed. "You look like a queen."

I tried to smile as she examined me from head to toe. Then I turned and saw myself in the full-length mirror on the bathroom door.

For a split second, I thought I was looking at Véronique again, and then I realized, this time, it was just me.

I really did look like a queen — or a duchess.

At any other point in my life, I would have been thrilled to wear such a gorgeous dress, like a real, honest-to-goodness member of the nobility. But now it just reminded me of what I was, and what my ancestor had done — and the terrible consequences her actions had brought about.

Mathilde went to the door and opened it. "She's done!"

Jules came in and stopped short.

My heart leaped to my throat as I stepped closer to him.

He stared at me, almost in wonderment. "I feel like I should bow to you," he said softly.

If I lived to be a hundred (or any age past sixteen), I'd never forget how it felt to have a boy look at me that way. Like I was the most beautiful thing he'd ever seen.

Audrey tapped me on the shoulder. "This is great, but you guys need to get going. Jules, how far is your car?"

"Very close," he said.

"*Bon*," Mathilde said. "Let's go."

"Wait!" I said. "One last thing."

I reached for the medallion and slipped it around my neck.

Audrey cringed a little. "Are you totally sure you want to wear that?"

"Yes," I said.

I wanted the queen to know I was there.

CHAPTER 21

THE PALACE WAS lit up like something from a fairy tale, with spotlights illuminating the gold accents on the edges of the roof. The front gates were open, and Jules slowed the car and rolled down the window to talk to a security guard holding a clipboard.

"Colette Iselin," Jules said.

The man scanned the list, then shook his head.

"Maybe it's under Norstedt?" I said, and Jules translated.

The guard flipped the page and nodded. He handed Jules a piece of paper and waved us through.

We were in a line of cars, slowly creeping toward a long red carpet set up between a set of velvet ropes. Partygoers emerged from the cars ahead — most of them were dressed up almost as elaborately as I was, the women in ginormous dresses and elaborate hairpieces and hats, the men in frock coats and even bigger hats.

Watching them, I got chills. It was easy to imagine ourselves in some parallel universe, where people came to parties at marvelous palaces. I supposed, in a way, that's how Hannah's life was shaping up to be. With as much money and as many connections as she had, she could look forward to a lifetime of being handed out of limousines and sashaying down long red carpets, while admirers looked on as she passed them by without so much as a careless glance.

Whereas this was probably a once-in-a-lifetime event for me. Might as well make the most of it.

Jules parked, then came around and opened the door for me. He reached for my hand and helped me climb out of the little car. The piece of paper the guard had given him was my ticket. He pressed it into my hand.

"I think we're in time," he said. "Anyway, it certainly doesn't seem like there's been a murder yet."

Yet. The word chilled me.

"I'd better go," I said.

We stared at each other for a minute.

"I will park nearby," he said. "As soon as you have a chance, call me. Mathilde put her phone in your purse. Just hold down number one and it will dial me."

"Merci," I said. There was a little quiver in my voice.

"Be safe, Colette. Please."

I nodded, but I felt like speaking would give away how freaked out I was — to him and to me.

He hadn't let go of my hand. He raised it to his mouth and kissed it lightly.

I gave him a small smile and pulled away. "I have to go."

My head held high, I walked toward the entrance.

A security guard took my ticket and let me pass through a set of massive double doors. After that, it was a straight shot down the red carpet all the way to the Hall of Mirrors.

At the entrance to the hall, I stood in silence, looking around.

"It's so beautiful," the girl next to me whispered to her date.

Beautiful didn't even begin to describe it. Without crowds of tourists, the room looked like it must have looked three hundred years ago . . . gorgeous, elegant, and transcendent. The light from the chandeliers made the golden walls glow, and outside the windows, the last purple clouds of twilight were fading to indigo. There were no party decorations. They weren't necessary.

As my eyes swept the room, I had the odd feeling of not being completely sure where — or when — I was. Girls grouped together in giggling clumps, whispering and gossiping, leaning back and forth in a way that made their skirts swing flirtatiously. It could have been the year 1785.

Enough looking around.

I had to find Hannah and Pilar.

Voices hushed slightly as I made my way through the crowd, and I knew I looked like a *duchesse*. Somehow, Versailles was a part of me, and I was a part of it. Being there suddenly felt as natural as being in my own living room.

I scanned the room as I went, hoping to catch a glimpse of Hannah's pale-green dress or Peely's mauvey-purple one. The room wasn't stuffed with people, but there were enough guests that I had a few false alarms — glimpses of similar gowns being worn by other women.

Maybe I was too late. Maybe the ghost had already gotten Pilar alone and —

No. I couldn't let myself think that way.

I paused to take a glass of water from one of the refreshments tables, and when I turned around, I caught sight of Hannah and Pilar across the room. Peely waved to me excitedly, her eyes wide with disbelief. Then she pointed to herself, mouthed something I couldn't begin to understand, and turned away.

"No, wait!" I called. I rushed over to where she'd been standing, but she was gone.

"What are you doing here?" The icy voice coming from behind me was Hannah's. "I uninvited you. And where did you get that dress?"

I turned around, looking over her shoulder. "Where's Peely?"

Hannah's face darkened. "She went off with some French guy. She saw a fancy piano and just about lost her mind. So he offered to let her touch it or something. You know how dumb she gets about that stuff."

"But where did she go?" I asked.

Hannah drew back. "Why are you acting insane? I'm totally going to tell them you're not allowed to be here."

"Hannah!" I grabbed her roughly by the sleeve. "Are you not listening to me? This is *important* — it's literally life and death!"

She jerked away and leveled a death glare at me. "You have no idea what's important, Colette."

"What's that supposed to mean?"

"Oh, just a little concept called 'the truth.' Ever think about trying it?" Her lips curled into a sneer.

The truth? Did she mean about the ghost? Or about . . . everything else?

"Colette! I can't believe you came! You look miraculous!" Pilar had come back. I turned to her, so relieved I couldn't speak. She was gaping at my dress. Then she glanced up and saw Hannah's face, and her happy smile faltered.

"Oh, this is good," Hannah said. "I'm glad we can do this together."

"Do what together?" Peely asked.

"Hannah, don't," I said. "I'll go. I just came to talk to Pilar for a minute. Then I'll leave."

"No, Colette, stay." Hannah gave me a snide, narrow-eyed smile. "I think a costume party is the perfect place to expose someone as a giant liar."

"Peely, can you just come with me for a second?" I asked. I took hold of her arm and turned it over. There it was — the dark smudge of the key symbol.

"What's wrong? What are you looking at?" Clearly, Pilar couldn't see the mark. She gingerly pulled her arm away and glanced at Hannah as if she were asking for permission. "Who's a liar?"

"Our dear friend Colette," Hannah said. Then she turned to me. "I know everything. I know that your dad left your mom. I know your mom works at the mall. I know you're on scholarship and you just moved to some crappy apartment. And hello, all of your supposedly vintage clothes? Most of them are from, like, Sears."

I stared at her. I'd had nightmares about a moment like this . . . except even my worst nightmares weren't even close to being as painful and embarrassing as reality. I'd always worried that Hannah would treat me with disdain if she learned the truth. But the expression in her eyes went way past disdain. . . . It was hatred.

"I've known all of this since like three months ago," she said. "I've just been wondering if you were ever going to stop lying about it. You know — since we're your *friends*."

Pilar turned to me, open-mouthed. "You're on scholarship?"

"I was going to tell you," I said. "But I was waiting for the right moment."

"You've been lying to our faces," Hannah said. "For almost a year. And then you lied about Armand."

I opened my mouth to defend myself, but the thing is . . . she hadn't accused me of being poor, or of having a mom who worked in the mall — she'd only accused me of lying. And she was right about that.

I'd been lying to them for almost a year.

My face flushed as I turned away.

And then I saw her in one of the mirrors —

The ghost.

There was no mistaking the queen, though once I'd caught sight of her, all of the costumed women in the room seemed to be involved in some elaborately choreographed dance to keep me from being able to see her again.

I'd swing my head and catch a hint of her reflection out of the corner of my eye — and then find myself looking at just another partygoer.

I turned to Pilar. "Peely, don't go anywhere by yourself tonight, okay? Promise?"

"What's wrong with you? Pilar, don't promise her anything." Hannah glared at me. "You're over, Colette. You're completely cut off. Especially after tonight."

I let my glance travel across the room as I searched for the white plumes of the queen's headpiece. And I said, "I don't care."

"Excuse me?" Hannah said.

"You're *excused*, Hannah," I said. "And I don't *care* if you cut me off. You're a terrible friend. Actually, you're a terrible person."

"You're both being crazy," Peely said. She looked as if she might cry. "I thought tonight was supposed to be special."

"Oh, grow up," Hannah said.

"Don't talk to her like that," I snapped. "Like she's a little kid."

Hannah took a half step forward. "Don't you ever try to tell me what to do."

I really didn't have time for this. But I stood my ground. "Hannah, I promise you that from this day on, I'm going to say exactly what I want to say to you at the exact moment when I want to say it —" I stopped and looked around. "Where's Pilar?"

Hannah screwed up her face in an angry scowl. "What?"

I grabbed both of her arms. "Where did she go?"

Hannah shook me off. "How should I know?"

I ran away, darting through the crowd, searching for Peely and, at the same time, trying to keep an eye out for the ghost.

Every time I saw the queen reflected in a mirror, I would turn and see a living, breathing human standing where she ought to have been.

She was playing with me, taunting me.

I made my way down the entire length of the hall that way — turning my head back and forth, frantically spinning to try to catch another glimpse of the ghost.

I got all the way to the end of the Hall of Mirrors.

Peely was gone.

CHAPTER 22

I STOOD LOOKING helplessly past the velvet rope that led into the next room. The guard gave me a knowing look, just reminding me he was there.

"There she is!" Hannah's voice, clear and cold, cut through the rest of the sounds as she pushed her way toward us. "She's not supposed to be here! I uninvited her!"

The guard looked at Hannah curiously . . . and then he walked away from his post to go see what her problem was.

"*Thanks, Han,*" I murmured.

For the moment unwatched, I slipped around the velvet ropes and through the darkened doorway on the other side.

The ghost stood in the center of the room, a haughty look on her face.

Then she disappeared. On the floor where she'd been standing, I could see a little purple feather — the same kind that had fallen from Peely's hat in the penthouse.

The queen wanted me to follow her.

And she was using Pilar as bait.

When I went into the next room, the door slammed shut behind me, and the lights came blazing on. The electric lights were made to mimic the candles used two hundred years earlier.

"Where is she? Where's my friend?" I called, looking at my surroundings in the dim flickering light.

My gaze stopped on a painting on the wall. It was the one from the postcard. *La Duchesse* sitting by a pond. Véronique.

I stared up at the face that looked so strikingly like my own and tried to imagine what she must have been thinking, what would have caused her to forsake her dearest friend.

I felt eerily calm, because there was no going back now, no choices left to make, nowhere to run. I was either going to find a way to save Pilar and myself . . . or I wasn't.

The queen had a plan. I just had to let her reveal it to me.

In the center of the room was a round table. I leaned over to study the intricate carvings at its center. There was a tiny pattern made of cornflowers, and then between every fourth or fifth flower was a key.

The table sat on a huge circular rug. As I walked onto the rug, I felt a change in the floor underfoot — as though there were a hollow space beneath it.

Suddenly, the rug rolled back in one quick motion, revealing a trapdoor.

My heart went all fluttery, and not in a good way. The queen was giving me directions again.

The door had a latch, which seemed to be locked. And then I realized that I had a key — my medallion. The tiny metal pieces on the latch fit into the hollows of the carved key, and tiny spikes stuck through the cutout cornflower.

I held my breath and turned it. The lock moved easily, not like it had been sealed for two hundred years, and I was able to lift the door open.

"Oh, God," I said.

Darkness yawned before me like the mouth of a lazy, hungry monster.

A set of stairs led down to impenetrable blackness.

I can't.

I stepped back and leaned against the round table for support, gripping its carved edges.

You have to.

I looked around the room. The doors were still shut — and I knew they wouldn't open for me. There were no other exits.

It was this or stand there like a lamb in line for the slaughterhouse — and miss my chance to save Peely.

On the round table was a candle on a little dish — the kind people in period movies carried up to their bedrooms at night. Somehow, the candle had been lit, like it was waiting for me.

You made it through the Catacombs. You lived through the elevator ride.

This was much worse . . . but it was also much more important.

I grabbed the candle from the table, took a deep breath, and stepped down onto the first step, then the second, then third — pausing to remove my medallion from the lock and pull the trapdoor closed.

I descended the rest of the stairs, while from overhead came the heavy thud of the rug unrolling over the trapdoor.

For the first minute or so, I was too busy trying to drag air into my lungs to take stock of where I was.

Finally, I managed to calm my breath and look around.

This was a tunnel, but it was nothing like the Catacombs. It was more like an extension of the palace. The walls were papered with a beautiful Asian-inspired pattern. Though much of the paper had begun to curl at its edges, the colors, never exposed to daylight, remained brilliant. The ceilings were easily a foot above my head. The floor was green-and-white-marble tile, and every few feet was a wool rug — eaten threadbare in places by moths, but still mostly intact.

I kept throwing glances over my shoulder, but the queen hadn't appeared behind me.

The farther I went, the worse the conditions in the tunnel became. I seemed to be heading out under the palace grounds, because in places the seams between the wall and ceiling were split by the winding, wandering roots of a tree. There were damp spots where the wallpaper had mildewed and peeled away, and some of the tiles were cracked and chipped beneath my feet. Eventually, all traces of the fancy, manicured space were gone, destroyed by time and neglect, and I was surrounded by nothing but rot and ruin, the smell of damp dirt permeating the air. I kept trying to think what it reminded me of — until I remembered my grandmother's storm cellar.

My heartbeat echoed off my eardrums, and I could feel myself start to panic. *Go, go, go.* I had to concentrate to keep the bright flashes in my vision from tripping me up.

The ground grew damp beneath my feet, turning the hem of my dress black and wet with mud. I must have been passing near one of the ponds.

Soon the water was ankle-deep, inky and opaque in the darkness. There was no way to know how deep it would get — if part of the path had decayed into a muddy pit, I would be sucked in, trapped. But I had to keep going. I trudged onward through the murky, freezing mud, my ice-cold feet squishing in my shoes. Mathilde's dress was ruined beyond any hope of repair, but I pushed the thought out of my mind.

I paused at one point to listen more closely to a sound on the edges of my hearing . . . a slow *whoosh*.

It sounded almost like . . .

I let the light of the candle stray to the tunnel behind me. It hit the surface of the muddy water — and the bits of light seemed to quiver.

The water was moving.

Breathless, I stared at the same spot, trying to figure out what I was seeing.

The *whoosh* grew noticeably louder. . . .

The water level was rising.

With a burbling sound, a wave of dark water surged down the tunnel toward me. Suddenly, instead of being ankle-deep, it went halfway to my knees.

I didn't have time to think. I needed to get out of there — but first, I needed to ditch the massive dress before its weight pulled me down. I tore at the buttons of the bodice as I began to run. What had seemed like a harmless burble sounded like a full-on roar as I struggled to lift my feet.

Finally, I was able to free myself from the top of the gown. Then I grabbed at my waistline and gave a tremendous, merciless tug. With a ripping sound that would have broken the heart of anyone who loved clothes, the skirt split from waistline to knee. I shoved it down and climbed out, leaving the dress slumping in the mud like a melted Wicked Witch.

Now I wore a simple white cotton underdress with a lightweight skirt that I could gather and hold in one hand. Which I did.

And then I ran.

Even as I went, I could tell that the water was getting higher and higher, as though someone had released a floodgate. Soon it would be up to my waist . . . and then my chest . . . and then my neck . . . and then . . .

I was a decent swimmer, but what good was swimming if the water went all the way to the ceiling and left me with no air?

I think I would have opted for a swift decapitation over the feeling of being lifted and pressed to the dirt ceiling above, choking for a few last swallows of air, my lungs finally filling with freezing water. . . .

Just when I was beginning to think there was no end — no end I would live to reach anyway — there was a sharp turn to the right, and fifteen feet after that, the tunnel dead-ended. In front of the dirt wall was a splintery wooden ladder that led to a trapdoor overhead.

I hesitantly put my foot on the bottom rung of the ladder and let a little weight press down on it.

It snapped in two. The pieces disappeared into the murk with a splash.

"Awesome," I said, tying the skirt of my dress into a knot.

I stepped onto the second rung. That one held.

I had no choice but to wrap my hands around the rough wood and hold on tightly as I made my way up the remaining six rungs, slivers embedding themselves into the skin of my fingers and palms. The fifth rung snapped like the bottom one had, but the rest held. At the top, I gingerly let go of the ladder with one hand to push up on the door.

The whole thing gave way under the pressure of my gentle push. The boards plunged into the water below as I whipped my head away to protect my face from falling splinters of wood.

I managed to drag myself out of the hole, panting and gasping for air. The water in the tunnel below churned and bubbled like oil. I stared over the edge at it for a moment before looking around. I was in the center of a small square room, and above me were the sparkling stars and shining moon. At first I thought it was a courtyard, and then I figured out that the roof had simply given way at some point. The walls were pale-yellow plaster.

I was in Le Hameau.

A single door led out of the room. I reached for the knob, but it opened ahead of me, without being touched.

Through another door ahead, I could see the great room with the hearth and the black-and-white-tile floor. There was no sign of Peely, so I crossed the room and went into the round turret where I'd gotten stuck my first time at Versailles.

Upstairs I found a long hallway, with rooms coming off one side. At the very end of the hall, an open doorway glowed with the golden flicker of candlelight.

When I reached it, I stood and stared.

This had been a playroom. It held several small child-size beds, and one larger bed — as though the queen had slept here, surrounded by her children. The walls were still lined with shelves, though most of them were empty. There were a few broken wood and metal toys scattered around, and debris littered the floor.

The feeling of loss was so thick you could practically breathe it in. I thought of the innocent children who'd been torn from this place, separated from their parents . . . locked up — in some cases, until their deaths.

My thoughts were interrupted by a thin, tinkly, metallic tune, graceful and haunting. Once upon a time, it might have struck someone as playful, but in this desolate setting, it echoed in my ears like a funeral dirge.

The sound came from under the big bed, so I knelt and looked for its source.

I found a small wooden music box, polished to a gleam under a half-inch layer of dust, which I wiped away.

I tried to open the latch, but it was locked.

I set it down and looked around the rest of the room. The walls had once been a pale peach-orange. Now they were splotched with gray and streaked with black mold. On one wall was a painting of Marie with her children, the canvas roughly slashed. The queen wore a flowing blue dress and wore her hair simply, in loose, powdered-gray curls around her collar. A blue-and-white-striped cap perched on her head. The children were similarly plain, in the royal equivalent of playclothes. They all sat close to one another, and Marie's eyes gleamed with maternal pride.

Suddenly, the eyes in the portrait gleamed brighter.

The ghost came swooping toward me, and I staggered backward, collapsing onto the big bed. The ancient mattress sagged around me like quicksand, trapping me on my back, a cloud of dust billowing in the air.

The ghost hung in the air over me.

"*Tu te souviens?*" she whispered.

I racked my brain for the translation. . . . *Do you remember?*

"*Tu te souviens, Véronique?*"

"I'm — I'm not Véronique," I stammered. "But I'm sorry. I'm so sorry that they betrayed you — please don't kill me!"

She sneered at me, and a red line slowly made its way across her neck.

273

"Je ne vais pas te tuer . . . maintenant," she whispered.

What did that mean? *I'm not going . . . something, something now.*
She wasn't going to kill me now?

Until she broke my heart?

The wound on her neck grew wider, and ghostly red blood
began to ooze out of it and drip down. I instinctively cringed
away from it, but nothing landed on me. Opening my eyes,
I saw the drops of blood vanishing in the air inches above
my face.

As the queen hovered over me, seething, her skin turned from
rosy pink to pale gray, as if death were overtaking her. Her
teeth rotted and fell out of her mouth, disintegrating in the air
just like the drops of blood. Eventually, her hair grew stringy
and came out in clumps, and her flesh decayed and flaked off in
small pieces, which disappeared in midair.

And then she was gone.

I lay on the bed — or rather, in it — my chest heaving.

The room was silent, except the sound of my huffing and
puffing.

Had I done it? Had apologizing really been enough?

I flailed around for a minute like a beetle stuck on its back,
finally managing to roll to one side and heave my legs off the
bed frame. There was a Colette-shaped indentation in the old
mattress.

I picked up the music box and dusted it off. Holding it in my
hands, I wandered out of the room in a daze, trying to figure
out how I'd get back to the main palace.

But first I had to find Peely.

I had just started to descend the staircase when I heard a sound below me. My first assumption was that the security guards had tracked me down.

But the sound wasn't footsteps. It was music — the same song the music box played, only louder, less mechanical-sounding. I couldn't tell exactly where it was coming from, but I followed it to the bottom of the stairs.

I pulled open a door off the great room, revealing a bashed-in dinner table with several broken chairs upended around it. I walked toward the old hutch standing against the far wall. Behind its shattered glass doors, the shelves were covered with the remnants of whatever beautiful dishes had once been inside.

I paused and listened. . . .

The music sounded as if it were coming from *inside* the hutch.

As I stared, the whole thing swung smoothly away from the wall — as if it weighed twenty pounds instead of several hundred.

Behind it was a door with a latch like the one on the trap-door in the floor of the palace — made to be opened by my medallion.

I carefully set the medallion in the latch and turned it. The door opened away from me, revealing another set of stairs.

This must be the safe room.

The music came from inside.

I went to the bottom of the stairs. The room was shrouded in darkness and smelled like warm sewage, but I could hear the music plainly.

And now I knew where it was coming from.

"Pilar?" I asked. "Are you down here? Are you all right?"

The music didn't stop. But I heard a weak voice say, "Colette?"

"Where are you?" I called. "We need to get out of here."

She didn't answer — or stop playing.

I started to walk in the direction of the music. The bits of the room visible in the pale light spilling from the door seemed like snapshots of a once-beautiful place ravaged by time. The wide wooden planks of the floor were warped and cracking from age and moisture. The intricately woven Persian rugs were stained gray by mildew and the legs of the furniture were splitting from the water leeching up through the floor.

I found Peely in the far corner, sitting on a small bench, playing a violin. The music that came from the bulging, warped instrument was distorted and ghastly.

"Colette, I don't know what's happening. . . . I can't stop playing." Her eyes were bright with terror. Even as she spoke, her hand guided the bow, and she gently swayed with the rhythm of the song. She moved like a marionette being controlled by some unseen hand.

"Don't worry. I'll help you," I said, turning to go around the small sofa that separated us.

But my path was blocked.

The ghost of Marie Antoinette stood in my way.

I held my hands up, as if that would keep her away from me — and in the pale-blue light that radiated from the queen's face, suddenly, I saw it. The black key-shaped mark on my own wrist.

"La fille de la famille Iselin," the queen whispered.

It was finally my turn.

CHAPTER 23

THE GHOST RAISED her hand in a sharp, sudden gesture, and the room around us glowed with the light of candles and lamps — only instead of golden firelight, these flames were blue and silver and white. The room seemed to grow colder, as if the supernatural radiance sucked the warmth and life out of the air.

The full horror of the situation was on display, a once-beautiful sanctuary reduced to a tomb.

"This was supposed to be our refuge," the queen said, her voice a harsh whisper. "But we were never safe here. They all betrayed me . . . but Véronique's sin was the worst. Because I loved her like a sister.

"We had no place to go. No way to escape. And no one came for us . . . except the murderers." She took a step toward me. "Do you know how it felt — to try to bring my children to safety and then to find that the one I trusted the most had run away without me? Had saved herself and her family and left mine to . . . to die."

"Marie, I'm so sorry —"

"You may call me *Your Majesty*!" she snapped.

"Your Majesty . . . I apologize very much for what my family did to you. But I can't do anything about it. I can't change the past. I wish I could."

"You can do something," she said. "You can do what Véronique should have done. . . ."

I took a step back from her and found myself in a corner of the room.

"You can die," she snarled.

Without warning, she picked up a heavy vase from one of the tables and hurled it at me. I managed to duck out of its path but felt it pass inches from my face.

I took the moment to scramble past her toward the center of the room. She picked up one of the upholstered chairs as easily as if it weighed a couple of pounds. I dove behind a sofa as the chair sailed overhead, smashing into a cabinet that had been filled with porcelain figurines. The whole thing fell backward with an enormous crash.

My main objective was to get Pilar and myself out of the room alive. But the queen wasn't going to let us go without a fight. How do you fight a ghost?

The queen chased me around the room, upending tables, flinging paintings from the walls, and trying to bash my head in with heavy antique sculptures. But she grew less focused by the second, as if the effort of trying to kill me was using up her energy.

Should I try to go for help? If I summoned the guards, they could rescue Pilar while I distracted the ghost.

I made it to the stairs — taking a heavy hit in the leg from a crystal punch bowl — and ran to the top, reaching for the doorknob.

"Very well," the queen called. "Leave her alone with me. But I promise that if you do, you will never see her alive again."

Slowly, I turned around. The room looked like a tornado had ripped through it.

Pilar was still playing, terrified tears rolling down her cheeks.

"I'm sure that she will understand," the queen said, "why she is dying for the sins of her friend."

I took a slow step down the stairs. "She's completely innocent. She doesn't deserve to be a part of this. Let her go and I'll stay . . . forever."

The ghostly blue lights around us flickered.

The queen's haughty glance turned spiteful. "If I wanted only to kill you, I would have done it before now."

"Then what do you want?"

Her eyes narrowed. "To show you how it feels."

"My friend has nothing to do with this."

"Ah, I see," she replied in a cold, mocking voice. "You know how to be loyal under *certain* circumstances."

"I only know I don't want my friend to get hurt."

She glided toward me and stared up from the bottom of the

steps. "I was your friend once, Véronique," she hissed. "And you did not care if I got hurt."

"My family sucks," I said. "I get it. But Pilar is innocent. You wouldn't hurt an innocent person, would you? She's just a child . . . like your daughter."

She flinched.

I gritted my teeth. "And I'm not Véronique. My name is Colette."

The queen didn't answer.

"I know what it's like to be betrayed," I went on, not sure if I was doing the right thing or not. Can you reason with a murderous ghost? "I understand how much it hurts, but Pilar never did anything to you. You said yourself, Véronique was the worst. So please leave my friend alone and you can do whatever you want to me. Then maybe you can . . . rest in peace, or something."

She seemed to consider what I said. When she spoke, her tone was stubborn and haughty. "I cannot rest. For me, there is no peace. . . . All that is inside me is hatred."

Then she did something I didn't expect her to do. She disappeared and reappeared next to Pilar, swatting the violin from her hand. Pilar stared at her, awestruck, and tried to stand up. But before she could take a step, she collapsed to the ground.

"Yes, you care for your friend very much," the ghost said. "Perhaps your punishment will be to watch her die."

"No!" I shouted, vaulting down the stairs three at a time. My feet got tangled in my long skirt, and I tumbled down the last few. By the time I got back to my feet, Pilar was being dragged across the room.

The queen dropped her on the ground in front of the massive bookshelf.

"Véronique made me suffer — but she never had to see it," she said. "*You* will not be able to pretend that this is not your fault."

She raised a ghostly hand toward the shelves and they began to tip forward.

I didn't even have time to think. I charged across the room and threw myself at Pilar, half pushing and half rolling her unconscious body out of the way. A millisecond later, I felt a terrible impact on my body, like someone had punched me — only they were punching every muscle and bone at the same time.

And squeezing the air from my lungs.

I was pinned beneath the huge, heavy bookshelf.

I couldn't feel my feet or my hands, so I figured that, at the very least, my back was broken, if not my neck.

I drew in a breath of air, and it was as thin as if I'd drawn it from a straw.

My head rested limply on the ground. I couldn't really move to look for the ghost, but I figured she would be around somewhere. Watching. Waiting. Eager for my death.

The swish of her skirt, pale pink and translucent, appeared in my field of view, and I closed my eyes. "Just do it fast, please."

The queen knelt next to me, her face as anguished as the expression her statue wore at the Basilique. "Véronique, *why*?" she wailed. "Why did you betray me, when I trusted you to the depths of my very soul?"

I didn't know how to answer. And my vision was growing dim. . . .

CHAPTER 24

I AM STANDING with my back to a wall, shaking. A wave of nausea passes over me and I bend over to throw up. Reynaud Janvier appears beside me.

"You locked the sanctuary door?" he asks. "And took the key?"

I can hardly breathe through my sobs, but I manage to nod.

"Good," he says. "Tomorrow, you will go home and tell your husband and father that your family must be in Belgium by Sunday. That was all the time they would give us."

I can hardly hear his words. My thoughts are too full of my friend, my dear one, my queen.

Suddenly, I change my mind. I stand up straight and prepare to run. I can get through the tunnel and unlock the door. And then they will be safe —

I can do it. If I hurry, I can make it in time.

But Reynaud shoves me back roughly. "Are you crazy?" he growls. "This is not just about you, Véronique."

He will never let me go to her. He would murder me first.

I collapse on the floor.

We are in the kitchen at Le Petit Trianon, the six of us. We will spend the night here, and then, when the crowds of enraged peasants have dispersed, we will scatter like seeds in the wind. Tonight is the night we have planned for.

Tonight is the night they will come for her.

I will spend the rest of my life hating myself for what I have done this night. I will have three sons, and I will drive them away from me, because I do not deserve to be loved. They will leave me, and my husband will be cruel to me until he dies, and then I will spend my days alone.

I will never forget my sorrow or my guilt, and God will punish me by giving me a long, lonely life.

By the time I am eighty-four years old, I will dream every night of cornflowers and of my queen and her dear children. I will envy those who were tried and executed during the Revolution, for they never had to live and hate themselves as I have done.

Finally, I will grow sick, and my broken heart will give up. In my dying moments, as I choke for air, I will think of her face, and the faces of her precious, innocent children, and I will pray the only prayer I have prayed for more than sixty years.

I will pray that she may someday forgive me.

My grave will be a modest one, my tombstone a simple granite marker without my name, without my birth or death years. On it will be only two words — the two words that defined my wretched life. . . .

* * *

As I began to come around again, I heard a faint voice in my head. Not the queen's voice, but a familiar one. Speaking in French — but I understood her words.

Tell her this, the voice said. *You must tell her this for me, or I will never rest.*

I coughed, a hacking, ragged cough that burned my lungs as if they were on fire. I forced my eyes open. My vision was blurred, but I knew the queen was still nearby.

"Your Majesty," I whispered. I forced out the words, trying to ignore the pain in my chest. "I have a message for you . . . from Véronique. . . . *Je regrette. Je suis profondément désolée.*"

Through a veil of pale light, I saw the face of the queen above me. Tears streamed down her cheeks and faded out of the air above my eyes.

"She was . . . sorry." I had to pause to draw strained breaths between my words. "She was . . . so sorry."

The queen closed her eyes. *"Ma meilleure amie,"* she said. *"Je te pardonne. Et je pardonne tes enfants."*

Marie looked down at me, touched her lips gently to my forehead . . . and then she disappeared.

CHAPTER 25

A BURST OF coolness traveled through my body like electricity, quickly blossoming into a pulse of pain. I gasped, feeling my arms and legs suddenly spring back to life.

"Colette?" Pilar cried, rushing over. "Are you okay? Do you need me to —"

"If you can help me," I said, air rushing back into my lungs, "I think I can get out."

She came closer and looked down at me in horror. "That thing must weigh a thousand pounds."

"Yeah, but . . ." I wiggled around a little and found room to move. "Here, take my hands and pull."

She hauled me out, and after I sat for a minute and caught my breath, we looked under the shelves.

Tipped on its side, supporting the weight of the giant piece of furniture, was the queen's music box.

It began to play.

"Um, Colette? I don't think I know where we are. Or how I got here. How did all these candles get lit?" She looked around at the lights, which were growing fainter. "And . . . how did you learn so much French all of a sudden?"

"What?" I asked.

"You were speaking French," she said. "For, like . . . the whole time."

"Let's go, and I'll try to explain when we're out of here, okay? I'll tell you everything, I promise."

* * *

We left the cottage and stood out in the night air for a minute, watching the flashlights bob around in the distance.

"I think they're looking for us," Pilar said.

"They definitely are."

"Well . . . we could go out the back way," she suggested, pointing off to our right. "I saw it on the map the other day. See the cars? That's a road."

I nodded. "Good idea. I just need to do one thing."

I reached around my neck and took off the medallion. Then I walked to the edge of the pond and threw it into the water. It landed with a soft *plink* and sank out of view.

Then we started walking. And as we walked, I started talking.

I don't know exactly how much Peely believed, but she listened to the whole thing and then didn't say a word. She just patted me on the shoulder.

"I was so afraid you were dying," she said.

"Me, too."

She stopped and faced me. "So this does have something to do with Armand? And the murders?"

I nodded. "But I think those are over."

Then I remembered to check for the mark on my arm — it was gone. So was the mark on Pilar's. I could breathe again.

When we reached the road, I asked Pilar to use her phone (Mathilde's was buried forever in the tunnel) to call Jules. She answered his panicky questions and told him where we were. In three minutes flat, he pulled up and drove us back to the hotel. We explained everything to him, and he kept looking at me, taking my hand, like he couldn't believe I was real.

"I'll have to find a way to pay for the dress," I said. "And your sister's phone."

Jules shook his head. "Don't worry about it."

"I'll pay," Pilar said from her spot in the backseat. "You ruined them saving me."

"Thanks, Peely," I said.

She gave me a little smile. "You're welcome."

At the hotel, we went to Audrey's room, where she was waiting, her fingernails chewed to nubs. We told her the whole story, and as she listened, her mouth dropped farther and farther open.

"Just to be clear," she said, when I'd finally finished. "You're not just messing with me?"

But by the look in her eyes, I could tell she was joking. That broke through a bit of the stunned shell that had hardened around me, and I was able to laugh — just a little.

"But it's over?" she said.

"I hope so."

Pilar sat up and folded her hands in her lap. "I know I'm not very smart, but —"

"Stop saying stuff like that about yourself," I said.

"Well — about ghosts and whatever, I mean," she said, but I could tell she was pleased. "But I was there, and I saw her, and I think she's done murdering people. She looked really peaceful at the end."

Audrey sighed. "That's good."

I tried to hold in a giant yawn, but it forced its way out. "I think I need to take a shower and get some sleep."

"You should stay here," Audrey said. "That way you don't have to face Hannah."

"Oh, *Hannah*." Pilar frowned. "I forgot about her. I'm not looking forward to dealing with her."

I wasn't, either. Audrey's offer was beyond tempting. But I wasn't going to send Peely up there alone.

We rode in the elevator together. When Peely knocked on the door, Hannah opened it.

"Well, look what the cat dragged in," she said.

"Hannah," I said, "shut up."

"Pilar, I think your *friend* needs to learn some manners."

Pilar stopped in the hallway and looked at her. "Hannah," she said, "seriously. Shut up."

CHAPTER 26

I WOKE THE next day unsure of what had really happened the night before. Was the mark on my arm really gone? Yes. Was I really alive? Yes. Had I almost died and then been saved by the ghost of Marie Antoinette?

Yes, to all of it.

It was our last day in Paris. We had to leave for the airport at four o'clock.

Pilar and I headed downstairs to the café for breakfast and found Audrey in the buffet line, waiting for crêpes. When she saw me, she gave me a knowing glance and a smile.

After Pilar got her plate and started walking toward the exit — to eat in the penthouse, I guessed — Audrey stopped her.

"Sit with us," she said. It was almost a question, like she expected to be snubbed.

But Peely's eyes lit up. "Yeah, okay. Hannah's being a total pill."

Brynn showed up a minute later, and then we all sat down to eat — me, Brynn, Audrey, and Pilar. The conversation was slightly awkward, since all Brynn knew — all anyone from our group knew — was that there had been a falling-out at the party the previous night and I was no longer in Hannah's good graces (to put it mildly).

But it was still a nice breakfast. Pilar, when she realized nobody was counting her calories for her or planning to criticize her every dreamy thought, relaxed and talked as much as the rest of us.

As for Hannah? She was up in the penthouse suite — alone.

*   *   *

Jules came by the hotel later, and he and I went out walking. We stopped at a little café for an early lunch. He asked a million questions — he wanted more details about the night before. I told him as much as I could remember.

"So there are tunnels under the palace," he said.

"*Oui*," I said, taking a bite of my *croque-monsieur*. "They go all the way out to Le Hameau."

"And yet they have never been found?"

"They have now," I said. "But I doubt they'll still be there the next time someone thinks to look for them. I'm pretty sure they flooded."

"Such a shame," he said softly. "All that history . . ."

I didn't reply, but I was thinking that it wasn't such a shame. To Jules, it might have been a fascinating piece of the past, but to me, it was a reminder of the horrible things people could do when they were scared or selfish.

After lunch, he told me there was somewhere he wanted to

take me. We got on the Metro and rode it for a while, holding hands but not really speaking. We got off at a little station a few miles outside of the city.

"Where are we going?" I teased. "To meet your grandparents?"

He smiled mysteriously and kept walking.

Finally, we turned into a small graveyard next to an old stone church.

"Here," he said, pointing to one of the graves. "I had heard of it before — it is famous, in a way, because of the mystery. Now I know what it means."

We stood together, looking at the modest stone, which read JE REGRETTE.

I sighed for the past, and for the future — for poor Véronique and for the question of whether my family could shake off the effects of a blood bond that seemed to make us genetically predisposed to use people for our own gain.

I'd made the right choice, saving Pilar last night. But in the face of the years of shallow choices I'd made, that didn't seem like much to go on.

Then I thought of Charlie and how he was always looking out for Mom.

If he could do it, maybe I could, too.

* * *

On our way back into the city, we got off the Metro at the Villiers station — near the former Errancis Cemetery. After paying my respects to Véronique, I felt like I owed at least as much to the queen herself. I braced myself for the chaotic construction site.

But as we rounded the corner, we found that the street had been almost totally filled in. A single worker drove a small backhoe carefully around the torn-up asphalt. The construction was complete.

Maybe the queen really could rest in peace now.

* * *

Jules walked me back to the hotel. It was hard to say good-bye. I cried a little. We promised to email each other and to try to meet up again next summer — either in France or in America. But I wondered if what had existed between us was destined to be just a passing moment in our lives.

"It seems so Parisian," I said, through my sniffles, "to find someone and then have to say good-bye so quickly."

He cupped my face gently in his hands. "It is not Parisian," he said. "It's just life."

"I know, but . . ." I let my voice trail off.

"Colette, you are so different now than you were on that first day. You have changed so much. And I am a part of that. So I am happy."

It was true. I'd wanted Paris to change my life. . . . I'd just had no idea how dramatic the change would be. And Jules was a part of that, as much as the ghost had been.

"But what about you?" I asked. "What difference did I make for you?"

He smiled, his eyes crinkling. "Besides convincing me that ghosts are real? You are the only girl I've ever kissed on top of the Eiffel Tower. And I swear, you are the only girl I will ever kiss there. So every time I see it, I will think about you."

I nodded, wiping my eyes.

"Plus, Mathilde will never let me forget how nervous I was when you came to eat dinner with us," he said. "And you know the secret of my brief career as a poet."

I smiled in spite of my sadness.

"You are special, Colette," he said softly, lifting my hand to his lips and kissing it. "You can forget *me* someday, but do not forget that."

And then he kissed me . . . and kissed me . . . and kissed me. And I knew there was no risk of my ever forgetting him.

*　　*　　*

Pilar gave her first-class seat to Madame Mitchell and rode in the back of the plane with the rest of us. I was shocked, but Peely didn't seem to think it was such a big deal.

"I didn't want to sit there and listen to Hannah lecturing me the whole flight," she said.

I was beginning to get the feeling that Pilar wouldn't be putting up with much of Hannah's lecturing at all from now on.

We landed and went to baggage claim, where Mom and Charlie were waiting for me with a sign that said WELCOME HOME! and, under that, in tiny letters Mom hadn't noticed, STUPIDHEAD.

I hugged them both and pointed my bag out to Charlie. He picked it up off the belt and rolled it back to our car while Mom peppered me with questions about the trip.

I tried to answer them all, but she got so excited that they all ran together into one sustained request for information, and I had to promise her I'd talk all through dinner and well into the night if that was what it took to satisfy her curiosity.

She did want to know about the murders. She'd followed the news about them all week.

"I was worried about you," she said, "but I didn't call about it, because I knew you'd be mad at me."

"She knew that because I told her so," Charlie added. "You're welcome."

"Well, Paris is a huge city," Mom chimed in. "Statistically speaking, I knew you weren't in danger."

"*I* showed her the statistics," Charlie said. "You're welcome again."

I gave my mother a little smile, grateful she didn't have to know everything that had really happened. "All's well that ends well, right?"

She inclined her head. "That's been my motto for a year. I'm just glad you're home."

We pulled into our space in the parking garage, and Charlie lugged my bag up the stairs.

"I know this will be a disappointment," Mom said, "after being in a fancy hotel all week. I just want you guys to know that I'm going to get us out of this apartment as soon as I can."

"Mom," I said, "stop worrying. It's great."

"It's . . . great?" she repeated.

I looked around the main room. She and Charlie had made a lot of progress while I was gone. "Yeah, you guys fixed it up super cute. We'll be fine here, won't we, Charlie?"

Charlie looked confused, then smiled at me. "*Très magnifique*," he replied.

Mom looked as if she couldn't quite believe it.

"You must be hungry," she said at last. "Do you want to unpack while I make some dinner?"

I shrugged. "Unpacking can wait. I'll help you cook. Charlie, you can hang out, too."

She headed to the kitchen, glancing at me over her shoulder as if I were some apparition that might disappear. Then she pulled out a pot and a package of ground beef.

"How does spaghetti with meat sauce sound?" she asked.

"Yummy," I said, and Charlie nodded.

As she cooked, we all talked, and I described as much of Paris as I dared. Then we ate, and afterward we sat around the table talking, like Jules's family did.

"So," Mom said, as we carried the dishes into the kitchen, "how does it feel to be back?"

"Wonderful," I said. "It feels wonderful."

*　*　*

Later that night, I was in my bedroom, unpacking. Charlie came in and sat on my bed.

"Are you just being nice because you're tired or something?" he asked.

I laughed. "I don't think so."

"Okay, good."

He looked around. Normally, I wouldn't have even let him into my room, so this was a new experience for him.

"Um, hey." He stared at his hands. "I'm sorry I scared you in the garage before you left."

"Have you been feeling bad about that the whole time?" I laughed and patted his shoulder. "You're forgiven. Not like I haven't been mean to you for the past, oh, fourteen years."

He laughed, but it was the kind of laugh that meant I'd spoken the truth.

"You know, Charlie . . . we don't have to do that anymore."

"Do what?"

I took a deep breath. "I don't know, hate each other? Maybe we could just start getting along."

"What, starting now?"

I shrugged. "Why not?"

"Okay." He gave me a small smile. "You must be tired."

"Yeah," I said. "I'm so turned around, I can't even tell what time it is."

"I'll let you go to bed, then." He stood and then leaned over me and gave me an awkward little hug, which I returned as well as I could. "You want me to take that back downstairs for you?"

He was looking at my desk, where Great-Grandma Colette's box was still sitting.

"You know what?" I said. "I'll do it myself." After what I'd been through, the storage closet no longer seemed so scary. And I liked the idea of sealing the box back up and stashing it far out of reach, even though it was free of the medallion.

Some things deserved to be locked away.

Charlie nodded and left my room, wishing me good night as he closed the door.

I went to the bathroom to brush my teeth, unpacking my toiletries with one hand while I brushed with the other. I knelt to put my makeup bag under the sink, and when I stood up, I stared into the mirror.

I waited for the swimmy, woozy feeling to take over, for Véronique's face to show up in place of my own. But even though I stared for a full minute, I only saw myself.

I hope you've found peace at last, Véronique.

I knew that I would always be looking for her. Every time I looked in a mirror, I'd expect to see her face. Véronique was part of me. What she'd done was part of me. But . . . what I'd done, what I'd chosen, was a bigger part.

I returned to my room, slipped beneath the covers, and fell asleep before I had time to wonder if I was tired.

I dreamed of small, curving streets paved with rough stones; of the perfume of flowers and sweet pastries in the air; of beautiful buildings rising up on every side of me; and of a feeling of magic and history beneath my feet.

And my dreams felt as real as a memory.

HISTORICAL NOTE

WHILE MANY OF the details found within this book are based on actual locations and historical accounts, the Order of the Key, its members, and its role in Marie Antoinette's life (and death) are completely fictional. In reality, the queen's dearest friend, Princess Marie Louise of Savoy, the Princess of Lamballe, was executed for her stalwart loyalty to the royal family.

ACKNOWLEDGMENTS

MANY THANKS TO Aimee Friedman, David Levithan, and the other wonderful people at Scholastic who helped to make this book what it is: Natalie Sousa, Janet Robbins, Rebekah Wallin, Erica Ferguson, Becky Shapiro, Stacy Lellos, and Tracy van Straaten.

Thanks to Matthew Elblonk (as ever) for his encouragement, patience, and guidance.

Thanks to the friends, readers, fellow authors, teachers, librarians, parents, and booksellers who have been so supportive of my books over the years.

Special shout-out to the lads (you know who you are).

And finally, infinite love and gratitude without end to my family, especially my husband, Chris, my sister Ali, and baby G (who kindly put off being born by a few days so Mommy could meet her deadline).